Escaping Humanity
The Exceptionals Book 1

Sarah Cass
Mary Terrani

Urban Fantasy

Sarah Cass
www.authorsarahcass.com

Divine Roses Ink Publishing
www.divinerosesink.com

A Divine Roses Ink Book
Urban Fantasy
Paranormal Romance

Copyright © 2018 Sarah Cass & Mary Terrani

Cover design by Sarah Cass
Edited by Megan Koenen & Annie Farrell
All cover art and logo copyright © 2018 by Sarah Cass

PUBLISHER
Divine Roses Ink
http://www.divinerosesink.com

Other Books by Mary Terrani

Decking the Halls

Books by Sarah Cass

The Tribe Series
The Tribe
The Wolf
The Chief
The Raven
The Dominion Falls Series
Changing Tracks
Derailed
Dark Territory
Runaway Train
Home Signal
The Lake Point Series
Santa, Maybe
Deep-Fried Sweethearts
Stalled Independence
Witch Way
A Thorough Thanksgiving
Eve's New Year
Heartstrings & Hockey Pucks
Luck of the Cowgirl
Stars, Stripes & Motorbikes
Free Falling
Love for Hire
Haunted Hearts
Stand Alone Novels
Masked Hearts
Leap

Dedication
For Mary Terrani

To Sarah,
Thank you for helping me bring this world and these characters to life. It's been a long road getting here, but I am so proud of what we have created. I couldn't have done this without you. The adventure has only begun and I cannot wait to see where it takes us. Love you.

To Mom and Dad,
Thank you for always being there to push me in the right direction no matter where my dreams may take me. I was blessed and hit the parental jackpot when I was given to you. Mom, thank you for all your help and encouragement with this project and editing this for Sarah and I. Having you on the team made it that much better. I love you more than I can say.

Dedication
For Sarah Cass

To Mary,
Thank you for putting up with me working on twenty gazillion projects while trying to help you with this one. Your six years of patience with me have finally paid off. I'm so excited for where this world is going, and the new paths it's giving us. You are my best friend, and I'm so happy to share this with you. Love you.

In 2023 all major cities have been nearly destroyed.
Everything is in chaos.

In an attempt to make a 'super soldier' a consortium of the world's top scientists designed a virus that swept across the globe. It turned ordinary humans into mutants.

After almost ten years of covert operations to destroy the virus, and the results of their blunder, the military leaders began an all-out war. One that ended in total disaster.

Japan is under water, California joined it not long after. New York was nearly leveled. All forms of communication are gone or severely compromised. The internet is almost non-existent. Cell towers are down everywhere and even in areas where there are towers, getting a signal is near impossible.

Military powers around the world are rounding up what they call 'Infected' humans. Torturing and killing the mutants they created. Now the Exceptionals are gathering. Trying to find a safe haven and rebuild some semblance of a life in a world turned upside down.

The governments that created them are hell-bent on destroying them. Will they survive? Only time will tell if they are successful in *Escaping Humanity*.

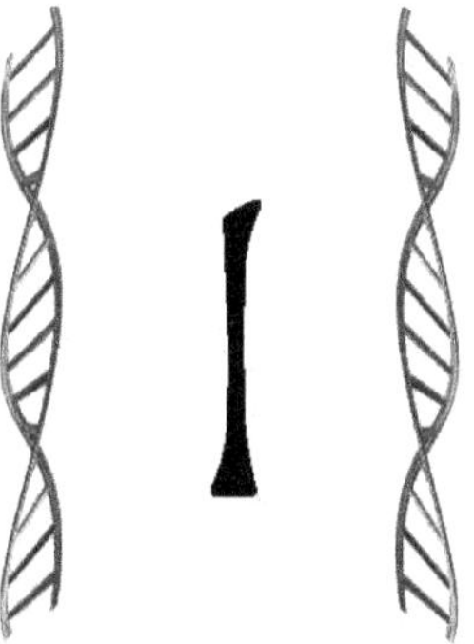

Annie rubbed her temples to ward off another burgeoning headache. The pain stretched behind her eyes until she thought they might pop out. Right when she thought it couldn't get worse, the pain would then deepen until she couldn't move for hours for fear of setting off another wave of nausea.

Such attacks had become more frequent and more of a nuisance. She popped a couple of pills in hopes of heading it off at the pass. From her spot at the kitchen counter, the shadow of a large bird flying past drew her eye to the picture window. Strange, as so few birds hung around any longer without the easy handouts from humans.

She rubbed her arms against the renewed sense of disquiet. When she'd returned to her apartment something had felt off, as if someone had been there, inside the apartment. Now this bird, wherever it had gone.

She was being ridiculous, of course. If the army had come by for another of their sweeps, they would have moved on, not gone inside. They had ways of detecting if there was a person inside, after all. Otherwise, her apartment was non-descript, and though in one of the few buildings that hadn't been decimated, she would have known if a thief had been scrounging around. No thief would leave her apartment as neat as she kept it intentionally.

She shook off the odd feeling and closed her eyes as she leaned against the frame of the large picture window. The window had been a huge selling point when she'd rented the apartment a few years back.

Before the war, the thought of being able to sit in her chair reading a book while looking out over Central Park had been too good to resist. Anymore it was just a constant reminder of how badly New York had been hit.

The whistle of the teakettle pulled her out of her thoughts in time to see a figure emerge from the shelter of trees in the park. Dismissing them as one of the many scroungers that roamed the streets and park, she moved to the stove. Once the water was in her mug she dropped in the tea infuser, splashing herself in her distraction.

Unable to help herself, she moved back to the window to focus on the person in the park. The knots in her stomach tightened. Not only did the man not appear to be a vagrant, he was staring right at her window.

For a moment, he appeared to be speaking to someone, but Annie couldn't see anyone else with him. Her body shook from a mix of nerves and a chill so she drew her mug close. The steam rose in lilting curls of heat, but her hands failed to feel the warmth emanating from the cup. More often than not her hands were always cold anymore.

As she took a sip of her tea, the man seemed to vanish in a blink. While disturbed by the disappearance, she was also relieved. Instead she focused on what was left of Central Park stretched out before her. The pond and zoo had been spared, but the carousel had not been as lucky. The charred remains still lie exactly as it had been right after the attack.

A knock at the door startled her. "Who the hell could that be?"

Anyone with half a brain after the War knew better than to answer the door without good reason. However, you always checked immediately in case it was the army. She set down her mug to check who it was. When she looked out the peephole her confusion doubled. On the other side of the door was the man she'd seen moments ago in the park.

While common knowledge told her to step away, some deeper instinct told her otherwise. She battled the disparate instincts as she studied the man through the doorway.

The man leaned closer to the peephole and spoke. "I know you're there. I see your shadow under the door."

"What can I help you with?" Curiosity rose up and she stepped to the side, opening the door a crack. If the man on the other side of the door wanted to hurt her it didn't really matter. Whether death arrived in a few months or this moment, her fate was still the same.

"Anna?"

A laugh bubbled up at his use of her birth name. "I haven't been called Anna since I was a little girl. What are you, a bill collector or something?"

"Not a bill collector, I think those went away with the War." Despite the humorous bend to his statement, the young man showed no amusement in his features at all. A serious, stern downturn to his eyebrows oddly seemed to add to his attractiveness.

"I think bill collectors will always exist." Anna shook off the out-of-place attraction.

"I came by earlier, but you weren't here."

"Did you come in my apartment?"

"How could I? The door was locked."

"People find ways."

A low sound almost like a growl ground through the silence. "Anna. Stop fooling around."

"Maybe you are looking for someone else. We've never met before." Her grip on the door remained firm. "I can't imagine what you would want with me."

His gaze darted back and forth down the hallway before he looked at her again. "Can I come in? I promise I'm not here to hurt you."

"Isn't that the line of every murderer?"

The harsh lines of disapproval, anger, and stress, softened and she could have sworn she saw his lips twitch in a brief smile. Had to have been her imagination, because a moment later he shook his head and the amusement was gone. "This is important. Your life depends on it."

Indecision ran through her. She didn't think he was there to hurt her, and honestly, if he was, she didn't think she could stop him from forcing his way in anyhow. A door clicked open down the hall. Rather than have one of her remaining neighbors asking about the man outside her door, she opened it wider. "All right then."

As he entered, she hoped she wouldn't have any need to defend herself. Though she was more than capable of defending herself quite assertively, it would likely knock her out for a while. He scanned her apartment, and she thought she saw him take a deep sniff.

Once he was inside, she shut the door behind him. "What's so urgent? And who are you?"

"I don't have a lot of time to explain. I need you to come with me." James vibrated tension.

"You're joking, right? I don't even know you. First, you stand outside and stare at my apartment like some creeper. Then you just show up outside my door. Now you want me to go with you? Not gonna happen." Annie rolled her eyes. "And people wonder why they say men are dumb."

"I can explain on the way, but it isn't safe for you here." One step forward for him equaled a step back for her.

"Hmm, stranger on my door step with some mystery danger he wants to protect me from. You have some candy to go with that too? I think I'll take my chances here." She took another step back wanting to put a little distance between them.

"You might not say that if you knew what was out there." He didn't advance this time. "Or what has been in here."

"What the big bad wolf? I can handle myself." The regret of having let him in her apartment built. "I think you should go."

"I'm not leaving here without you."

"And that's supposed to be comforting? Make me want to go with you? I think you need a few pointers on how to pick up women." Granted she didn't need a weapon if she really needed to defend herself but she hated using her mutations. They made her as uneasy as the cancer growing inside of her. They also got people killed.

"I know you were infected, and had the gene that turned you into an Exceptional. In other words, you're a mutant." This time he did come towards her. He stopped right in front of her but he didn't touch her. "It's not safe here anymore. We need to get you someplace that is."

Everything came to a screeching halt. Everything that is, except the headache that had been growing exponentially all day. "You need to leave." The last thing she was going to do was admit to him what she was. People that admitted they had been infected were rounded up and killed.

"I am not going anywhere without you."

"Who are you? Why are you here? I have more important things to worry about than whatever fairy tale you are spinning." Her fingertips rubbed along her forehead.

"My name is James. I promise I will explain more as we go."

The frustration was evident on his face. Not that she cared at the moment. "Why should I trust you?"

"You can trust me because I'm just like you." He said exasperated.

"You're dying too?" The words tumbled from her mouth before she could stop them.

"No, I'm an Exceptional." He did a double take. "Wait what?"

"I'm dying." It came out a little softer this time. Saying the words made it even more real. The doctor telling her didn't hit as hard as hearing the words come out of her own mouth.

"Shit, that wasn't in the plan."

"Yeah tell me about it."

Well if everything hadn't just gotten exponentially complicated. Most missions James had been on went smooth. Exceptionals were scattered everywhere now, still being picked off by military that had been kept safe in hidden locations when the worst had hit.

James' own home had been destroyed—the reservation that had housed not only a large Lenape tribe, but also many mutants. His parents, fighting on the front lines had been blown up in front of his own eyes. The loss of them had been almost too much for him and his brothers and sisters to bear. Only the thought of keeping the people they held dear together had made any of them move forward.

Now what was left of the tribe gathered in Montana. They had started rebuilding a life there. One that had become a sanctuary for many. The Lenape had always accepted those who had developed gifts from the virus, so keeping the easy rapport had made sense.

His mom's old friend Warren had returned to the states with his wife Abigail. Since then, they'd been working to find as many mutants as possible to take to safety before the military found them. It was his job, along with his sister Ilana, to gather them up and bring them back.

Now there was this one. Anna. The young woman in front of him was an Exceptional, her response to his statement had been proof enough even if she didn't say it aloud.

Dying? That added a complication they hadn't planned on. While Abigail was an excellent doctor, medicine had been scarce and not easy to come by. They had to rely on the land for the majority of it. Raiding abandoned hospitals was their next best bet, but they were running out of those.

Perhaps it was a case of mistaken identity. None of the records Warren had found in regard to Anna had revealed any doctors. "Are you sure?"

Her scoffing laugh was enough of an answer, but she elaborated. "Yes, I'm sure. Or do you think I made it up to make you go away?"

"Well that would be stupid. It would make me more determined to get you out of here. Somewhere that you can be cared for."

"So, you'll take me somewhere that I don't know, with people I don't know so I can die with an audience of strangers? No thanks."

"No. So that maybe you can get help." He couldn't stop the sneer that formed. "Or would you rather stay a spoiled brat and be killed in far worse a way than whatever you think is killing you?"

"Excuse me?" While moments before she'd been almost trepidatious, a hint of fire now showed under her tired features. Even more when she moved towards him, "You don't know anything. Just go away or I will make you."

A smile tugged at his lips, but he kept it in check. "I'm not leaving without you. There are people out there that will torture and kill you just for being a mutant. Spirits forbid the military gets a hold of you. I can take you somewhere safe and we have an excellent doctor."

"I have absolutely no reason to trust you."

"No. You don't. Just…hold on." He pulled out the ringing cell phone in his pocket and flipped it open. Keeping in mind the woman in front of him, he used Warren's code name, "Yeah Cy? What did you need? There's been a complication. It's taking too long to get her out of here."

"A cell phone? There's no active tower here!" Anna moved towards him, her eyes glued to the device.

James hand rose to keep her at a distance and to silence her. "No, she's giving me trouble. Not frightened and desperate like most of them. She doesn't understand the danger she's in. There are troops everywhere in this wasteland of a city."

"How could she not know? I thought everyone knew after the War." Warren's voice raised a few decibels; his disbelief clear. "That's what the damn War was about!"

"Look, I'm not paid to psychoanalyze the nutcases."

"You're not paid."

"Exactly." James looked over at Anna, feeling a lift of satisfaction at her scoff of defiance. "She doesn't trust me."

"You've got a mug like your Dad's. I'm not surprised. Put her on the phone for me."

James quirked a brow, but held out the phone. "Anna. Cyber wants to talk to you."

She snatched the phone out of his hand. "Hello?"

James didn't let on that he could hear every word. He walked to the window and looked out as Warren started to talk.

"Hello, Anna. Have you figured out my trail yet?"

The lingering silence almost brought a chuckle out of the depths of darkness James always carried these days. Almost. That and the way her nose crinkled up as she concentrated.

"I'm not sure what you mean." Anna recovered but too late for them not to know she was bluffing. "What trail? There's a strange man in my living room that showed up unexpectedly promising me medical treatment that doesn't exist anymore. Another one on a cell phone in an area with no towers or working lines."

"Don't play dumb. It's beneath your capabilities. Have you figured out how I got this cell phone to work? Have you followed my trail all the way to where I am?" Warren did chuckle into the line, but he kept it respectably short.

"Not all the way," she whispered as if it would mean James wouldn't hear her. "I'm tied up somewhere around what used to be Chicago. Where are you?"

So, Warren had been right. Her gift was the same as his— an ability to communicate with computers and through the Internet using just their brain.

A smile came through in Warren's voice. "Despite the ground destruction in Chicago, many of the lines and towers survived. It's easy to get a signal twisted around there. That's why I always use it as a hub. Don't feel bad. For every hack you try, I've already got a counterattack in place. You're not supposed to be able to get past Chicago."

"Bet my father could get through it." Anna muttered under her breath. She straightened up as she started to pace in the living room. "How do you know?"

"If you want to know that, you'll have to come and see for yourself." Warren wasn't an idiot, he knew James could hear. Without changing his tone of voice, he spoke, "James. What's the complication?"

"You mean besides the ground troops heading our way?" James still didn't turn around, but he could almost feel the daggers being glared into his back when she stopped pacing. "She says she's dying. I have no confirmation of the fact."

"I am." A hint of a sob echoed through her voice, but then it vanished. "I don't need a doctor to tell me that."

"I see. Well we have an amazing doctor here Anna. Managed to procure a decent amount of equipment and medicine as well. Let us try to help please." Warren sighed, "How close James?"

"Two miles. Give or take."

"He's rarely wrong Anna. As annoying as that is I think it's best to take your chance with James over the troops." Warren's tone was warm, but concerned. "The military will do whatever it takes to rid the earth of all of us. You don't want them to catch you."

"I've passed their sweeps before without incident." Despite the lack of conviction in her voice her chin jutted out proudly. When James turned around he saw not only that but how wide with fear her eyes were.

"Maybe you would this time. But what about next time? Each time gets much harder when you are trying to hide it."

James shook his head, "I'm done with pleasantries, Cyber. We need to get out of here. They know my face and we'll have trouble."

"Okay!" Anna gasped when he advanced towards her. "I'll go. I need to pack."

"No time. Give me the phone. We're leaving now."

For a moment, it looked like she'd be stubborn. Then she handed him the phone with a frown, "And just how are you going to get us out of here without them catching us?"

"I have my ways. Now move. We have clothes and food at the reservation."

"Wait I need one thing."

It took every ounce of effort not to shout or scream at her to move. Instead he gave a short nod, "Thirty seconds."

It only took her fifteen, a large purse that might have been called a small suitcase slung over her shoulder. "I'm ready."

"Good. I only have one rule. Until we get there you do as I say. Remember, your life depends on it."

"Doesn't mean much to a dying woman, does it?"

Ilana perched on the stone banister of the steps in front of Anna's apartment. On the surface, she kept her features stoic, almost bored, just as she'd been trained. To anyone that passed it appeared that the only thing of interest to her was the dirt under her nails.

On the inside, however, she laughed her ass off. James' internal dialogue about the young woman they were attempting to 'save' was just too much.

Damn it, she's a stubborn one. What the hell does she have in that bag? Could we be tracked because of it? After a pause, his attention turned to admiration of her assets again. *For someone that's dying she's got one hell of a figure.*

Ilana sighed and picked at some actual dirt beneath her nail. James might be a great warrior, an excellent tracker, but underneath it all he was always disgustingly male. Tired of the drama, she shut down the telepathic energy to let the silence take over. As amusing as some of his thoughts could be, she really wasn't in the mood to watch porn. Plus, when he switched back to suspicion again, and he always did, it would make Ilana paranoid.

She hated being paranoid. Yes, they lived in a really shitty time. There were very few people you could trust. Yes, she was fully aware of every danger lurking around every corner. Yes, she knew all too well how much the minds of the military had been corrupted into believing Exceptionals were an evil insidious race. They went as far as to call them 'the infected' as if they were zombies instead of the next evolution of man.

Before the War had gone from covert military action into an all-out war, Ilana had been anything but paranoid. There'd been a time when dark depression hadn't threatened every moment of lightness and sunshine. There were days before she was nothing but the Guardian, living only to protect her tribe and kill those that would kill them.

While her parents had been born human and become infected, every single one of their many children had been born Exceptionals. Ilana had been the most unique of them all. Instead of one mutation, or even two, Ilana had been able to call on any of the mutations her family members had. At will. Just as easy, she could push it away like it had never been there.

She'd been pegged as a Guardian of her people. The embodiment of an ancient tale of a shape shifter born to protect now come to life.

Believing that, Ilana knew, she'd been spoiled. Rotten as the day was long, she'd been a difficult child for her mother.

The War changed all of that.

Guardian. What a joke.

She hadn't been able to stop the destruction of her tribe's lands. Nor had she been able to save her own parents. Tears welled and she used her brother's water mutation to rid herself of them.

"Illy." James' voice was soft, rich with concern. The hand he set on her shoulder was warm and comforting. "I left you alone too long again."

James understood. His own self-loathing over what had happened to their parents rivaled her own. The surprise of his appearance made her control slip. A tear rolled down her cheek. She forced a smile when he wiped it away with the pad of his thumb. "I'm fine, Jimmy. This her?"

In a brief thinning of the dust cloud that darkened the sky, the woman's blond hair shimmered with a hint of red. At first her blue eyes were wide with shock, most likely over James' different nature toward Illy, but then they narrowed in suspicion.

"Yup. She insisted she bring a bag. Think you can haul this load?" James grinned.

Ilana smirked despite Anna's anger-flushed skin. James' intent had been to make Ilana smile, not insult the woman behind him. Even if he had managed to do both with a skill she almost envied. "Be nice, Jimmy. She's got no idea what's going on. Although with her mutation, I have no idea how she couldn't."

"The War." Anna straightened like she was putting her backbone into place. Admirable, even though clearly an act. Without reading Anna's mind, Ilana could see how worried and afraid she was. It was something they were all too used to seeing these days. Everyone they rescued wore the same thin lips, wide eyes, and pale flesh of fear. "New York City is pretty much dead. I can find signals out, but so much information is controlled or encrypted beyond my capabilities."

"Cyber." James and Ilana said at the same time.

They both laughed. James nodded at Ilana. "Exactly. I'm guessing whatever intel Anna got a hold of was all military propaganda. Cyber is intent on protecting everything else from those that would use it to hurt us."

"So, you want the world to think the military is right?" Anna huffed. "Because if he's blocking all that information, no one is getting it."

"He's trying to make sure Exceptionals are safe. There are more military troops now than mutants, or even humans. General Steele has all the power. More than the President, who's only a figurehead these days." Ilana sighed. "We have to be careful who gets their hands on what until we have a better idea what position we're in."

"For what?" Anna's eyes widened again. She already knew.

"To fight back." James lifted his chin, his lip curling in an eager grin. "To pay back the bastards that created us only to destroy us all."

"You look excited at the thought that the War might not be over." Anna shifted her bag and took a step away from him. "Haven't we had enough?"

Ilana pursed her lips. They didn't have time for an argument, or to explain everything yet. "James. Is the distraction set in place? We should head out as soon as possible."

Before James could answer a loud scream echoed through the remains of the buildings all around them. James grinned as gunfire and high-pitched female laughter followed it. An explosion shook the ground. "Sounds like she's got it covered. Why didn't you check yourself?"

"Because I didn't want to hear your sick and twisted thoughts, thanks for asking. You okay to get back to the plane?" Ilana rolled her shoulders, preparing for what she had to do next. In a blink, she pulled on the one mutation she was born with and could never dismiss. Shape shifting.

"I'm fine. I'll probably help out Caiman and meet you back at the rendezvous point." James bounced and ran off.

"Fine. Just remember—you could still be killed." Ilana shouted after him, even though he'd already disappeared from view. Her back stretched and pulled, her body making room for what was to come.

"Failure is not an option." James' yell echoed back to them, followed by more laughter and gunfire.

"Well then, Anna." Ilana tried to smile while keeping her eyes from rolling at the insanity of her siblings. "Are you ready to get away from the chaos?"

Anna clutched her bag to her chest, staring where James had disappeared. What little color had been in her face was gone. Pale as a ghost, the dark circles under her eyes added to the effect of death. Maybe she wasn't wrong. Maybe she was dying.

Ilana moved closer and touched Anna's arm. "I know this is all overwhelming, Anna. I also know that James is a total idiot and handled this poorly. I mean, really most people keep to themselves these days. Post War, showing up at someone's house and asking them to just let you in that you didn't know is insane. Caiman and I came too late to stop his idiotic move there. I promise, we are the good guys. If there is such a thing."

Anna trembled, but nodded. "He's a jerk."

"Let's get moving. Those two will only be able to distract the soldiers for so long. Once they scatter, our chance for escape will be lessened."

"But how will we leave?"

Ilana chuckled and pulled her shoulders forward as the wings she'd been preparing for sprouted from her back. Under Anna's wide-eyed gaze, Ilana stretched them to their full length.

Once they were free, they flapped instinctively. "We're going to fly."

"What the hell?"

"Yeah. I get that a lot. There's a lot you must learn. Don't worry, I'm stronger than I look. We'll get to the plane long before those two animals do." Ilana stepped closer. "I know it's weird being picked up by a girl, but it's going to happen."

Anna's weak protest was ignored as Ilana scooped her up. Ilana bent her knees to prepare for flight. She flapped them once, twice, to prepare the young woman for the sound and sensation. "Don't hold your breath. That makes it worse."

With that final warning, she shoved off the ground. They shot straight in the air, hitting the dust clouds as fast as Ilana could. It wouldn't help them survive if any of the soldiers saw them before they hit the cover of the dust clouds.

Ilana didn't need to see in order to fly back to their plane. Her sense of direction was impeccable. To her fortune, Anna had gone completely still. If the woman had fought there would have been a much bigger problem. Instead, they made it to the plane quickly, with no trouble.

The barn they'd hidden the plane in sat next to a burned-out field. The barn itself was scorched and half collapsed. Ilana yanked open the door of the barn. "Our plane is inside. It's nothing fancy, but it gets us where we need to go. Cyber's trying to build us something much nicer and stealthier, but parts are hard to come by. James will be along soon."

"Seriously. What are you people?"

"Exceptionals."

"I know that. What *are* you."

Ilana's amusement faded. "We're what the military created with their virus, Anna. Thousands of mutants created because they wanted to make super soldiers and instead spread a virus across the planet. In return for their blunder, they tried to find us all and kill us. You were there, you should know this."

"I don't remember. Not all of it." Anna pulled her bag close. "I mostly remember the end, and the time before. The War itself is hazy except the day New York City was destroyed."

"When we get back home you can get a full history lesson from Cyber far faster than I can explain it here and now unless you want a violent insertion of memories via telepathy."

"No." Anna shook her head violently. "I don't think I would like that."

"Good choice." Ilana smiled in what she hoped would be a comforting gesture. "Right now all you need to know is that we are the ones fighting for survival for all people. Exceptionals are far from the insidious species the military paints us to be. We're the victims of a virus. We just want to survive. To live. Like everyone else. Now please get on the plane. Hold onto the armrest, this plane has no stealth. We'll be in for a bumpy ride."

"I'm already on a bumpy ride."

"It'll get worse before it gets better."

Abigail paced the length of the room, turning an envelope over and over again. She knew she should pay attention to Warren's side of the conversation with James. Only Warren's mention of an amazing doctor stopped her in her tracks. The reasons behind saying such a thing could only mean something happened to be terribly wrong. So what else was new?

"We need to be ready when James gets back with this one. She says she's dying." Warren turned his chair to face her.

"What are we dealing with?" Her demeanor shifted to business. The distraction of the envelope faded to little more than trembling hands. When faced with a challenge, she did as she always did best, faced it head on.

"Not sure. All I know is there were troops closing in on them." His already grim frown deepened. He rose. "James said they had to go. From here it's up to him, Ilana and Caiman to get her home."

"I'll see what I can scrounge up test wise. We're running dangerously low on supplies again." She let go of the envelope with one hand to run it through her hair. "ETA?"

She jumped when he laced his fingers with hers. He held a hint of a smile, but the underlying concern she could sense thanks to her personal mutation clouded the warmth. His lips brushed across her forehead. "Is it the new girl? James and the others will get them out in time. They always do."

"It's not that." Her gaze drifted down to the envelope still gripped tight in her other hand. "I got this delivery today."

"Delivery?" His brows knit together. The concern poured off him in waves she couldn't block thanks to her own nerves. "No one is supposed to know we're here."

"The important people do," she whispered.

Warren's fingers danced along her cheek before he tucked a lock of hair behind her ear. "Gail. Focus."

"Sorry." She squeezed her eyes shut to steady herself as well as block the emotions around her. The shock of what she'd found in the envelope had jarred her normally strong and steady shields. She blew out a breath and handed him the envelope.

"Playing card?" Warren's eyebrow quirked as he removed the seemingly normal item from the envelope. He had yet to realize the implications. As he flipped it over in his fingers, he shook his head in confusion. "Someone sent you a playing card? No, wait. This isn't a playing card. What is this?"

"It's a tarot card." Abby bit down on her thumbnail.

"Since when do you know tarot cards?"

"The compound. Talisa had a deck herself. She did a reading for me once. Of course, I researched it after. Tal and I did together, actually." Tears nearly choked her. Guilt welled once again. They'd been so far away for the attack that had stolen so many of their family and friends from them. Their best friends, Tal and Roark especially. Even now the guilt pecked away at her soul.

"I miss them too, baby." Warren pulled her close. He kissed her temple, a soothing action that eased some of her trembling. "So, you were delivered this card and it reminded you of them?"

"Partially."

"Gail, what aren't you telling me?" He stepped back enough to level his gaze with hers.

"It was a soldier—who delivered it, I mean."

"One of Steele's men was here? He could go back and tell Steele where we are."

Abby wrapped her arms around herself against the rush of anger and paranoia that poured off him. "No need to worry. He barely made it to the edge of the perimeter. Dead before he hit the ground. Don't think it was natural causes, but it wasn't our men."

"And they found this on him?"

Abby didn't need her shields down to know the amount of tension pouring off her husband. "No uniform…no weapons. Just the envelope with my name on it."

"That makes no sense. Who would send you something like this?" Even in his tension, he ran a hand along her arm in an attempt to comfort her.

"It's a message. From Talisa." She held up her hand to stop his protest. "Before you tell me I think that just because I miss her, you're wrong. I know you're wrong, because of that card. It was Talisa's card."

"How is that possible?" Warren looked every bit as confused as conflicted as she felt. "There were all sorts of these decks before the War. Are you sure?"

"Positive." She worried her bottom lip between her teeth. "Talisa and I made this deck ourselves. It doesn't even look like a regular deck. We changed the symbols and no one else knew about it."

"I'd say. I don't remember any dream catchers in the Minor Arcana." He chuckled softly. After a shake of his head, he sighed deeply. "Only Talisa would think of something like that."

"The dream catchers are the pentacles." She traced her fingertip over the image of a wolf standing in the middle of the card. "The timber wolf is the king."

"So, this is the King of Pentacles?"

"It is. I helped her create the deck. We worked on it in our room." Her heart dropped at Warren's skeptical expression. "You don't believe me?"

"I want to. I really do. It's just…." He sighed. The brief smile vanished, replaced by a deep frown. "James and Ilana were there. Even with Roark and Tal's abilities, I don't see how they could have survived. I'm monitoring every channel I can. If they were still out there I would have picked up some sort of chatter by now."

"You think I don't know that?" She snapped. To stop her hands from shaking, she clenched them. "I'm a doctor. I know damn well it should have killed them instantly, even with their mutations. Hell, Joe regenerated and I don't think they ever found all of him."

He reached for her, but she turned to walk to the door.

"I should have been here." Her voice dropped to a whisper. "I should have been here to help."

"Wait a minute. Back it up, Gail. There's nothing you could have done. What we were doing for those kids overseas was just as important. That was the key to finding out what the virus did to all of us." His arms circled her waist. "We could have been killed too if we had been here."

"What if they are alive? Charlotte still sees the threads that tie us all to them. Warren, what if this is her way of telling us that she and Roark are alive?" Tears welled in her eyes. "I'm so afraid to hope, but I'm the only one that knew about this deck."

Warren rubbed her shoulders. "Okay. So, let's say this *is* from Tal. What does it mean? For the two of you, does this card have a special meaning?"

"Most of the meanings are the same. Typically, the King of Pentacles means stability, power, security, and abundance. The wolf, the king is a father figure who takes care of others. It can also mean completing a task." She fixed her gaze on the card again. As she stared, she flipped it back and forth to search for any other clues. "What are you trying to tell me, Tal?"

"I want to believe this more than anything. Not just for us to have our friends back, but for James and the others to have their parents back." He scrubbed his hands over his face. "And to have two of our best fighters back."

"What do we do? Do we tell the others?" Abby pulled away to pace the room. "If it's true we have to find them and bring them home."

Warren stepped after her as she walked the length of the room several more times. "Gail."

"You think I'm crazy, don't you?"

"No. I don't." He cupped her cheek. "You're hopeful. That's rare these days, but it isn't crazy. We do have to take certain things into consideration, though."

"Such as?"

"On the off chance they are alive—this could be a trap." Warren sighed. "This could be Steele's way of flushing us out."

"What if it's not, though? What if she sent this because they need us?" She held onto his hands so tight he winced. "I can see it in your eyes. You think I might be right."

He smirked. After a minute his features softened. "The only reason you see that is because we've been married so long. I don't know how he'll react to the possibility, but you know we need to tell Chance."

"Are you sure?" She released her grip on his hand. Relieved he actually believed her hope flowed over her. "He's been saying he thought she was alive since right after the explosion that took them from us."

"That's the part that worries me. We don't know how he'll react. Talisa was his best friend."

"She was my best friend too!"

"Woah." He lifted his hands in surrender. "I didn't mean anything by it, baby. We all felt the loss in different ways."

Abby leaned into him with a shaky breath. She accepted his soft kiss to her forehead and relaxed. "I'm sorry. I'm just on edge."

"Don't apologize. We've all been on edge for a long time." His body twitched. When she lifted her head, she found his tilted to the side. "Ilana and Anna are at the plane. Soon as the other two get there they'll take off. They'll be home soon and hopefully we can help her."

"I hope so too. Details on what she's dying from would be nice but I'll have to wait until they get here, I guess." She took a deep breath, desperate to change the subject. "Any word on the latest scouting trip?"

"Nothing yet. Chance said some of the plants they found have taken root and are growing well. I'm not sure what he's growing, though. Could be medicinal…or lettuce. Not real sure."

A genuine smile emerged. The twitch of his lips prompted her own laugh. "Maybe we'll get lucky and it's both."

"There's my girl." Warren tucked his finger under her chin. He lifted her lips for a gentle kiss. "We can hope we get both."

"That's all we really have right now—hope."

"And a tarot card."

The flight to the compound seemed normal, uneventful even.

As uneventful as escaping from soldiers chasing them, a woman that could sprout wings and fly, a decrepit old barn, and an aircraft that appeared to be held together by duct tape and bubble gum could possibly be.

Annie wondered briefly if bubble gum still existed. Contemplations like that were the best distraction she had as she kept her eyes screwed shut for the duration of the flight. One hand clutched the bag on her lap while the other dug into what was left of an armrest.

Solid ground. Was that too much to ask?

The other passengers talked the entire flight. No, they picked on each other. Now and then for a brief moment she could have sworn she heard a smile, almost laughter, in James' voice. Such a thing seemed unlikely. She held the conviction he'd been born scowling.

"Anna, we're here." James spoke close by. His voice stirred her to open her eyes. He towered over her, arms folded across his chest.

Mission accomplished and he still appeared permanently pissed off. "And where is here exactly?" Did he ever smile?

Annie rolled her neck from side to side in an effort to get rid of some of the stiffness.

"Montana. What's left of it anyway. As wide open and unpopulated as the state was, it didn't get hit as bad as states with major cities." He tapped his foot in a quick cadence against the metal floor. "We need to move."

"Right. You're the impatient one."

"Look, Anna…!" The growl re-emerged.

If James stood as the group's version of a welcome wagon, the reason for their dwindling numbers couldn't be clearer. "It's Annie. Please. Anna is my grandmother's name."

A scoff escaped his gritted teeth.

She pushed on the armrest, not at all surprised when it tumbled to the floor. Her eyes fluttered shut. "Sorry."

"It'll get fixed."

She muttered under her breath, "So much for finding my parents before I kick the bucket."

"Anna—Annie," he corrected himself. "You can't think like that. It could still happen."

"Right. Next, you're going to tell me Santa Claus, the Easter Bunny, and the Tooth Fairy are all downstairs." She pressed her lips together tight in an effort to reign in her emotions. Even with that, her fingers shook on their way to grab the strap of her bag. "I'm sorry. This whole thing is just…well I don't know what it is."

James' expression softened. "I know it's a lot to take in. I can explain more once we are inside where it's safer."

For the first time since they landed she realized they were alone. "Where are the others?"

"They had something to take care of."

So, they left her stuck with tall, dark, and angry? Great. "Lead the way, then."

Off the plane they wound up on a broken-down street. Several houses lined what she imagined had once been a nice, suburban sort of street bustling with kids and soccer moms in their SUV's. Hard to believe it would have been only a year ago when the world had blown up. The way nature had already taken over, it seemed like ages since the street had seen any regular traffic.

They walked into the first house on the right without so much as a knock. She wanted to ask why they didn't stop in any rooms, but held herself back. Despite the fact that he led her straight toward a door that framed steps descending into a basement, she followed him.

She'd already come this far and really, where would she go? A maniacal sort of giggle filled with nerves and humor over the craziness bubbled to the surface. "You pull me from my home to a place in the middle of nowhere and the first place you take me is a basement. This isn't serial-killer worthy at all."

"Hard to have serial killers with so few people to kill…and not everything is as it seems, smartass." The barest hint of a smile graced his features before he wiped it clean away.

"Careful. You almost smiled there. I might begin to wonder if you were feeling well or not." Another laugh reached for the surface. "Sorry. If I don't laugh I'm liable to end up thinking I'm in an episode of the *Twilight Zone*."

James jogged down the steps without turning around. "We all do whatever we have to get by."

He led her straight to a dead end. The room looked like any normal basement before or after the War. Shelves with boxes and canned foods lined the walls. A few bags here and there on the shelves and floor lent to the general idea of a still-functioning home.

Then James reached through a few of the boxes and things got weird again.

The wall moved. It swung inward to reveal a wide metallic corridor. The bags remained on the floor where the shelves had been, but with a simple step over them they'd be in whatever that place was. Before the wall had moved, Annie had seen no sign of a seam in the wall at all.

She blinked several times. "And this day just keeps getting weirder."

"You haven't seen the half of it yet." James motioned for her to go through ahead of him. "Every house in the area has an access port like this."

"Everyone is underground?"

"Not everyone. We take turns staying topside. We're still human, we still need sunlight." He paused at an intersection in the tunnel. "That leads to the house next door."

"But it looks so deserted up there." She scanned the tunnel as they kept walking. After walking a few feet, a familiar sensation hit her like a ton of bricks. Once she hadn't felt in a while. A rush of energy that left her near giddy. Computers— lots of them. "You have a full functioning computer network."

"Yeah. No getting any ideas, though. Cy has them locked down tight. You won't get anywhere no matter how hard you try."

"No ideas. It's just an odd feeling after not being able to feel it for so long." She trailed her fingers along the wall. The construction impressed her. "The tunnels haven't always been here, I'm assuming. So how did they get here?"

"We have a few mutants that are good with that sort of thing." He shrugged as he punched in a code to open the next section. "We have a few…uh…containment cells in here."

"Containment cells? I thought you said you were the good guys." Annie took a step away from the door. She searched for another path they could take.

"Would ya chill out?" He rolled his eyes. "We're not gonna lock you up. Some mutants are more dangerous. California sank to the bottom of the ocean because of an Exceptional that got really pissed off and lost control. Although he kinda went down with the ship so to speak."

"Why do we have to go through this way?"

"It's faster."

Somehow she doubted that. She couldn't help but suspect he took new people this way to make sure they knew containment was a possibility. She proceeded with caution down the corridor, but found herself drawn to a cell.

Inside a woman rocked back and forth in the corner. Her hair sat askew, disheveled only slightly less than her clothes.

"What's her story?"

"That's Lucy. She was a fortuneteller with a traveling carnival. Went completely insane during the War."

"What's her mutation?" Annie couldn't drag her gaze away from the woman in the corner of the cell.

"When she looks at someone she can see their future. She couldn't handle it, especially seeing so many deaths no matter where she went." James shrugged beside her. Without another word, he pulled away to move down the hall.

"That's kind of sad, don't you think?" Annie stared at his retreating back. With no answer, she turned back to the cell. Lucy's gaze lifted to meet hers with such intensity, Annie gasped.

"You have no future. Not supposed to be here. Borrowed time. Yes, borrowed time." Lucy paused before she tore her eyes away and resumed her rocking.

"Thanks for the vote of confidence." Annie deflated, her shoulders sagging. "Anything else creepy I need to see?"

"This is nothing. Don't you remember the telethon a few years back?"

"A telethon? You're kidding me, right? Our own freaky-freak version of Jerry's Kids or something?" She didn't hesitate to leave the containment cell area the second he opened the door. He led her into another hallway.

"So, you didn't see it?" He spun to face her, his eyes wide, features pale.

She ran her fingers self-consciously through her hair. "No. Never heard of it."

"Wow. An Exceptional with a talent like yours shouldn't be so obtuse. What's your game?"

"No game." She fought the urge to back away under the accusatory stance he took. "My parents didn't like to see me in the middle of the debate. I looked human, unlike some of the Infected—"

"Exceptionals," James snapped. "Don't ever demean our position like *they* do."

"So-orry." She straightened her shoulders. "So, I was to act human! We avoided the debates, all of it. We all laid low. Unlike some people, I don't feel it's necessary to provoke others. Including my own parents."

James flinched when she said 'parents'. He shook his shoulders like ridding himself of a nasty thought. Then he spun away and moved again. "Doesn't matter. We're going to make sure you're thoroughly checked. Can't trust a computer Exceptional as obtuse as you."

She straightened her shoulders against the clear insult. While her first instinct was to snap back a retort, she bit her tongue. When she had a hold on her anger, she spoke again. "So this telethon? Why did you bring it up?"

"Didn't work out too well." Whatever sharing mood he might have had was clearly gone. He didn't bother to elaborate any further. He inclined his head down the hallway. "We're almost to Cyber's office. I know you're anxious to meet him."

"I don't know if anxious is the word I'd use."

"What word would you use?"

"Curious."

"Curiosity killed the cat, ya know."

"Good thing I don't have whiskers, then."

James strode down the hall toward Warren's office quick as he could. The sooner he passed Anna off, the sooner he could go let off steam. Something about being near this woman made his already taut nerves shatter.

For her part, Anna still laughed under her breath at her own little joke. Apparently tension made the woman giddy. Either that, or she was cracking under the pressure. Around the compound such a thing wasn't exactly uncommon. Hiding from the world after being nearly destroyed wasn't exactly great on the psyche.

"Here we are." He pushed open Warren's office door. The brief relief he'd felt at passing Anna off, flew away when he found an empty office instead of Warren. "Damn it."

"What?" Anna followed him into the room, a soft gasp interrupting the smile she'd still been sporting. "Oh my."

James left the door open, surprised at his own amusement by the sight of her enraptured by Warren's wall of monitors, and half a dozen keyboards, and then the four laptops. Only time he'd seen such joy at the sight of technology was on Warren himself.

In a heartbeat, James shook off the amusement and hardened his thoughts again. After everything he'd been through, he didn't need the distraction of a woman hell-bent on cracking his hard-earned shell. He lifted his cell to text Warren, but Warren beat him to the punch, the incoming text buzzed through before he'd opened his messaging window.

Something came up. Be there soon as we can.

"Damn." He shoved the phone back in his pocket. "Cyber's been delayed. Have a seat, we'll wait here. Not there, over there."

Anna's smile faded at his direction, but she took the seat he'd pointed to, well away from the wall of computers. If she was as talented as Warren, it wouldn't matter much, but he preferred her distance in case she wasn't.

James took Warren's seat and folded his arms across his chest. Rather than face the girl, he stared at the door, willing Warren to appear.

"So, are we going to sit in sullen silence?" Anna broke the tension-filled silence. "Or do you want to tell me about this telethon?"

"Silence." James didn't flinch away from the door. Nervousness clawed at his militant calm. He'd trained for years to be a warrior, and to embrace the calm his well-crafted nature tried to deny him. Every bit of that calm had blown to smithereens with his parents. Now he clung to the tension that kept him alive, his heart beating, and his outward appearance of stone.

"Really? How long do we have to wait?"

He gritted his teeth and tried to ignore her, but her knee bounced rapidly. His sensitive ears picked out each tiny squeak of her sneaker on the floor.

"Wow. You really mean silence. I can't do that. I'm nervous."

"I'm not your babysitter, I don't care."

"Actually, you are my so-called babysitter, unless you want to leave me alone in a room full of computers." When he finally looked her way, the goofy grin on her features was completely contrary to the nervous twisting of her hands.

"Or I could just sit you in a cell while you wait." The joke was the opposite of funny, he knew it—yet she giggled. He sighed. "You really want to hear about the stupid telethon?"

"Yes. Please. Anything but leaving me in silence."

"Fine." James sighed. "The telethon. It was supposed to raise money and awareness as to what we really are. So maybe they'd stop calling us the 'Infected'. Also, the hope was to raise money for those hurt by the military, and their families. It was all my mom's idea."

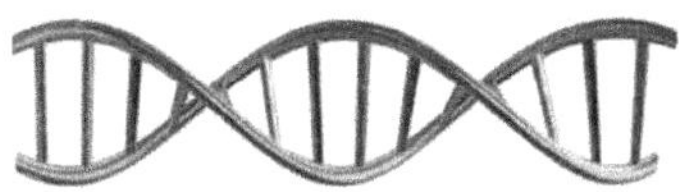

Five Years Earlier

"No. I don't want this to be a parade or a freak show for the viewing public's pleasure." Talisa slammed down her clipboard. "We aren't a circus side show. This is serious. Any day now they could launch an all-out attack to try to wipe us out."

Roark walked up behind her and rubbed her shoulders. "I agree, Li—but we also have to make some bit of a show. There has to be at least a few of the infected that have physical alterations for the world to see."

"Stop saying that. I *hate* that. *Infected* has such a negative connotation." She pressed her hands into the table, but her shoulders sagged as Roark continued to rub them. "We aren't infected we're…that's it! We're the 'Exceptionals', not the 'Infected'."

Roark chuckled. "I like it. I bet Abby will, too. Now back to the cast."

"I won't let it be a freak show," she protested. "We're better than that."

"Everyone has volunteered." Roark sighed. "They know what they're getting into."

James' hands clenched together and his low growl filled the room. "This whole thing is a freak show. Why don't we just fight already? I'm sick of the subterfuge. You've got Cyber running so many pathways for this thing, the entire country is wired for battle. I'm sick of hiding and cowering."

"James." Talisa's tone switched in a flash. The frustration melted into concern and warmth he knew she reserved for all her kids. She smoothed her hand along his head before she rubbed his back. "If we go into an all-out war, the destruction could be extreme, especially with the skills of the Exceptionals and the weapons of the military. Right now, our best defense is counteracting the propaganda. This telethon will take a huge leap in that direction."

"We're taking every precaution to make sure every inch of this telethon is safe." Roark straddled a nearby chair, meeting

James' gaze level. Despite his apparent calm air, James knew his father was as tense as James was. "Cyber is running all interference, making everything un-hackable by even the best military minds. There are P.O. boxes all over the country in the offices where our best In—sorry, Exceptionals are working. If this fails, you might just get your wish."

"It's not a wish," Talisa snapped. "We don't want a war. It would be too vast. Too many innocent lives, human and Exceptional, would be lost. I like a good fight as much as either of you, but I don't want a war."

"No one does." Roark rubbed his hand over his face and heaved a sigh.

"It's going to happen." James shrugged off Talisa's hand and rose. "Don't delude yourselves into thinking this freak show is going to do anything but make them angrier. It will make them hunt us down even harder. I'm supposed to be protecting our people!"

"And you do protect them." She sat on the edge of the table. "But we have to do whatever we can to make people know what we really are. How we were created."

"Look at everyone here, James." Roark gestured to the office window. The crew was setting up for the first hour of the telethon. Humans and Exceptionals greeted each other like old friends. Some took their seats behind phones, others showed off their infection-given talents. "They all have hope for something better. We need to foster the hope, not the fear."

"You've turned into such a weak old man," James snarled. "I remember when you both used to fight first and bother with science later."

Before James could blink, his mother had him pinned to the floor. She snarled in his face with her full animal in force. The animal had come out in most of her family in some fashion when the infection had first spread, which gave them each better hearing and senses, and a crap-load of a temper.

Talisa's arm pressed into his trachea, cutting off his air supply. "We lost a lot of good people that way. I almost didn't live the last time we tried to fight first. If the day comes that we need to fight you know your dad and I will be on the front lines. Right now we are doing whatever we can to keep you and your siblings safe for as long as we possibly can! You need to stop being such an angry little brat and start using the brain I created you with!"

"Li." Roark pried her off James. "Let him breathe."

Air rushed into his lungs so fast, James coughed until the tingle of healing took over and all the pain subsided. "Damn it, Ma!"

Roark's growl mimicked Talisa's. "Remember, son. We've been fighting since before you were created. You have the need for battle in you, but you haven't had to live with nearly half the consequences we have. I hope you never have to."

"I hope I never get as weak as you two have." James spun on his heel and stormed from the office. For extra measure, he slammed the door behind him.

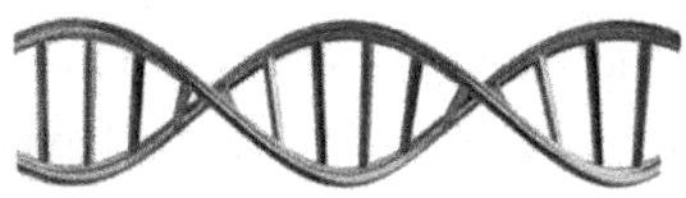

2023

James clenched his jaw, glaring at his fists where they pressed into his thighs. The consequences he'd ended up facing were far worse than he'd ever expected. Worse than his parents had ever expected. "I was right. Everything escalated after the telethon. Within a year the War began. Small skirmishes grew into larger battles. Then a year ago the global militaries sent out the mass destruction efforts."

"And your mom was right about the innocent lives," Annie whispered.

"To say the least." James straightened and tugged the phone from his pocket. After he'd sent off a quick text, he hopped to his feet. He had to get out of there before she stirred up any other emotions he'd have to burn off in practice battle with his sister. "Gotta go. Cyber will be along soon enough."

"Wait. What?" She rose, her features pale. "I'm just supposed to sit and wait?"

"Something like that. I don't care what you do. Just know that every move you make is watched." James stormed to the door and closed it behind him. The memory was too much, he never should have shared. He couldn't be around anyone like her while he dealt with it. She was a stranger, an unknown, and it had to stay that way.

"That was rude, big brother." Charlotte touched his arm. The concern in her eyes made him keenly aware of how much she'd heard. "Go on. Caiman is waiting for you in the training room. I think after that, you need it. I'll wait with Anna."

"Annie. She wants to be called Annie."

Talisa double-checked the test tubes lined up in a perfect row. Across the impenetrable glass she noted Roark's equally precise set of test tubes. Today would be the first of their biggest deceptions yet. The last thing they needed was a mistake.

During the first months of their captivity, they'd tested Steele's resources. They'd learned he had someone that spoke Lenape and could translate if they used their native tongue. Through intentional mistakes in formulas and results, they'd learned they were still the most brilliant minds he had within his grasp.

All of this meant they could develop a new alteration to the initial infection right under the man's nose. Thankfully they'd developed a sort of secret code years ago when they first realized Steele was after super-soldiers, not a cure for diseases like cancer.

It had taken another two months for them to perfect the secret communication for their current predicament. As an extra measure of cruelty, Steele had locked them in one large room, separated by a clear, impenetrable glass. They were watched constantly from above and with cameras located strategically around the room. The bathrooms even had a camera, although they allowed a measure of privacy with the toilet.

Every single day she worked beside, and talked to, her husband, but they hadn't touched even a finger in almost a year. It was enough to drive Tal to distraction, seeing her husband every day like this.

"Tal?" Roark stepped up to the glass. As they did often to approximate closeness, his hand pressed to the glass. "You all right in there?"

"Just missing you." She set her hand against the glass opposite his. "Call it wallowing, if you want."

"I wouldn't, because that would mean I wallow, and men don't wallow." He winked and leaned closer. "Are you ready to test the K-five and G-fourteen's today?"

Steele sanctioned experiments were always G's. Their own personal experiment was under K, although they always ran one of Steele's alongside it to fool the riffraff. K-five, if it worked as their formulas suggested, would be a game changer on many levels. She nodded. "Ready."

Roark tapped the glass with his palm before stepping back to his lab table. She followed suit without hesitation. There was no time left for speculation. Her measurements had to be precise, or she could end up with some very bad side effects.

For almost two hours they worked in virtual silence. She remained painfully aware of their guard dogs behind the darkened sheet of glass above them. Though certain the men were often half-asleep, bored with the science speech of her and Roark, the cameras were ever vigilant.

During the past few months they'd come to realize that their guards during the morning shift were the most careless. No one expected them to pull something when Steele was on the premises, or during normal business hours.

For some reason, they were convinced Roark and Tal tried things in the evenings and overnights. Maybe because they spent some hours whispering in Lenape and English. Sometimes sweet nothings, sometimes formulas. Other times they'd get up and do some late-night calisthenics around the lab.

Their Exceptional status, as Tal preferred to call it over Steele's demeaning 'Infected' title, left both Tal and Roark with animalistic alterations to their cell structure. Increased senses, stamina, and healing were some of the best attributes of the change—if you weren't holed up in a cage somewhere. They used that as the excuse for the random eruptions in movement and workouts they performed. All to keep their guards, and Steele, on guard at odd hours.

As per norm, Roark finished at the same time as Tal. They leaned on their lab tables and locked gazes through the glass. Tal smiled, her mood bolstered by the results she'd seen under the microscope. "Race you to the pill press."

"Eat my dust, Li." Roark laughed as he grabbed his own powder presses. He got to his tablet press a second after Tal, and she already had one die in place.

"You're getting slow in your old age, dear."

"Maybe I thought it would be best to let my wife win."

"You've never let me win a day in my life. You're too much a pain in my ass." She chuckled and lined up the presses into place. Inside the press was a partly filled cast that she'd skimmed over for weeks as she'd built the formula.

Every month they tested their multivitamins for unwanted drugs Steele might slip them. This past month, Tal had re-pressed all but one. Over the past few weeks she'd added bits and pieces of the formula. Today, as she dropped the last of the powder in, it would be complete.

She intentionally bumped the press she'd filled too far with today's addition. With her gloved hand, she brushed the powder into the die beside the hole, and then set the press into place.

The pill created from that powder would do nothing but create a placebo effect of increased mental stamina in the person that took it. The mix was totally harmless until mixed with what she'd put in her multivitamin.

"Mental stamina," Roark interrupted her thoughts. "For you. Speed for me."

She knew he said it aloud for the cameras watching them, but it annoyed her. "I'm not a child. I know that."

"Smile for the camera, baby."

Tal grimaced and made a face at the camera in the wall. "That work?"

"It does for me." He chuckled and closed the door. "Ten pills in the chute, half and half."

"Ten pills in the chute. Half placebo, half true drug." None of the drugs they created would ever work. The last thing Tal or Roark would ever do was actually help Steele. Still, they did enough to make the soldiers think they worked. All effects were always temporary, but enough to keep Steele from killing them and finding new brainiac's to solve his problems.

Roark started his press. Tal followed right behind. As the pills started to come out, Roark counted off. "One. Two. Three. Four. Five. Six."

Tal cupped her hands under the chute to catch her pills as they came out. A habit she'd adopted months before when they'd first started their attempts to change her existing DNA alterations. Steele either wrote it off as a quirk, or didn't notice. Either way, it had helped her get four whole first round tests complete.

Although she was perfectly content with her animal side and her fire abilities were killer-fun, they were useless to getting to the outside world. One thing would help, without a doubt.

Telepathy.

She had no idea if Abby had received her message, or if the soldier had died long before he'd reached their compound. He'd been half dead when he'd gone out the door. Steele had been infuriated at his disappearance, so he might have had the man killed.

"Nine. Ten."

Tal shook her head to clear it. She returned her attention to the pills in her hand. To appear as if she were counting them like Roark, she shifted them around. As she counted, the final pill slipped into her hand and she cupped them together. "Ten here, too." She walked back to the lab table where the pill bottle waited to be filled.

Roark dropped his pills into his bottle and closed it.

She slipped the pills in her cupped hands so they would pour out slow. Intentionally, she pinched her finger close to the palm so the tiny pills she'd made for the soldiers would spill out, while the larger multivitamin would get caught.

While he pretended to not pay attention, more focused on his notes, Tal knew he was focused on what she was doing. The pills were intentionally mixed up, the only difference being a letter on top. They didn't want Steele to know which was the placebo and which was the—well, placebo, but a functioning placebo. They'd reveal that after. All Steele was supposed to do was note which soldier got what marking. In the end, they'd even reduced the matter to putting five different symbols on the pills.

To further Steele's cluelessness, and help keep his observations on course, they never wrote down what was what, just relied on their own memories.

With the pills in place, she popped the lid on and grabbed her pen. She wrote her own notes, then dropped the pen into her pocket along with the pill. "Ready for delivery."

"Think these will work?"

"Has anything?"

"Not yet, but have hope."

"I always do."

Chance focused on the two exceptionally large roots that burrowed deep into the earth before him. Bits of dirt and debris flew back toward him. Initially the expansion of the tunnels hadn't been scheduled for another week or so, but after his talk with Warren and Abby he had extra energy to burn.

The tarot card now in his possession gnawed at his soul. Question after question swirled and twisted in his head much like the roots he controlled. Talisa had teased him often when it came to his choice of meditation methods.

"You wanted to see us, Chief?" James' voice barely cut through the sound of the roots burrowing ever deeper. "I thought we weren't starting this section yet."

"You aren't the only one that needs to blow off steam from time to time." Chance continued digging without turning around. "How did the mission go?"

"We got the girl out." Caiman joined the conversation, her typical bored tone firmly in place. The girl had two positions when it came to Chance's dealings with her: bored and pissed. At least today she was on the bored side of things, for now. He'd hate to see her starting in pissed and then hearing his news. "There were a few complications, though."

"What kind of complications?" The roots slowed at the news. Complications were never a good thing in their world such as it was.

"Says she's dying. Char is with her now. Guess Abby's gonna look her over or something." Caiman went the extra step of a deep yawn. Her sense of compassion needed serious work. Without Talisa, that would likely never happen.

"You're awful quiet about this one, James." Chance turned to face the two children of his best friends. The roots stopped their digging and came to rest on the ground behind him after a simple twitch of his fingers. "You're usually more vocal about the new ones."

"Not much to tell." James shrugged, his arms folded across his chest, one foot propped on the wall behind him. "Doesn't know a whole lot. Barely remembers the War, doesn't remember the telethon at all or anything like that."

"Interesting." Chance wondered how an Exceptional couldn't remember everything.

James attempted to appear as bored as Caiman, but a hint of something more lingered in his features. Almost like he had one ear listening for the woman. "What came up earlier?"

"That's what I wanted to talk to you two about." A smaller vine next to Chance wrapped around the water bottle on the floor to lift it to his waiting hand. "Seems we had a delivery today. Well, Abby did."

Caiman's eyebrow lifted. The simple action reminded Chance just how much Caiman and her twin Charlotte looked like their mother, Talisa. "Delivered? Didn't realize the postal service went back to work. Then again, roads such as they are was it the pony express?"

"No. No mail trucks or mustangs here. A soldier showed up."

"A soldier?" James pushed off the wall, a low threatening growl under his words. "Why didn't anyone tell me?"

"I'm telling you now, aren't I? Relax." Chance straightened against the hint of possible subordination from his warrior. He folded his arms across his chest. "He had no uniform on, and was unarmed. The only thing he had on him was a sealed envelope with Abby's name on it."

"And *in* the envelope?" James inquired.

"A tarot card." Chance stuffed down his own emotions in an attempt to keep them in check. In all honesty, the whole thing bothered him. Despite Warren and Abby's explanations, he couldn't get over how it happened.

Why would Talisa send a message to Abby and not to him? Sure, the message had been risky, but he'd been best friends with Talisa since they were children.

"One of Lucy's friends?" James interest deflated. "What does it have to do with anything? And why's it got your panties in a bunch?"

"He's got a point." Caiman spoke up from her corner. Though her comments spoke of curiosity, she picked at dirt under her nails. "A playing card? What's that got to do with anything?"

"Abby swears it's from Talisa." Chance paused to let the information sink in. "She said it is part of a deck she and Tal made when they were both working in the program for Steele."

"That's impossible." James hit the metal wall hard enough to make it ring. His sister cringed at the onslaught of the tone. He growled and paced the length of the corridor. "We saw them blown up in that explosion. We know what happened. Why the hell would Abby drag them out of the grave like that?"

"It's not like she's saying it to screw with our head, James." Chance tried to keep the calm head he was supposed to be so famous for. "She's just as torn up about this but swears it's the same card."

"Anyone could have sent it," Caiman interrupted.

"Abby says no one else knew about the cards or what they meant to them. Not even Warren or Roark." Chance blew out a shaky breath, his head drooped. "I'm inclined to believe her. I didn't know about them and there wasn't much Tal and I didn't share."

James raked his hand through his hair. "So, if it's true then what are we doing about it?"

"If we were doing something about it right now do you think I'd be working on the expansion?" Chance smirked.

Caiman frowned as she looked between her brother and Chance. "So, we're doing nothing about it because…why?"

"Because we don't have enough information yet. Warren is looking into it, but he's also dealing with Anna at the moment." Chance downed half the water in the bottle.

"We have an obligation to look for them," James snapped. Tension radiated off him so much Chance could have sworn the floor shook with it.

Chance's temper flared over his usually strong control until the vines on the floor behind him quivered. He held a firm, almost-angry stare down against James. "You think I don't know that, James? You think I don't think about your parents every single day? We cannot go charging in somewhere if we don't know where that is. Warren will work on it soon as Anna is settled."

"What's the point of processing her if she's dying?" James' words flew out with venom, but immediate regret filled the young man's complicated gaze.

"Shall we just feed her to the wolves too?" Chance sighed against the onslaught of anger. He'd expected it from James, who always was so angry anymore. "Don't you think I want to go out there and find them? To bring them back here if it's the real thing?"

"No. You want to stay down here and dig a damn tunnel and *meditate*." James' fire had returned, full of frustration over having her hands tied.

"James." Caiman laid her hand on her brother's arm. In an unusual, and curiosity-piquing turn, she seemed to be calm about the whole situation. "Stop. We're supposed to keep the family together. Tearing the Chief apart isn't doing that."

"I'm right there with you both. I want nothing more than to bring them home as soon as possible. I want to see Charlotte flip us all the bird while telling us she told us so." Chance scrubbed his hands over his face. Charlotte had never once believed her parents were dead. "I know you're anxious but we have to wait until Warren gives us the go-ahead."

"Why can't he multitask while he's processing Annie?" James's fists remained clenched.

"I'm sure he is." The fact James used a nickname for their new arrival didn't slip past him, but Chance decided to let it slide for the time being. "Just like you have to keep your siblings together it's my job to keep what is left of this tribe together. I promise you the moment we have something we will act on it."

Caiman briefly nodded. "Who else is being told?"

"I'll tell Charlotte myself once she's done helping Abby with Anna and the others are up to you. It is not to go beyond the family, though." Chance had a passing thought of another who had lost family in the defining battle of the War. "And please don't let it get back to Ariel. She wasn't having a good day."

"Fine. We'll wait until Cy has more." The scowl on James' face left little to the imagination as to how he felt about the whole situation.

Chance reached over to give James' shoulder a light squeeze. "We all have promises to keep James. Sometimes we just don't get to keep them the way we wanted to."

Charlotte cracked the door with an obligatory rap of her knuckles to announce her arrival. She flashed a quick smile at the woman inside before she stepped in the room. "I should apologize about my brother. Unfortunately, he never developed tact."

Annie looked up with her own smile hesitant. "It's fine. He seemed pretty upset when he left. It's my fault for asking about the telethon I guess. Is he okay?"

"Even if he was upset, leaving the way he did was rude. There's just been a lot going on around here today." She shrugged. "Entertaining isn't one of his strong suits. He much prefers action over decorum."

"Entertaining? Is that the new polite term for babysitting? I mean, that is why you're here isn't it? To keep an eye on me until this Cyber guy and your doctor can find time for me," Annie snapped. She let her eyes flutter shut as she sighed out her frustration. "Sorry. This isn't your fault. I'm a little bit on edge here and my head is killing me."

Charlotte reached over to squeeze Annie's hand. She felt for the girl. Yes, things were crazy in the compound, but not an hour before Annie had been ripped from the life she had known and brought into the middle of chaos. "It's fine, really. I know this is a lot to take in. By the way, I'm Charlotte. It's nice to meet you, Annie."

"You know my name?"

"James told me." Charlotte stood and held out her hand. "Come with me."

"James told you?" Shock was clear on Annie's pale features as she took Charlotte's hand.

Charlotte swiped a quick text to Warren to let him know they were going to get some medicine for Annie's headache across the hall in the small clinic. It wasn't the full-blown hospital wing, but they had supplies laid in there. "Yes."

"Huh." Annie followed her across the hall in stunned silence.

"Well, he told me you prefer Annie over Anna." Something more than just discussing the telethon had bothered her brother. In the past, he'd never got attached to anyone they brought in, or really anyone for that matter. He was much like Caiman in that aspect, who only really felt attached to her husband and their mother. The mere fact James took time to fill Charlotte in on Annie's preference spoke volumes to her.

"Don't think he likes me very much." Annie's gaze dropped her to lap.

"That's just James. He covers up a lot with anger." Charlotte stayed in constant motion. She pulled out the supplies she'd need and lined them up on the counter in and almost OCD line. A behavior she'd learned from her parents. "Let's see what we can do about that headache, shall we?"

Annie's head snapped up. She winced at the sudden motion. "How are you going to help with that?"

"Abby isn't the only doctor here." Charlotte flashed a grin as she grabbed her pen light. "I'm just going to take a look at your eyes first, okay?"

"Wait. You're a doctor? We're the same age." Annie blinked rapidly at the revelation. The moment the light hit her eyes she squinted against it.

"Try to keep your eyes open. I'm sorry. I know it hurts." She jotted down a few notes on the pad next to her. "And yes, I'm a doctor. I took my GED at fifteen and started college right away. Finished my residency not long before the first big attack."

"Wow." Annie flinched when Charlotte shone the lights in her eyes again. "Sorry. I'm trying. Light only started to hurt here recently."

Charlotte continued to alternate between taking notes and examining the woman in front of her. "Don't apologize. Abby will look you over more extensively, but I can tell something is definitely going on here. We've been able to get a lot of equipment scavenged down here over the last few months. We have a full-blown hospital wing though some supplies are scarce." She placed a reassuring hand on Annie's arm.

"I guess Mr. Personality left out the part about me dying. I've been learning to deal with it." Annie's shoulders slumped. "I doubt there is anything you guys can do."

"We'll see what the tests say. Anything is possible." She focused on her notes to ensure they were thorough. Her heart constricted. The way her eyes reacted to the light told her a good portion of the story. If a brain tumor or something in that realm were present then Annie's assessment was spot on.

"What does your husband do?"

"I'm sorry?" Charlotte tensed at Annie's question.

"Your husband. He a doctor too? You're wearing a wedding ring."

Innocent questions from their new addition appeared to hit sore spots with the people she met. Annie had no way of knowing, so Charlotte did her best to not react with much emotion. "He was. He was an amazing doctor."

"Was?" Annie's question laced with curiosity and sadness wove into Charlotte's heart.

"I lost him in one of the attacks." Once again, her heart shattered into a million pieces the moment she spoke the words aloud.

"I am so sorry." Annie fiddled with a loose thread on her shirt. "Gee, I'm just batting a thousand with questions that upset people today."

"It's okay. There's no way you could have known."

"C-can I ask what happened?" She held up her hands quick as if in surrender. "I totally understand if you don't want to talk about it."

"About a year ago." Charlotte's voice shook. "We'd gone on a mission to help some of the children affected by the virus. We separated so we could get more accomplished. The goal was to get back here to the compound quicker."

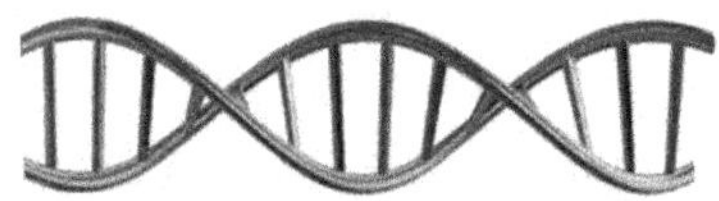

September 12, 2022

"Neil. I don't know if that is such a good idea. We can both go to Indiana and then head to St. Louis from there." Charlotte knew her husband was well aware of her feelings on the matter. She absolutely hated the plane.

"If we each go to one we can get them both done and be on our way back to the compound that much quicker." Neil tucked an ebony curl behind her ear.

"Call me crazy, or paranoid, or whatever. I just don't have a good feeling about this." The dread twisted and gnawed at the pit of her stomach. Deep down she knew separating was not the right plan.

"I'm not thrilled with the idea of you being in harm's way at all, Char, but we need to take care of these kids." Neil cupped her cheek and pressed his lips to hers in a soft kiss.

Charlotte kissed him back but extracted herself from the embrace a moment later. "You do realize how sexist that sounds, right? I'm the one with offensive mutations and I can read the people around us if I need to."

The smile on Neil's face was all-too brief. He wrapped his arms around her waist to pull her close. "It's not sexist. You are my wife and I want you safe, it's nothing more than that. I don't want either of us out there any longer than necessary."

"I still don't like it." She wrapped her arms around his neck. Her lower lip edged out in a pout. "Why can't one of the other doctors go to Indiana? We could go back to the compound and book some time in the underground spring."

"As much as I would love that, baby—these children need our help and you know it. Neither of us would forgive ourselves if we didn't help them." His lips brushed along her neck with a feather-light touch. "However, when we get back from this mission some quality time in the spring sounds wonderful. Just the two of us."

"Keep that up and I'm not letting you go anywhere." A soft giggle floated between them. Pleasant tingles from his kisses eased her frayed nerves, and she suspected his Exceptional ability had something to do it. She gave him a pass on the manipulation this time. "We need some time just for us after these missions."

"You don't know how tempting it is to take you up on you keeping me prisoner is." He shook his head with a sigh. "We need to get going if we're going to meet our contacts on time."

Tears welled in Charlotte's eyes. She did her best to push them aside. Their missions were essential to the well being of the Exceptionals her mother had fought so hard for. "You're right. I hate it, but you're right." Her arms tightened around him to hold him just a minute longer.

He didn't fight her hold. His fingers trailed down her back, soothing her with the simple touch.

"I can't lose you too." A few tears slipped past her control to etch down her cheeks. "We still haven't found my parents. I wouldn't survive if I lost you too."

His trembling lips pressed against her temple. "I promise you. I will be fine."

"Don't make promises you might not be able to keep." Charlotte released her hold enough to search his eyes. "You do what you need to do, no more. Then you come right back home. Come back to me."

A sad smile pulled at the corners of his lips. "I promise you I will do everything I can to come home to you and we'll have that time to ourselves."

Charlotte hugged him so tight she feared she might break him. "I love you…so much."

"I love you too." He extracted her arms from around him. Before he pulled too far away his lips captured hers.

She threw her arms around him again as the kiss communicated everything neither of them wanted to verbalize. When they did separate she forced a smile to hide how much she wanted to break down right there. "I'll see you soon."

Neil trailed his fingertips along her hairline. "I will always come back to you, Char. Always."

September 17, 2022

Charlotte alternated between leaning over the microscope and jotting down notes on the pad next to her. She had returned from St. Louis the day before. Upon arrival, she'd thrown herself into work as a distraction until Neil returned from his mission.

"Hey Shorty." James walked into the lab. His hands shoved deep in his pockets, and his grim expression didn't match the jovial nickname.

"Feel like cataloguing the genetic mutations with me big brother?" Even though Charlotte had been born before him, James had been created so that he had always appeared older than her.

"Not exactly." He leaned against the counter beside her. "We need to talk."

"That's not usually a great way to start a conversation." Charlotte set her pencil down after she made one last mark. She turned to face him. "What's wrong?"

"There's been another attack."

"Spirits, no! Is everyone okay? I didn't feel anything from Elan. Are Lucas and Illy okay?" Her eyes widened as she waited for him to drop whatever bombshell he had come to hit her with. His avoidance of eye contact and fidgeting frayed her already taut nerves. "James. Tell me. Where was the attack?"

James shook his head. "Maybe you should sit down."

She snapped her fingers in front of his face before he'd finished his sentence. "Stop dragging this out. Just tell me. Making me wait is only going to drive me crazy."

"Indiana."

Charlotte inhaled sharply. Tears slipped free before she even realized she was crying. Deep down she knew what he was going to say. She didn't want to hear it, but she had to. "Where in Indiana? Not Neil. Please James. Please tell me Neil is okay."

His arms encompassed her before her legs gave out. He led her to a nearby chair. "You don't understand. It wasn't a part of Indiana. It was all of Indiana. The whole state has been decimated. We haven't been able to locate him yet, but the house he was supposed to be at has been completely leveled."

"*No*. He's not dead. Don't you dare say he's dead!" She fought against him. Her fists pounded on his chest, his shoulders, anything she could reach. "I would know. I would know if he was dead. I'd see it."

"I'm so sorry Char." James took the beating without complaint. "We'll keep looking, you know we will, but odds are…."

"Shut up! Stop acting like he's dead. My husband is not dead. The thread is still there. It's still here, I can see it. I can." She sobbed, repeating the phrase over and over again as James rocked her.

September 21, 2023

"So, he died during the attack?" Annie winced as Charlotte pulled the needle from her arm after filling several vials with blood.

"No. He's not dead."

"But I thought you said…."

"He's still out there somewhere. He promised he would return to me and he will." Charlotte busied herself with labeling the vials. Everyone in her family kept trying to convince her otherwise, after all she still saw the threads tying her to her parents and there were tons of witnesses that had seen them die. Still, she believed. "I should have stayed with him."

"But then you might have been lost too, or worse."

"You've never been in love, have you?" Charlotte gathered the vials together. She did her best to keep her tone neutral. Despite still being able to see the thread between them, moments of doubt over whether she'd ever see her husband again managed to creep in.

"No, I haven't. Just been me as long as I can remember. I mean since I left home. That's why I wanted to find my parents. To be with people I love before I die." Annie's confusion etched on her face clear as her pain.

"If I could turn back time I would have stayed. I would have made him come with me to St. Louis first and he wouldn't have been in Indiana during the attack." Charlotte forced a smile. "He'll be back."

"I hope you're right. That he's going to return to you." The hint of skepticism in Annie's voice was hard to miss.

"He will. He promised and he always keeps his promises."

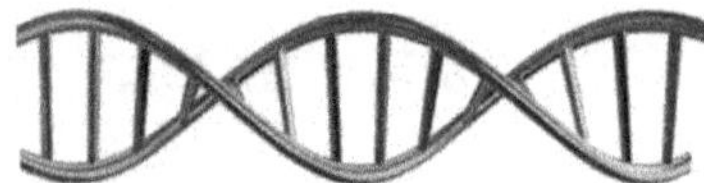

"Just what do you think you're doing?" As towering and impressive as his duplicate, Lucas loomed in Caiman's path, his arms folded across his chest.

"Don't screw with me, Lucas," Caiman released a feral hiss. "Just go back to your happy, blissful ignorance, your happy little wife, and perfect little life and get the hell out of my way."

"Fat chance, Tiny." James' voice came from behind her.

They'd tag-teamed her? A deep growl rumbled through her chest, and escaped in a pure feline snarl. "James. You know I can kick your ass from here to next week. Luke, you aren't even an animal, and your water doesn't touch me. What do you think you can accomplish?"

"Maybe getting you back into a clear-headed state of mind?" Lucas leaned against the wall of the tunnel. "Because James and I are certain you aren't in one."

Caiman forced herself into a relaxed stance, even as her skin thickened and turned gray in preparation for battle. Her nails grew into long, dark claws. She grinned when both men tensed at her transformation. They knew just how poisonous her claws were, even for those with better healing like James. "I'm not like you Luke. I can't sit there, close my eyes, count to ten and go off to la-la land talking to hallucinations. There aren't enough drugs in the world."

"You aren't going out there blind Caiman." In one swift move James moved close enough to make her claustrophobic reactions that much stronger.

"If they're alive, you know exactly who has them. You also know that if anyone can get in there, it's me. The old man still has a soft spot for me, his perfect creation."

James ignored her clear threat to grip her arms. With her thickened skin, she was only aware of his hold thanks to her line of sight, not by any physical sensation. "And he'll take you back and try to make you his again. When you don't join his team with a smile, he'll kill you. You know what that would do to Mom, you ungrateful little bitch!"

"*Enough!*" Lucas remained softspoken on most occasions, but when he wanted to he could pack a crap-ton of power behind his words. This was one of those times. "We aren't here for you two to show how well you fight. Caiman, you promised Mom. You swore that you would never go near Steele again."

"It was a different time." Caiman narrowed her eyes and let a claw sink into each of James' wrists. As an animal, he would eventually heal, but her poison would lengthen the healing and the wound would burn like hell. Once his eyes widened, she grinned and shoved him off toward Lucas. "And they weren't in a Steele trap. I have to get them!"

Both men looked at each other. For all intents and purposes, they were identical, but the expressions they wore were as opposite as who they were. Lucas had been born and raised as natural as the day is long. His personality had always been calm, collected, the perfect temperament for his eventual chosen path as medicine man.

James was his opposite in every way. Talisa had created him under duress, forced to make him hot tempered—so angry he could almost be called unfeeling. A world-class fighter, he might have been what he'd been created to be if Talisa and Roark hadn't found him. So instead of becoming the world's best soldier, he was the head warrior of what was left of the tribe and of the Infected's fighting force.

She knew as the pair stared at each other they were having a discussion. Lucas had the exceptionally rare talent of telepathy. Only a handful of the Infected had been rewarded with such a talent.

"Lucas." James growled. "I can't let her. I am bound to Chance's orders. Mom and Pop's, too! They made us swear we would keep this family together no matter what."

"That's what I'm trying to do." Caiman backed away from the pair. "And I'm not bound to follow Chance's orders like you. I do what I want."

"It's suicide." James lunged for her. "I won't let you. I should lock you in a cell."

"You think the threat of a cell scares me?" Caiman snorted. "I thought you knew me better than that by now."

James' growl cut off. In the next moment Lucas was in his place in front of her. Lucas ignored her claws and thick skin, drawing her into a hug. "Caiman. We all want Mom and Dad back. That doesn't mean we're willing to give you up to do it."

Caiman closed her eyes, but fought the draw of the hug. She shoved him back. "Love and affection doesn't do it either, Lucas. You just don't get it. Neither of you do."

"What's going on here?" Out of the shadows came the only face that was welcome to her. Unfortunately, it was also the least welcome. Of all the people that would fight her plan to go save her parents, Danny was the only one who had the power to stop her.

James knew it too if his shit-eating grin was any indication. "Well, for one—your woman was about to try to head out of here to save our parents. Didn't plan to tell anyone about it either. Not even you, Danny boy."

Caiman growled and lunged for James.

Danny grabbed her arms, but stayed behind her to avoid the claws. "Babe? Is he serious?"

"Asshole." Caiman snarled at James.

Lucas nodded toward Danny. "Yes, Daniel. We just got word this morning that our parents might not be dead after all. Caiman has it in her head that she is the only one who can save them."

Caiman took a swipe at Lucas, knocking away Danny to run down the corridor. She could hear him calling for her, but she didn't stop. With speed and sure footedness, she raced through the corridors toward the closest exit.

Soon as she could, she burst out of one of the houses. Danny wasn't far behind her, but it didn't matter. She just had to get out of the confines of the tunnels. Despite her claims that a cell wouldn't affect her, she was far too claustrophobic for tunnel living.

"Elan." Danny wrapped his arms around her and pulled her back against him. "Babe. Look at me."

"No."

"Elan."

"Stop calling me that!" She struggled against his grasp, but then a flood of memories filled her head. The tears of Talisa rang through her head, images of Talisa reaching out and screaming. *My baby.*

"Babe. She loved you."

I couldn't bear the thought of losing you to that man again. Please, Elan. Stay with your brothers. Promise me. Talisa had been trying to keep Caiman from going to kill General Steele once the truth of what he'd done to her and her parents came out. At the time, Caiman's first goal had been to kill the man she'd once considered like a parent.

Caiman fought against Danny's grasp. "Stop. You said you wouldn't do that to me!" Danny's ability to manipulate memories, to keep a person confined in the emotions of them could be valuable. But she had some scary memories and made him swear to never use it on her. Ever.

"I'm sorry, babe. I just thought you needed to see Talisa's argument too." Danny turned her toward him. "I know you want to save them. If they are alive, I can't blame you for that one bit. Going in there just ain't smart."

"I'm the only one General Steele will let close." Caiman relaxed despite her better judgment, and her skin returned to normal. Being able to feel Danny's touch relaxed her the rest of the way. "There's no other way."

"There's always another way." Danny kissed her forehead. "Your parents are some of the smartest people I know. Bet they're working on something now."

"Danny."

"Yes, Elan?" Even though he was the only one that didn't receive the threat of death for calling her by her real name, it still hurt every time she heard it.

"They've all lost so much. I helped start this hell they're going through." Caiman kept her gaze on the floor, even when he tried to force her to look up. "If I can save them, I have to. For the family they gave me. For them."

"They wouldn't want it if it meant losing you." He sighed. "And I ain't about to spend the rest of my life moping around like Charlotte and Ariel. So, you're not going anywhere. Not without me."

"I'm not risking your life."

"Then you ain't risking your own."

James slowed to a stop outside of the village. After the confrontation with Caiman he'd had to run, and run hard. The adrenaline and need for a fight burned strong as ever in his system, and he was unable to do a damn thing about any of it.

About Caiman.

About his parents.

About Charlotte's husband, Neil.

About the War.

About Anne.

He growled when the thought of the new Exceptional underground entwined with those of his family. Her presence unsettled his carefully fought-for calm. Winning his role as the tribe's head Warrior had been a long battle against the nature he'd been created with.

Every day he struggled with his demons, and any interruption in that struggle could be disastrous. Which meant she could be disastrous.

He sensed, rather than heard, his brother's approach.

Lucas stepped into the clearing soundlessly, one brow cocked. "I have never before known you to be so histrionic in your thoughts. Pessimistic, yes. Always battle driven, certainly. Never so dramatic."

"Get out of my damn head before I cut yours off." James snarled and lunged when Lucas dared to smile at him. "And wipe that smirk off your face."

"Mom may be alive but she isn't here to talk to. You're stuck with me or the Chief." Lucas didn't have the courtesy to flinch at James' challenge. He just sat on a nearby felled tree. "I might be able to help."

"You're not animal. You don't understand."

"I would be offended if I thought you meant that. I might not be animal, but I am a part of this family. I have seen enough to understand."

"And you can get in my damn head."

"I will remain out of your head if that is your preference. Just stop shouting at me and we can talk verbally."

James paced back and forth, the miles-long run had done little to actually help his overdose of adrenaline. "My control is wavering. I'll be letting down the Chief."

"You have not let anyone down."

James snorted. "I let down the whole tribe. Mom, Pops, everyone."

"Mom would slap you if she was here."

"Then she should be here. Besides, you can't tell me they didn't blame themselves. That would be the pot calling the kettle black."

"Only because it was their genius that created the virus that triggered the War. Mostly they blame Steele for lying to everyone not just about the reasons for getting the scientists together, but to the entire world about what the infection was."

"We aren't faulty or an army created for evil, we're Exceptional, and even ordinary people were turned. I know. I heard the rhetoric." James unsheathed his knife and flipped it in his hand. "Mom drilled it into my head enough trying to make me human."

"You are human. Just like me."

James snorted. "Just like you, eh?"

"With a few modifications, yes." Lucas grinned. "Not better, just different."

"Better."

"Different."

"Caiman won't listen." James turned his back on Lucas, unwilling to cave to friendly banter and calm down just yet.

"She never does. That is not what bothers you. Is it the new recruit?"

"Get out of my head."

"I am not in your head. I do not have to be to see it. Charlotte finds it odd as well. You took the time to learn her name. You never do that. You only care if their skills are compatible with your warriors."

James exhaled long and low, squeezing the handle of the knife tight in his grasp. "I don't understand it."

"What bothers you more? Her life? Or her inevitable death?"

With a deep growl, James spun fast and threw his knife.

Lucas didn't move a muscle, even though the knife flew right past his ear with only a centimeter to spare. "Both, then?"

"She is a distraction I cannot afford. I will lose my place if I lose control again."

Lucas rose without a word. He turned to pry the knife from the tree it had embedded in. "Do you remember what Mom and Dad told us about how they met the second time?"

The first time their parents had met their Mom had been young. When they met the second time she was a full-fledged adult. "Yeah. TMI to the max."

"Besides that." Lucas chuckled, but flipped James' knife around in his hand.

James knew the weight of his knife was off, he'd done that intentionally. He didn't want anyone to be able to pick it up and use it against him so easy. "I don't get your meaning."

"The instant connection."

"You mean lust."

"Sure, but more than that." Lucas stopped weighing the knife long enough to flip it in his palm. "They just clicked. They knew pretty fast they needed to be together, just took Mom a while to stop worrying about hurting Chief to tell him as much."

James sighed. "Thanks for the history lesson I didn't need. What is your point?"

"When you were given the animal trait, it increased the innate knowledge of your mate."

"Mate?" James scoffed. "Fat chance. I was created to be alone."

"No one was created to be alone."

"Tell that to the Chief."

"The Chief is destined for someone. The War has delayed, or maybe hastened, her arrival."

James stopped pacing to stare at Lucas. When he said things like that, they could only come from the Spirits they were so cryptic. "That made no sense."

"Now you sound like Mom."

"She always did hate the Spirits cryptic messages." James chuckled, most of the tension seeping away in the humor. "I still think that's crap. Steele wanted a hardened soldier. I was created without the need for a mate."

"Not having a need for one doesn't mean there isn't one. Maybe there is a reason you are bothered by this Anna's appearance in our midst. Your programming is warring with instinct."

"I think Caiman is right. You need to go back to your meditation room and get stoned. There's no way." James turned his back on his brother. Even with no warning, he wasn't surprised when the knife winged past him to embed in the tree he faced.

"Denial only leads to pain, brother. Look what it did to Kenzie and myself." Lucas and Kenzie had faced some tough trials on their way to marriage. Because Kenzie had denied their connection, they'd been forcefully separated and had to overcome a lot to get back to each other.

James sheathed his knife. "It's not denial, it's fact. I am calmer now."

"Go and meditate, brother." Lucas' voice drifted away. "However, you do it best. Find Caiman and fight if you must, but work this out. You'll only make it worse on yourself if you wait."

"It's worse on everyone." James muttered, though he knew Lucas would hear him through his thoughts. "We need to find Mom and Dad now."

Plans are being made. Lucas assured him mentally.

"Not fast enough. They may be our only hope. In Steele's hands, they might be our worst enemies. He holds the cards."

Annie had picked the skin around her thumbnail raw. As a little girl she'd adopted the nervous habit, and though she'd conquered it as an adult, the War had brought it full circle. Each tick of the second hand on the wall clock felt like an hour.

She kept her eyes downcast while Charlotte worked over at the counter. Despite Charlotte's reassurances, guilt ate at her already frayed nerves. "I'm really sorry, Charlotte. My specialty today seems to be bringing up sore subjects for everyone."

"Annie, relax." Charlotte took Annie's hand in her own. She gave it a gentle squeeze. "It's fine. I promise."

A light knock came on the door.

"Come in." Charlotte's smile was reassurance to Annie.

"Thank you so much for getting started, Charlotte. We needed to take care of something," A feminine voice said. Heels clicked on the floor in crisp steps.

A woman entered the room with a man right behind her, if Annie's guess were correct. The shadows on the floor were all she could see, she still couldn't raise her eyes so much. The time spent waiting to be examined had left her exhausted.

She might know cancer was the real culprit, but it was easier to blame the wait over the truth. Charlotte slipped away. Out of the corner of her eye she could see Charlotte writing more notes in a folder that looked vaguely like a chart.

"No problem, Aunt Abby. I'll let you all finish here. Her file is started, blood is drawn. You might want to do more testing for the headaches she's having."

"I appreciate your help, Charlotte. I'll finish up and we can go over the results together later." The woman replied. Something about her voice nagged at Abby's tired brain.

Charlotte ducked down to meet Annie's eyes. "You're in good hands here, I promise. Abby is the best there is."

Abby? The name clicked through her exhausted state finally. Abby had been her mother's name. What a coincidence. Annie nodded to Charlotte, and the girl left the room. Tears blurred her vision as she lifted her head. The whole ordeal had taken a toll. She managed a weak, "Hi."

"You must be Anna. I believe you spoke with my husband on the phone." Abby moved next to her to where Charlotte had left the chart. "Charlotte called you Annie. Do you prefer that over Anna?"

"Yes. It's Annie, please." She cleared her throat, which suddenly felt as thought she'd been chewing on a sandbox.

"It's nice to finally meet you, Annie." The gentleman spoke, a glass of water in his hands. He held it out to her. "While Abby is looking over Charlotte's notes, why don't we go over a few things really quick?"

"Sure, whatever you guys want." She took the water, grateful for the reprieve from her own thoughts. While the man took a seat in front of her, she gulped down half the glass. Despite her lack of fear being around this group of people, her stomach still twisted in nervous knots, threatening to revolt.

"James mentioned you don't remember much around the major attack, or the telethon beforehand."

Annie set the glass on the counter beside her. She pressed the heel of her hands against her eyelids in hopes of fending off the headache growing once again behind her eyes. When she pulled her hands away, she focused on the people in the room for the first time.

She froze as she drank in the sight of the man before her. A man she *knew*. With a gasp, she turned to the woman, cold shock coursing through her veins. Her gaze bounced between the two fast for several minutes. "I…I mean you…No. This can't be right." She flew to her feet fast, knocking the glass off the counter in the process.

Abby spun at the shatter of glass. "Annie? What is it? What's wrong?"

"You…and me…here…." Tears cascaded down her face. A mixture of shock and relief twisted her tongue in knots.

"Easy, Annie." Warren moved toward her slowly, his hands outstretched in front of him. "Take a deep breath, that's it. Tell us what's wrong. I promise we aren't going to hurt you."

"You don't recognize me?" Her heart plummeted into her stomach. She'd been searching for them for so long, but they didn't recognize her? Yes, it had been a while since she'd seen them last what with the War and everything—but it hadn't been long enough to make that noticeable of a difference.

"Why don't we sit down over here? We can talk about whatever has you so spooked." Abby set her hand on Annie's arm. "Today has been stressful. I know this is all a lot to take in."

"Abby is right. Once we finish here we can get you set up in a unit of your own. You'll have some time to digest everything then." Warren inched closer, but still didn't touch her.

"You…?" Annie's gaze ping-ponged between the two of them. No recognition showed on their features. Tears stabbed the back of her throat, threatening to choke her. "You really don't recognize me?"

"What do you mean—recognize you?" Abby's tone soothed gently, her free hand stroked Annie's hair in an all-too familiar gesture.

A wave of calm washed over her, and she knew it came from Abby somehow. Still, it doesn't touch her inner freak-out. "You're my parents!"

Warren and Abby both grew still. They turned to face each other, their eyes wide before they spoke in unison, "Your parents?"

"As in, I'm your daughter." Annie's eyes widened. The room seemed to lose all oxygen when they didn't respond how she'd expected. They hadn't missed her as she missed them? Her breaths grew tight, shallow. She tried to gulp to regain oxygen.

"We do have children." Abby hesitated, her hand twitching between a reaching touch and retreating away. "Two sons, actually. I never had a little girl."

Warren's eyes were as wide as Abby's. "We always wanted a daughter, but it wasn't in the cards for us."

Annie yanked herself away from the pair. "*No*. My name is Anna Maria Johnson. My parents are Warren and Abigail Johnson." Tears blurred her vision. She reached for her bag. The laptop she'd brought with her would prove everything. She could show her father all she had on there. Then they would remember.

"What are you doing?" Warren put himself between Annie and Abby.

"I'm getting my laptop. You can see everything." Her hands shook as she extracted the laptop from her bag. "I'm not lying. My screensaver is a picture of us at the waterfall we used to have picnics at."

Abby's breath shook as she spoke, "We'll run a basic DNA sweep. That'll tell us what we need. You do have the same mutation as Warren, so that gives credence to your claim."

"Mom, I have your molecule manipulation as well. Why would I lie about something like this? That's crazy! Daddy, I remember you teaching me to ride a bike!" Annie noticed a brief flicker of emotion when she called Warren Daddy, but then he closed off. Both appeared skeptical of her claims, as if they didn't remember everything she did. She shoved her sleeve up.

"Whatever you want. Take it all. I'll do anything. I know you're my parents. I remember everything. Why don't you?"

Abby pulled Annie toward her into a gentle hug. Her hand ran along Annie's back. Waves of calm seeped through the room. "Easy now. One thing at a time. Warren will look at your laptop. We'll do the DNA sweep on all of us and we'll go from there, okay?"

Warren blew out a breath. "Abby is right. We'll get to the bottom of this. And if we're not who you think we are, we'll help you find your parents. I promise."

Annie buried her head in Abby's shoulder, unable to keep herself from hugging her mother back tight as she could. In her heart, she knew her parents were right there in front of her, finally. Deep down she had no doubts. Abby was a brilliant doctor.

Perhaps there was hope now.

"Knock, knock, little brother." Charlotte rapped her knuckles on the doorframe.

"Come on in, Charlotte." Lucas sat still in the middle of his living quarters. His legs crossed and eyes remained closed in a meditative pose.

"Sure, it's okay? You look busy."

"It is fine. I did not think you would finish with Anna so quickly." Through his reassurances he didn't move from his position.

"I was just filling in while Abby and Warren took care of something. Were you able to extract James' head from his ass?" She made her way to the couch. A mug of tea sat there full, which she guessed Lucas had made for her. Flames danced along the surface of the mug to heat it. Once the mug grew warm between her hands she released her hold on the fire.

"He will need to straighten his own head out. I can only hope I assisted in that endeavor." Lucas tilted his head to the side as if he were listening to something. "The Spirits have told me little in regard to Anna. Her future is cloudy."

"That's reassuring." Charlotte sighed deep. Straightforward answers would be helpful with the puzzle of Annie—but so far none of that was happening.

"You know the Spirits do not hand over the answers easily."

"I know, but James…there is already a thread forming there. It's tenuous, but it is definitely there between them. If they don't acknowledge it soon it will snap like Joe and Ariel's did. I don't know that James will ever recover." Joe had perished in the same attack her parents were assumed to have died in. He and Ariel had a special connection and the violent nature of Joe's death had nearly destroyed Ariel.

"We will not lose him. We will assist him however we can." Lucas opened his eyes, his lips pressed together in a thin line.

Charlotte reached out to squeeze her brother's hand. "Kenzie with Ariel today?"

"Yes. Her mother is struggling. The anniversary was especially hard on her. She and her sister are trying to lift her spirits." Varying shades of grey pulsed through Lucas' aura that normally flooded with blues and greens.

"One day at a time. That's what Mom and Dad always said, right?" She mustered a brief smile. "This is one of your special tea blends. What sort of bomb are you about to drop on me?"

"You were right," he said simply.

"Care to be more specific than that? You know I'm right about a great many things." Charlotte smirked at him.

He took the mug from her to set it on the table. His hands came to rest on hers. "Mom and Dad are alive."

"Yeah, I know. I've been saying that since the beginning." Where was he going with this? She'd always maintained that her parents were still alive, out there somewhere. The only thing she couldn't do was figure out where exactly that was.

"Abigail received a delivery from Mom."

The range of emotion that spiraled through Lucas' aura made her momentarily dizzy. She pulled on humor to push aside whatever his emotions and her own were doing. "Did the mailman deliver my Fingerhut catalog too? What do you mean, delivered?"

Lucas shook his head. None of her stab at humor affected his own mix of emotions. "A man delivered it. He died just before he arrived at the first house."

"What was it? What did they deliver?" Charlotte knew Abby and her mom were close, but she didn't understand why she'd send a message to her and not to Pop. She made a mental note to check on him. Of her three parents, he would be the one that took things personally.

"A tarot card."

"A what? Tarot card?" That made no sense. "Are we sure it wasn't for Lucy?"

A smile tugged the corners of Lucas' mouth. "We are quite sure. The inner envelope was addressed to Abigail. She knew the specific card, and has said they created the deck together. Have there been any changes in our parent's threads?"

Charlotte pursed her lips in concentration. Layer by layer the auras of everyone in the compound dimmed. Left behind laid the tangled mess of threads that resembled her grandmother's knitting basket after a kitten decided to play with it. One by one she pushed aside the other threads until only those of her immediate family was left behind.

Like the bridge of a guitar the threads lined up next to each other before they veered off in different directions toward the people they were connected to. Each of those threads faded into the background as she picked out which family member they belonged to.

Her heart twisted at the sight of Neil's thread still shining brightly. She focused on it, wishing she could reach out and send him a message that she knew he still lived.

Tears stung her eyes as it too faded into the background until only Roark and Talisa's threads were left behind. Both threads shone bright and strong, not any more faded than they'd been before the attack, and still so close together it seemed as though they shared threads. "They are both still there and strong as ever."

"That is good to know. Plans are being made now to find them."

"Elan knows?" Once he nodded, she sighed. "Great. Could someone nail her foot to the floor before she decides to do something rash?"

"James and I have spoken to her. We still cannot guarantee she will not do something without the rest of us."

Charlotte closed her eyes to steady herself before she brought the rest of the threads and auras back into focus. The control it took to keep focus on specific threads for extended periods of time would eventually wear her down. She tilted her head to bring her parents thread back into focus as Talisa's thread moved in waves. "Something's wrong."

"What do you mean?" Lucas took a seat on the couch beside her. "May I?"

After a brief nod, she felt the familiar presence of Lucas in her mind. Sometimes having a telepathic brother had its advantages. Talisa's thread shook hard, small tears appearing as it beat against Roark's. "I've never seen them do anything like that before."

"I am unsure of what it means. I will need to meditate on it to see if the Spirits have any answers for what has happened." Lucas' hand remained firmed on her back.

"What the hell?" The thread shimmied violently before it dimmed to almost nothing. Tears burned the back of her eyes. She clutched Lucas' free hand tight. "Oh God! Mom! What happened? She was right there. She can't be gone."

"Wait," Lucas cautioned.

"Wait? Mom's thread just…." The words died on her lips as Talisa's thread pulsed brighter than it had ever been. A minute later it settled back into a slightly dimmer version of what it had flared to. "I know I'm repeating myself here, but what the hell?"

"I do not know Charlotte. We should tell the others. I will inform the Chief but I believe Abigail needs your assistance for some of the tests on Anna." Lucas hugged her close.

"Right. Multiple crises at once. Never one thing at a time." She leaned her head against his shoulder. "Do I have time to finish my tea? I really need it now."

"Finish your tea sister. We will not solve everything right now."

Roark's whisper crept into Talisa's sleepy awareness. "Li." The volume of his whisper didn't matter. Everything they said was monitored and analyzed, no matter how quiet. In a way, it helped—they'd been able to strengthen their form of silent communication and create code words and phrases. They were able to circumvent their orders and do more than their captors realized this way.

Everything about captivity sucked. The cruelest part, of course, was the thick wall of bulletproof glass between them.

For over a year Talisa had been denied the touch of her husband, her partner.

"Li, baby. Wake up." Roark pressed his hand to the glass in their usual morning greeting. "You know you don't want them to wake you."

Talisa sighed and pressed her hand against his where it lay on the other side of the glass. Tears filled her eyes, but she blinked them away fast so their captors couldn't see them. She forced a smile. "Morning, hot stuff."

"Ready for a brand-new day?"

Today would be the day, that's what he was saying. Their latest test would have to be today. They'd been working toward it for months. The forced smile curved into a genuine smirk. His excitement was a total lie, he was pissed as hell she'd insisted on being the guinea pig this time.

Considering the experiment was hers, she refused to test it on the man she loved. "As ready as I've been every day we've been living in this hell, my love."

So many things could go wrong. The depth of trouble could mean today would be her last day, her end. The fear didn't show on his features, but she swore she could feel it as if she was an empath like Abby.

Either way, his hand lingered longer than usual. "Then we should get to work before Mr. All-too-powerful ascends his throne."

For the bit of humor, Talisa allowed a laugh. She pressed her forehead to the glass. "Then let's get on with our daily routine. I'll meet you across the lab table."

"Same time, same place." Roark winked before rising. It was both an enjoyable show and a cruel tease that he stripped down on his way to the bathroom he'd been given.

With a heavy sigh, Tal slipped from her bed and went to her own bathroom for her usual morning routine. Everything was normal while she took her shower. Everything was normal while she shaved her legs.

While she brushed her teeth, nothing changed. Her daily multivitamin was the key for the new day. The bottle she grabbed with her wet hand, which proceeded to slip from her damp grasp and spill onto the floor when she tried to open it.

The simple act of a klutz gave her the excuse she needed to pick every single pill up in order to make sure she took the right one. The pill she'd altered to give her the drug. The pill that might even help her feel her husband's touch again.

She hadn't made it easy to select the right pill by sight, because it was meant to blend, but with the cameras on her, she didn't have a choice. Talisa snatched up the pills bit by bit, dumping them back into the pill bottle, still unable to find the right one.

Then she spotted it. A slight marbling inside the capsule not present in the other multivitamins gave away the medicine she'd mixed in. Every month Steele had their multivitamins delivered, and every month they insisted on checking them as a requirement to keep working. Tal and Roark wanted to be certain Steele didn't mix in any surprises in the same way Tal had done with this one.

Steele allowed the demand because he needed Roark and herself. Of course, that meant nothing was spiked, but they tested anyway. After Steele had made her Patient Zero without her awareness, they would always be wary.

Of course, it helped that their captors wouldn't expect them to try to kill themselves. Never mind that she was about to do just that.

Talisa dumped the rest of the pills back in the bottle before she set it back on the shelf. She tossed back the multivitamin and swallowed it with a sip of water before she could have second thoughts. From there, all that was left was heading back to work.

She grabbed her hair band and walked out to the lab, tying up her hair as she moved.

"Problem, Li?"

"Dropped my damn vitamins again. Stupid bottle is a pain in my ass." Tal winked at Roark and picked up her gloves. When she got to her lab table, Roark stood directly opposite her in front of his table, which was laid out identical to hers.

General Steele's voice boomed through the speakers before Roark could reply. "Roark. Talisa. How are my lab rats this morning?" Behind a darkened glass set up a floor above them to Talisa's right, stood the monitoring room where Steele watched them often. He never went into the field or to battle any longer. All his time was spent making sure they would wipe out anyone with a mutation, and turn his soldiers into the fighting machines he wanted them to be.

Tal pursed her lips and picked up a pipette. "Your wit is making me nauseous. You've kept me from being close to my husband for over a year. I'm just peachy, your highness."

"My, my, aren't we testy today? Come now, Talisa. You two are getting so close to a break through. Maybe then you can see your husband again. Maybe then you'll be normal." General Steele chuckled. "You know, as opposed to the freak show."

"You're the damn freak show," Roark muttered under his breath.

"I'm just not feeling well again today, General," Tal spoke fast before Roark could be reprimanded. "As I haven't the past week or so. It puts me on edge. Of course, it doesn't help that I miss my husband."

A sad smile lingered on Roark's features. "Feeling's mutual, baby."

She nodded to him before looking back up where Steele stood hidden behind dark glass. "I hope you have a soldier ready for testing. The latest pill test is ready."

Roark nodded. "We're keeping it small for now. We're testing to build strength and endurance. This test will focus on strength."

Which meant it would do nothing. None of the drugs they were developing would do anything beyond a psychosomatic effect. Just like they'd been told the original trials were to develop treatments and cures for cancer and HIV—they were lying to themselves if they thought anything like this would build strength or endurance.

The only thing that worked was the initial virus. The virus had activated a gene hidden in half the population, mutating them into something more, something exceptional. Steele hadn't seen it that way and was now hell-bent on destroying what was left of what he'd created. Despite wanting to destroy his initial experiment results, he still wanted to build a new breed of soldier.

Talisa sighed as she pulled the tray of pills out of the cabinet. Once again, there was one pill on it different than the others. One simple pill would add a boost to the rest of the plan, in this case for both her and Roark.

Before she could intentionally-accidentally spill these pills, the impact of her first pill hit without warning. Her heart started to race so fast she stopped dead in her tracks.

"Li?" Roark's pipette clattered to the counter. "Li, what's wrong?"

Light burst in her vision and her left arm tingled before it went numb. "Spirits," She whispered. The tray clattered to the floor and she dropped down next to it. Her vision blurred so she couldn't see the pills to pick out the right one. "Help."

"Li!" Roark pounded on the glass. "Damn it, Steele. Let me in there. Let me help her, look at her."

"How do I know this isn't a trick?" Steele's voice sounded distant.

The door to her cell clicked open and footsteps raced toward her. Hands checked her neck, but her heart wouldn't slow, it just kept pounding faster. Everything grew dim.

Roark might have been yelling, but it sounded like he was miles away. "Steele. Let me in there. If you don't, you'll lose the best mind you've got."

Black took over.

Silence.

Whispers of the Spirits.

Then pure, burning pain, accompanied by blinding white light. Tal screamed back into consciousness as the drugs worked through her body. Inside the syringe of adrenaline Roark had plunged into her chest was her own special concoction.

"Li. Li, baby, look at me." For the first time in forever, Roark was touching her. His familiar warm hands ran along her hair, her arm. "Baby, please. God, I thought I'd lost you."

"You almost did," She whispered.

His lips closed over hers before they could be ripped apart. To her surprise, when his tongue plunged into her mouth, the pill was there. With the simple act of the kiss it burst open, delivering the drug to her system as she swallowed.

She buried her fingers in his hair, holding him close. Normally she'd be embarrassed by the tears that slipped down her cheeks, but her relief was too great to care.

"That's enough. Split them up." Steele interrupted that relief and bliss, and had even lowered himself to enter her cell. "She's not dead. You can return to your room."

"She almost died, damn it." Roark's ferocity didn't reach his eyes when he pressed his forehead to hers. "Li?"

"I'm tired, Roark. So tired." She had no way to know if it had worked, until it did. One thing was certain, her near death wasn't a lie. It had really happened. "Please, General. Just this once. You can search us, we have nothing. You will hear everything we say."

They're up to something. I just don't know what. Steele's thoughts hit her without warning. The one voice precipitated a sudden influx of words and thoughts that pounded into her brain from all around them.

She couldn't have stopped her gasp if she'd tried, and she gripped Roark's arm. Their plan had worked, but she hadn't any idea how to control it. She forced herself to speak through the throng of other voices. "You need a few hours to test the pill. Please, please, please."

"Begging doesn't suit you, Talisa." Steele sighed like they were putting him out by her near death. "Fine. You will have an armed guard standing over you, so no funny business. You have two hours."

"Li," Roark whispered and pulled her close. Somehow from their awkward position he picked her up. It wasn't until she was safe on the bed that he let out a shaky breath she knew covered a sob. "Spirits. I really thought you were gone."

"I heard the Spirits. I was gone." Tal pulled his hand close to her chest, ignoring the guard standing at the foot of her bed. "I have missed you, husband."

"I have missed you, wife."

With great effort, she cut through the chaos of minds that plagued her. Roark's proximity let her focus just on his mind and thoughts. Unsure if it would even work, she tried to direct a thought as she had often felt Lucas do to her. *It worked.*

Roark smiled as he met her eyes. His thoughts were chaotic, but she picked out his clear excited yell of relief. She was now as telepathic as their son.

All that was left was to figure out how far she could reach. If she could find home, find the only other man as close to her as her husband, maybe she could read him. Chance would listen if she could find him. She had to try.

For now, though, none of that mattered. All that she wanted to do was focus on the fleeing moments of relief—and the long-missed warmth of her husband's touch.

Caiman paced outside the lab, her hands clenching and opening in a rapid, repeated attempt to release the stress. Action had to be taken soon, sooner than anyone seemed ready to, she knew it. Every instinct told her as much.

The problem lay with making it happen. No one in the compound would let her out if they knew. With two telepaths that happened to be related to her by blood, all her thoughts could potentially be at risk.

Lucky for her the life she'd led before she'd found her family made her capable of withstanding most telepathic intrusion. Hell, it had made her impervious to a lot of shit.

"Would you knock it the fuck off?" James' impatient voice boomed through the solid metal walls to reach her sensitive ears without a problem.

"Bite me, asswipe." She clenched her fist and let her Exceptional ability take over until her flesh thickened over her hand, wrist, and all the way up to her elbow. With the solid defense, she beat her fist against the metal door once, twice, and a third time hard enough to make her own eardrums throb in pain, and knew it would do the same to James.

The door slid open and James had her by the throat before she could react. He lifted her off the ground by her throat and slammed her into the wall. "I am busy. What the fuck is your issue, Elan?"

"Busy with what?" She didn't even feel the grip he had on her throat, due to the same thickening of skin she'd used on her arm. He, on the other hand, wouldn't be able to help notice the threat of her poisonous nails near his wrist. "Our parents are probably sitting in Steele's control and you're doing what? You don't even like the fucking lab."

"Seeing if Char has made any progress on Anne, damn it. You got a problem with that?"

"Yeah. I do." She gave him a solid kick in the stomach and landed on her feet with all the grace of a cat. She swiped her legs out quick to knock him clean off his own feet onto his ass. "This is our parents we're talking about, asshole. From what I've heard that one is already dead. What shit is that?"

"Don't say that." James snarled his way to his feet. He backed her into the wall, his lips curled, fire in his eyes. "She will not die."

"Fucking hell. You have *got* to be kidding me." Caiman recognized the scent pouring off of him like a skunk. When any of those infected with the mutating virus had an animalistic mutation, they were driven to a mate. When they found them, and the connection was threatened, a distinct musk was emitted. She couldn't believe of all times for James to get caught in heat it had to be when their parents had been found. "Fine. Whatever. Go do what you need to."

James blinked several times. His shoulders relaxed, clearly surprised she'd backed off so easily. "What?"

"I won't be able to get your brain out of the lockdown it's on. Of all the people I thought could help me, you aren't worth a shit now." Caiman shoved him across the corridor. She had to beat the shit out of something, so she spun on her heel to head to the workout room.

"What the hell is that supposed to mean?"

"I am *not* helping your pea brain figure out your base instinct, asswipe. You can't cheat off my homework. Go bother the hell out of Char, she might be sympathetic to your pathetic plight. I'm going to destroy some shit."

And plan.

Caiman needed a plan. She'd have to break her promise to Danny, but her parents were in danger and she couldn't ignore that. After all they'd done to free her from that life with Steele, she couldn't leave them in his hands to suffer.

Problem would be how.

Halfway to the workout room the rumble of burrowing roots nudged her senses. The Chief was at it once again. Part of her still believed it was all for naught. The bigger they got, the harder it would be to hide from Steele.

Plus living away from sunlight and fresh air was no way to live. It made her claustrophobic.

The only way to end things lay on another path.

They had to get rid of Steele, and any of the world's military leaders on his side of the battle. Instead of building a solid battle plan they'd lived on the defense since the world blew up. Defense. She despised it. Offense was always better.

She turned and followed the sound to where Chance worked. The light grew dimmer down the tunnel as she reached the end where they hadn't yet strung the electricity. "Mom would be so pissed off at you right now."

"That's not a surprise." Chance didn't halt in his work, his hands raised toward the root digging downward instead of out. "She often was."

"What the hell are you doing?"

"Building new tunnels."

"You're going down."

"We're trying to keep our footprint the size of the broken village above ground to account for the lingering electricity when we shut down the grid. Doesn't make sense to go out further, so I'm going down. We'll create a new floor below this, and another below that."

"Well look at that, the Chief used his brains for once."

"Do not test me, Caiman." He lowered his arms and turned toward her. "I understand you're upset about what's going on, but you aren't the only person in this compound."

"No, but Mom and Dad are the only ones that actually did shit to bring this War to an end. They would be pushing for the offensive. I bet anything they are from whatever hell he has them in." Caiman growled low in her chest. "And you know it's hell. Last time he got them, he forced Mom to make James. What other shit do you think he's doing."

"Don't you think I go through that in my head every minute of every day?" He folded his arms across his chest. His eyes narrowed as the roots he'd been working with quivered with a subtle threat. "Like I said I have more to worry about than you or your parents."

"All we've done for months is sneak around and hide. We've brought in more of the infected for—"

"Exceptionals," Chance interrupted. "Your mom doesn't like that word, *infected*."

Caiman smarted under the correction and curled her lip. "We'll never win this War by living in hiding. We're showing that Steele's propaganda is right, we have something to hide. When we don't have anything to hide. Steele wants people like us—no, like me."

"No, he doesn't." He gripped her shoulders and gave her a sharp shake. "He wants soldiers with super strength, he doesn't want those of us that are Exceptional. All he did was use you."

"At least someone did. I'm worthless here. I'm a guard dog in cat form. You have plenty of guard dogs. I was raised to fight."

"I know. We have no effective fighting force, Caiman. You, James, Kat and Running Bear don't make an army."

"Then train."

"Most of the people we bring in are scared. They aren't soldiers. All they want is peace." Chance's shoulders drooped. "I won't rob them of that. I won't send them to be slaughtered."

"You are robbing them of that by not letting them fight for what they want. We will be found; this compound will be destroyed along with everyone in it. You're failing them. You're failing us."

"I am doing everything I can, and I won't be questioned again. We are recruiting, we are growing, but these things take time. We don't have a built-in brainwashed lot of troops like Steele, and I won't brainwash anyone just to become stronger."

Caiman snarled and turned on her heel to storm away.

"Elan."

"You don't have the fucking right to call me that!"

"Your mom will be rescued. She wants her family safe. As long as she knows we're safe, she will continue to fight." He approached her, but didn't touch her. "I don't reveal all my plans and there are many. Don't make blind accusations."

"I'm not blind. I'm the opposite of blind."

"Have you been spying?"

"I've been doing what I was trained to do."

Danny pulled the door to Annie's room shut behind him. He raked his hands through his sandy blond hair in frustration. Unlike his twin, Ethan, he felt compelled to spend some time with Annie to get to know her. Even though the test results hadn't come back yet, there was a good chance she was their sister.

If she was dying, he felt compelled to get to know her before the end. To find her only to have her so close to dying tore through his heart. Despite the distance Ethan kept between himself and Annie, Danny felt his brother mourning.

None of the test results mattered except one answer, they wouldn't tell him anything he didn't already know. Steele's name was written all over this one, once again.

The man had etched himself into their lives so deep that he was tucked into every nook and cranny of it. To Steele they were nothing but a bunch of chess pieces to move around the board until he conquered them all and won the game. When the pawns dared to rebel, he destroyed the board with no care for what it did to the rest of the world.

Danny moved through the corridors on autopilot. His mind raced too much to focus on one thing. The constant flyovers. The soldiers and patrols everywhere. Perimeter checks with RB. Annie. Ethan. His parents and how they were dealing with the Annie situation. The loss they already felt so deep, even without the test results.

Elan.

Elan. That's who he needed right now. She'd help him refocus and get his head on straight. No matter the soldier she'd always been, somehow, she'd always had one soft spot with him. He could always count on her. He wanted, no he needed to see her now.

If he talked to her maybe she would have some insight on the situation with Annie. Anything at all that might help them. Help his sister. His family. He felt helpless with the entire situation.

He sure didn't possess the medical or computer knowledge his parents did and he had often told Elan he didn't have half the brains she did. She only refused to leave them in favor of fighting as she'd been trained. He only hoped she might know one thing, anything at all, from her time with Steele that could help. He had to try.

Soon as he entered the unit they lived in he called out, "Elan. Babe? You in here?"

The only answer he got in return was complete silence. Maybe she'd decided to take a shower. She'd mentioned using the workout room when he'd seen her earlier.

"Caiman?" He cringed soon as the name left his lips. He hated calling her that. Even though she insisted everyone call her that instead of her given name, he still didn't like it. He poked his head in the bathroom. "Babe. Come on."

Not in the shower, either? Damn it, where could she be? She had been absent during the security checks topside. Danny hadn't worried, as she'd said she was going to be working in the gym most of the day. Her frustration had been at an all-time high now that they had word her parents were alive.

Charlotte. She could have gone to see her own twin or gotten James to spar with her to blow off some of that steam.

He jammed his thumb into the comm button to contact Charlotte in the lab.

"Unless someone is bleeding out or burning, I'm busy right now." Charlotte's annoyed voice crackled through the speaker. Though she rarely had a flare of temper, when she did Char could easily rival her sister.

"Hey, sorry to bother you. It's Danny. I know you're working on Annie's test, Char…but I was wondering if Elan was in there with you." He chuckled at the unladylike snort that came through in response.

"Really, Danny? You know how much Elan hates the lab."

"Yeah." He sighed. "Knew it was a longshot. Maybe she's sparring with James."

James' voice came through the speaker. "Nope. I'm here. She might be in the training room. She said she was going to destroy some shit when I saw her earlier. She was in a damn mood and a half."

A knot twisted in his stomach. "Thanks anyway, guys. I'll check the training wing."

The comm went silent except for faint static for a minute before James' voice came through again. "Let me know if you can't find her."

"Yeah. Thanks. I'll check in with you guys later." He sighed heavily as he disconnected the conversation.

Danny scrubbed both hands over his face. "Not with Char or James, not in our room. Where the hell did she go? Back to square one. I need to check the training room."

He pulled his shirt over his head to change into a clean one. When he tossed the shirt on the bed he saw it.

A piece of paper lay folded neatly on his pillow.

His brow furrowed as he picked up the slip of paper. His name was written on the front in Elan's familiar flowing script.

The sick feeling he'd been fighting welled up inside him stronger than ever.

"What did you do, babe?" Danny sunk onto the bed staring at the note in his hand. The paper shook in his hands as he opened each fold in the paper with care. He hadn't realized he'd been holding his breath until he felt the burn in his lungs so fierce he had to let it out.

There were several lines on the note that had been scratched through until completely illegible. The end result left him with only three words. Three words that made his world spin.

I had to.

His eyes locked on the note, unable to tear away from the sickening sight. The hand not holding the note clenched into a fist at his side, the only sign of his distress at first. Then the hand holding the paper joined in by balling up.

Out of the corner of his eye he caught the glimmer of his wedding ring. Their promise to each other. To be there for each other, to shoulder all the burdens in their life together. She had broken that.

The knot in his stomach spun and grew into a ball of anger. He shot to his feet and grabbed the lamp off the nightstand. With a brutal yell, he threw it across the room. The shatter did little to quell his anger.

She'd snuck off without a word. Broken her promise. She'd waited until he'd been distracted and left. No excuses, no explanation, just a note that she'd 'had to'.

Danny spun fast, throwing his fist into his wall. "Damn it!" He swept one arm across the dresser, shoving all its contents on the floor. Pain radiated through his hand from the punch, but he ignored it in favor of the note still crumpled in his palm.

"Danny?" Ethan's voice drifted in from the living room. "Bro, what's going on?"

"Fuck off, E," Danny yelled back.

"Well. At least now I know why my hand hurts." Ethan leaned against the doorframe, arms folded across his chest. "Come on. You need to go get that checked out by Mom. Whatever you did, I'm pretty sure you broke it."

"What part of fuck off don't you get?" Danny seethed as he stared back at his much calmer mirror image.

"What's got your panties all twisted? Damn, man. I haven't seen you this worked up in a really long time."

Tension coursed through his limbs until he clenched his sore hand. He stood there taking ragged breaths, trying to tell his brother what had happened. "She's gone. Elan is gone."

Ethan's brow quirked. "What? You two have a fight or something?"

"No, but we're gonna." Danny tensed his jaw in silent circles for a few minutes. "She left to go after her parents. By herself."

"She what? Fuck. What is that wife of yours thinking?" Ethan straightened. "Let's go. We need to talk to Mom and Dad about this and your hand needs to be looked at."

Danny huffed, still glaring daggers at his twin. Even if he didn't like what she'd done, he understood. He hated that he understood, but he did. "Don't say that. You know she still thinks she has to make things up to everyone. She's had a hard-on for killing Steele ever since we found out what he really did to her and his parents."

Ethan pointed towards the door. "Shirt and then to see Mom and Dad."

"And if I don't little brother?"

"I'll just get Ilana to make you." Ethan shrugged. "Sorry the whole three minutes older routine doesn't work with me. I could just call Mom. Then there will be fussing and worrying and she's already a basket case over Annie."

"Yeah, I know. I just came from seeing Annie myself." Danny closed his eyes to try to steady himself. He took a few deep, bracing breaths before he opened them again. "You should spend some time with her, you know."

"We aren't talking about me, bro." Ethan took his own shaky breath.

"She could be your sister. You shouldn't let her die thinking you hate her." He grabbed a shirt from the dresser. Without thinking he yanked it on, and a curse erupted at the pain that shot through his hand. "Let's get this over with."

"Next time don't punch walls and I won't make you get it looked at."

"This twin connection is a real pain in the ass sometimes."

"I know all too well, bro. All too well." Ethan clapped his hand on Danny's shoulder when he was close enough.

The anger began to drain away only to be replaced with worry. "Maybe she took her cell. If she did, Dad can track her."

"Doesn't sound like her, but you never know. We'll talk to Dad and he'll be able to tell. She loves you, Danny. She'll be back."

"Can I ground her when we get her back here?"

"You can try, but it might be a bitch with those poison claws." Ethan punched in the code to open the door to the next wing. "Hey Danny, do me a favor."

"What's up?" Danny glanced at his brother, not sure where he was going with this.

"Don't ever tell me your wife has a hard-on again."

"TMI?"

"You could say that."

"How are you feeling, Li?" Roark trailed his fingers through her hair. Though the act was small and simple, he relished in each moment. To be so close to her for the last year but not able to touch killed him a little more every day. It was Steele's special brand of torture for them.

"Still a little shaky."

He couldn't help but glance at the clock. They only had ten minutes together before Steele separated them again. Knowing that felt even crueler than the year they'd been separated behind the glass. The brief reprieve intensified the pain of the separation that was about to be enforced again. He nuzzled her neck, memorizing every inch of her down to her scent. "You scared the hell out of me."

"You aren't the only one." Her eyes remained closed. To anyone else it probably appeared Talisa did little more than lay in his arms resting. The persistent presence in his head told him different. *I don't know how Lucas controls this.*

The thoughts focused on him easier than the first time she'd spoken. He knew she was struggling just based on their brief time together. Although they enjoyed being able to hold each other again, they'd been forced to help her get her new gift under control. He could only imagine how frustrated he would be if he'd been the one to get it. He picked one thought to focus on to help her get it clear and loud. *Our son has the patience of a saint.*

"Roark. Talisa." General Steele's voice interrupted them through the speakers. "I think it's time you—what? Are you sure?"

"Sounds like his highness has been distracted all of a sudden." Roark tightened his arms around his wife, dreading the moment he'd have to let go.

"Did something happen with the trial?" Talisa focused on the armed guard at the foot of the bed. "Did the pill work already?"

The gasp that followed the question sent a spike of worry through Roark. Talisa stiffened in his arms. "Li? Baby, what is it? Is the headache back?"

She groaned, her fingers pressed to the bridge of her nose.

He carefully peeled them away so he could search her eyes. With care, he tried to again direct his thoughts at her. *Baby what is it? What did you get from him?*

It's chaos. It hurts. She winced, but remained focused on him. *Steele is the worst. All I hear from the others is that his daughter has come home.*

His daughter? Who the hell are they talking about? An image of Elan filtered into his head. It took every ounce of self-control to not jump out of the bed and begin attack. He wanted to yell at Elan if she was here.

He turned his head toward the window over the lab where Steele watched them. Usually kept dark by Steele so he could see them and not the other way around, the window shone bright enough that they could see in.

There standing with Steele was his and Li's daughter, Elan. He tore his eyes away, a low growl rumbling through his chest.

Talisa had seen as well. Her nails dug into his arm, creating crescent-shaped welts. Elan wouldn't turn on them and return to Steele's side, would she? After everything they'd been through to get her back. Everything they'd done in order to heal their family. Elan wouldn't betray them like that. She couldn't, could she? Now more than ever it was imperative Talisa contacted someone back home.

Would you shut up? Talisa's voice slammed into his head like a freight train.

I didn't say anything.

I am hearing every little thought you are thinking. Beyond your panic over Elan, even. And while I appreciate the fact that you think you're lucky to have a wife that is both hot and smart—such thoughts are not helping me at the moment.

Properly chastised, he pulled the swirling thoughts in his head under control as best he could. He knew Tal needed him to help focus her new ability now, so he had to maintain control, even if it meant holding back his animal instinct.

Better, but not great.

He sighed to pull her closer. The only advantage they had now was that Steele was more preoccupied with Elan than with them. He glanced back up toward the window and immediately regretted it.

Elan embraced Steele like she used to embrace Roark. A combination of grief and anger welled inside along with an intense need to rip the other man limb from limb.

The glimpse into the room above them ended as the window went dark again. No order to separate them came, though. He pressed his lips to Talisa's temple. "I guess whatever is going on up there is more important than us."

"I guess so." Her voice cracked with the underlying grief they both shared at the turn of events. She could cover her emotions with the underlying fact that she had nearly died. He didn't have that luxury.

The door to the room opened and it was his turn to bite back at a gasp. Steele entered the room, something he never did. It didn't take long to figure out why. Elan followed him in, and Steele looked every bit the proud peacock. The man was getting braver.

"I thought you two might be interested in seeing who decided to join us. In exchange for coming back, she has offered to give us the location for the base of operations for your infected resistance." Steele grinned broadly. "Aren't you proud of her?"

Elan examined her nails, apparently uninterested in the whole exchange. "It's not like they care, Poppy. You're the only one that cares about me."

Talia lay still as a stone in Roark's arms. He couldn't read her, and she directed no thoughts at him to help him with her state of mind. He felt alone. Naked. And an intense need to rip Steele's arm off and beat him with it.

"That's not true Elan." Deep down Roark wanted nothing more than to run to their daughter so he could hug her, and shove his fist through the satisfied smirk on Steele's face at the same time. Despite his healing ability, he wouldn't make it far enough to do that with all the armed guards in the room.

"Can I go train with some of the other soldiers? I'm feeling a little rusty." Elan didn't spare a glance in their direction. She didn't even acknowledge that Roark had spoken to her.

Stars danced in Roark's field of vision. White-hot pain hit him out of nowhere and shot up his spine. It took every ounce of effort to remain still. Talisa collapsing had been one thing; if he did it as well they'd know that he and Li had been up to something. He kept his eyes screwed shut tight, his lips pinched tight between his teeth while it passed.

As the wave of pain passed he became aware of something new.

Water.

He cracked open his eyes briefly, only to widen them in surprise. A small cyclone of water churned near the ground. From what he could tell the thing was growing, and he had a good idea it was him doing it. *Shit, Li!*

Roark? Are you okay? What happened?

I think the drugs finally kicked in with me. Look behind Steele.

Fucking hell. There are cameras everywhere! Stop it now.

I didn't do it on purpose.

I don't care. Stop it before someone spots it!

Roark closed his eyes and focused. He could now feel every molecule of water in the room in vivid relief. He pulled back on his vented anger as quick as he could, until he was sure the cyclone was gone.

"Of course, you may go train, princess. Please don't kill any of the soldiers this time. I do need test subjects, remember?"

"I'll try my best." Elan kissed Steele's cheek with a smile so bright, Roark had to believe it was forced.

"It's definitely shaping up to be an excellent day. Your pill tests went very well, you two had a little time together, and my princess has come back to the fold." Steele almost came off like a cartoon villain twirling a mustache in his glee. "Yes. I'd say it's been a successful day."

"Yes." Talisa's voice dripped in sarcasm. She pried her nails free of Roark's arm. "It's a red-letter day."

"Time to say goodbye now." Steele's grin turned sinister. "Well, not exactly goodbye. I just won't allow any more touching. I can't take any further chances with the two of you."

"Come on, Steele. Keep a guard on us or something. It's not like we're going anywhere." Roark growled up at the other man. "She died today. She needs to be monitored."

"No. It won't be happening today. Give me a few more successes and we'll discuss such a possibility. Say your goodbyes."

Roark pulled Talisa tight against him. "I will miss you, wife."

"I will miss you, husband."

His lips captured hers in a deep, desperate kiss. He slipped his fingers into her hair as his tongue danced with hers. Every second counted. Who knew when Steele would let them this close again. Being separated from Talisa again after seeing Elan back with Steele had shaken his resolve.

Then his wife's thoughts entered her mind.

Our daughter is impossible to read, but I did get one thing. Abby got the card.

Tal stared at the vials before her, desperate to remember what she'd been doing. After four days with her new ability in full force and she still struggled with her focus and control.

It wasn't that she was so much surprised at how difficult it was to master telepathy, it was just very difficult to pretend she was totally fine. Somehow, she had to maintain her regular levels of work and speed to ensure Steele remained oblivious to the new development.

However, the regular intrusion of others' thoughts had proved far too distracting for her to perform well enough. The first two days the excuse of her brief excursion into death had been sufficient. Unfortunately, two days was all the leeway they'd allowed.

She blew out a long breath and leaned on the table before her. Across from her, Roark worked as normal. He kept one eye on her at all times, she knew all too well.

At first, she'd focused on his mind to attempt to gain control. In the end, his myriad of thoughts turned out to be nearly as chaotic as her own so she'd had to stop that pursuit. Even so, she was so familiar with his thoughts even without the telepathy, that the telepathy only strengthened that bond and she constantly heard his thoughts along with those of the others.

"Fucking hell," she muttered.

"Problem, Li?" Roark set down his pipette to focus on her.

"It's the formula." In her scramble for an excuse, any excuse, she latched onto the easiest reason to pause work.

"What?" Roark wondered what the hell she was doing calling attention to the formula, she knew because she heard it loud and clear.

"We didn't account for the first round, which proved so successful." The effective placebos they'd handed over to Steele last time were designed to work on a crazy-long time release. In about three days they'd fail, but they'd planned to blame it on the new round of drugs. She was ruining it by saying this.

His eyes narrowed in response. "No, we didn't."

"I know we didn't, but at the same time, we did." The idea struck her to really mess with Steele. She grabbed a dry erase marker and walked to the glass separating them. Thankfully she'd learned to write in reverse during their time there.

"What are you doing?" Roark followed her to the glass.

Buying time, she muttered into his brain. Under his watchful eye, she scrawled a formula onto the glass. While she wrote, she lied her ass off for the camera. "We accounted for one dose. By the time we get this to them there will be a buildup in the system."

"Right, but if we…." Roark's voice trailed off as he studied the formula like he was seeing her point. He moved closer to run his hands along the formula. *What for? It won't work anyway.*

I've almost got this under control.

No, you don't.

Fine, I've almost figured out how to reach our daughter. She's a stone wall. Tal scribbled a few more notes. "What if we link it this way?"

"No. I think we should do this." Roark grabbed his own marker and crossed off her newest equation. He wrote a new one right beside it. Through the glass, he met her eyes. *What about home? Chance?*

We are so far, they are but echoes right now. I'm trying, but there's a lot going on here I can't get, yet push away. Tal stepped back to study his equation, which was a sound temporary placebo. "You're right. It makes more sense to come at the speed from that angle. Let's get back to work."

"Sounds good. I need to dump this one." Roark followed procedures for destroying a sample. *Do you think you will be able to break through Elan's barriers? Lucas couldn't without great effort, neither could Illy.*

She is my daughter. To Tal that was reason enough. She simply had to break through whatever Elan used to block them. "Dumping mine. Best to start from scratch."

Roark remained silent while she worked, and met her back at their matching lab tables. He nudged his head toward the glass.

Tal took the hint and wiped the formula clean from her side. Opposite her, Roark wiped at his own formula. She couldn't help but grin. "Wax on, wax off."

Roark chuckled low. "That's an oldie but goodie."

"Just popped into my head." She grinned with him and offered a wink. "Maybe one day we'll be able to have a date night again."

"I'd like that. If we were back when the world was right, where would we go?" Roark lined up his supplies in careful order. He finally broached the subject again, *is her being our daughter enough? Steele has tricks we haven't figured out.*

It is. I have faith it is. She loves us. I know she does. I've seen that much, and I'm using that to get in. It will work. Tal closed her eyes and took a deep breath as if considering his question. She pushed forward a small smile to echo the nostalgia they were trying to project, all while shoving away the overbearing thoughts of others. "That is a tough question. There are so many possibilities, so many things we've done together."

"Dinner at Petit Soleil?"

"Oooh, yes." Tal met his gaze at the memory of their favorite restaurant to visit on their nights out. "You always did know how to romance."

"Not always." He chuckled. "Our first hookup was far from romantic."

"True. You did sort of just walk into my life again and next thing you know there's a bit of wham-bam-thank-you-ma'am." She giggled under his scowl. "What?"

"You were equally at fault, and I think we scarred Warren for life that day. No warning, he just walked in and found us screwing like bunnies."

She lost any control over her laughter, busting out loud at the memory. All thought of work or attempting to break through her daughter's defenses got lost in the humor of the moment. Across the glass, Roark seemed to be in the same predicament, gripping the edge of the table to keep upright.

After a few minutes, she managed to gather some level of control to her laughter. She wiped at the couple of tears that had spilled. "Wow. I didn't even know I needed that."

"Neither did I, but it sure felt good."

"Not as good as reliving the memory, but I guess it'll have to do for now."

"I guess."

She reached out to set her hand on the glass, glad to see him match the gesture. "Someday. Right, baby?"

"Someday. Promise?"

"Promise."

Warren tapped his thumb on the laptop before him faster than the computer could process his commands. A week of waiting for test results had worn his nerves thin. The amount of equipment they had managed to scavenge was impressive but a test like this took longer than all the other tests combined they had run. None of those tests confirmed Annie's claims of having cancer. All of which made him even more suspicious.

While he appeared to ignore the door shutting behind him, he spoke to Abby as if he'd seen her come in. "How is she? Who's with her?"

Abby rested her hand on his shoulder, then slid it down his arm and pressed down to stop his thumb tapping. "Illy is keeping an eye on her while she's resting. Danny visited with her for a little while but her headache was getting bad again."

"I want to say it's impossible. We'd know. I would know." He stared at the lines of code flying across his screen, but turned his hand over to grip hers. "But I think after everything we've all gone through we know that nothing is impossible. We'll need Charlotte's help, maybe even James. We have to be sure— one hundred percent."

"I know," Her whisper was shaky. The grip she had on his hand left her white-knuckled. "I know—in my head."

"If she is—you know she could be a plant." Logical as the statement was, and even though he'd said it to keep her head level, his own stomach churned at the idea. The lunch he'd enjoyed earlier threatened to make a return visit. That thought is what kept him from spending much time with her. "Steele could have sent her just to find us. If the general has Tal and Roark, they could have made her like they did James."

"Even if all of that is true, would that make her any less our daughter?" Abby left his side. She strolled by the 'window' that was little more than a TV screen designed to give the illusion of outside. "Say Tal and Roark did this, that they created her. They would have used our DNA to do it. So that means she is our daughter as much as James is their son."

"And that wouldn't make her any less of a plant. Steele would do anything to get inside these walls and accumulate the kind of knowledge she could, Abby. We can't ever forget that. Even for DNA."

"Not DNA, our *daughter*." She sighed. "I understand the risks, the dangers. That doesn't make me want to love her any less if she is. Can't you look at her like that instead of a possible threat? Spend some time with her. Did you see her eyes? They're your eyes, Warren."

"Don't you think I want that?" Warren strode to her side and turned her to face him. "Don't you think I want nothing more than to just chalk it up to one huge blessing that stumbled into our lives? After everything that's happened, how can I? Look at what happened with Kat. Steele had everyone convinced she was his daughter, including her! She almost destroyed Tal and Roark."

"So did Caiman, but they are both here now and part of this family. They both want to see their parents again, like every other one of their kids. Why can't we have that with Annie? It's possible to break through Steele's programming if there is any."

"Both Caiman and Kat had to go through a lot of shit to get where they are now. A harsh and painful detox, if you will, from that bastard." He cupped her face in his hands. "If she is our daughter, I will do everything I can to reach that point, but I can't go into it blindly. I won't. I won't let you get hurt like that. We've had too much pain already."

"That's why this has to work. It's why Tal must be alive. We're due some joy, damn it. I'm so tired of the pain."

"Abigail." Warren sighed and pulled her close. Each of her sobs twisted his heart until he could hardly breathe. "The basic scan will help. I'm remote scanning her computer now. We'll get our answers. I promise."

"Sorry." Abby sniffed. With a strong swipe of her hand she tried to remove the tears from her cheeks, but more escaped. "It's been a long week."

"My little empath hasn't been blocking well, has she?" He tucked a finger under her chin. "You promised me you wouldn't try to ease everyone's pain and stress at once any longer. It wears you too thin."

"They got such a blow this week, I had to help. I didn't know we'd get one, too." A subtle tremble of her lips keyed him into her continuing struggle to maintain decorum. "Not to mention Chance's sense of betrayal—that Tal would contact me before him."

"Yeah, well she knows Chance. She knows that he's taking on too much responsibility already as it is. That's probably why." Warren smiled and brushed his lips across hers. "Don't you go feeling guilty for the choice Tal made."

"I'm sorry. I just…I don't know." Abby sank onto the bed. "Annie. What if she is? And she's really dying? To find our daughter only to lose her again? Warren, I know that's just the sort of thing Steele would do. I just can't think that she would hurt us. Did you see the look on her face when she saw you?"

He'd never forget that look so long as he lived. The pure joy and relief. If she'd been looking for them for a long time, he wasn't surprised she'd not been able to find them. Then she'd called him 'Daddy'. The lump reformed in his throat before he could stop it. "One step at a time, Abby. First, we need test results. We need to find out if she is our daughter, and then we can focus on what's wrong with her."

"The initial DNA sweep should be back soon." Her lip turned white between her teeth. "After that we'll start the more in-depth scans. If we need to dig deeper with her DNA, that will have to be on Char or James."

"James won't touch it, you know that."

"Maybe he will for this. If we really think she's like him, why wouldn't he?"

"You know why." Warren tucked a lock of hair behind her ear. "No matter what intelligence Tal gave him, the anger wins every time. Seeing another clone might just send him off on another surge of violence. Plus, he swore he'd never touch another science tool with his parents gone. They were the only reason he ever bothered to use his brain over his brawn."

"He has to get over that! Char can't do this all alone. My knowledge is only helpful to a certain point. I never took the in-depth study that Tal did." Her nails dug into his hand. "He has to make an exception."

"Abby." The computer beeped and immediately Warren saw the results in his own mind without looking at the screen. He closed his eyes as the ramifications became more real.

"Warren?"

"Basic sweep says she's ours. Our daughter."

"Our daughter."

"And she's dying. I don't think it's cancer, Abby. Not even close."

Annie clenched her teeth against yet another needle sinking into her skin. The effort to not jerk away from the damn thing resulted in a hiss escaping. The doctors she'd dealt with during her illness before the War had never been her favorite. Needles, however, topped the list of her least favorite things.

"Sorry, Annie. I just need another vial or two. I won't have to stick you again today, promise." Charlotte flashed an apologetic smile. "I'm a little distracted today."

Annie couldn't help but laugh. "Distractions and needles aren't usually good things to mix. Is something wrong? I mean, beyond what appears to be the norm."

"There's still no sign of my sister."

"I'm sorry. I know that's tough—but why is it worse today?"

"It's not. I just have a feeling. Around here, if you have a feeling about your twin, it's pretty spot on. Something bad is going on. I don't think things are going like she'd hoped." Charlotte sighed as she switched to the next vial.

"You should be worrying about that, about finding your parents. You shouldn't be spending so much time worrying about me." Her eyes stayed glued on the needle penetrating her skin.

"Based on your test results, the sooner we start this, the better. I can get tests started on you do something to help." Charlotte secured a Band-Aid over the hole after she'd removed the needle. "There isn't much I can do in the search for my parents right now. Others are working on those details."

With a small smile, she rested her hand on the other woman's arm. The pain building behind her eyes made her feel the opposite of her statement, but she'd learned years ago to face facts, and her illness on her own. "Charlotte, please. It's okay. I don't think I'm going to fall over dead right this second. You should be concentrating on that, not trying to save a lost cause."

"Annie?" Charlotte's voice laced with concern. Her hand settled over Annie's. "What is it?"

"Nothing. I just...." The fire sprinkler on the ceiling had to become the most interesting thing in the room to look at. Her eyes fluttered rapidly to stave off the tears. "When I thought about what it would be like to find my parents, this is far from what I imagined."

"What did you imagine?"

"I thought they'd want me, you know. Maybe even be happy to see me." A tear ran down her cheek against her control. The whole week had been way too much.

"They do want you. You're their daughter."

"No. They don't. He doesn't, at least." Annie blew out a gust of frustration. "Mo-Abig-hell, I don't even know what to call them! Warren can barely stand to look at me."

"You have to understand. This is a lot for them to digest. You have a lifetime of memories, they don't. I wish there was an easy fix to all of this for you."

"Hey, Shorty. We're shutting down the grid in a...." With a click the room went black a moment after James stepped into the room. "Okay, make that now. Steele is doing flyovers."

"Good. That means you can't work. Go be with your family, Charlotte." Annie stood, hands outstretched to guide her while she waited for her eyes to adjust.

"Are you okay to find your way around?" A warm light filled the room. When Annie turned, Charlotte held a small ball of fire in her hand.

"I'll be fine. I told you, I'm not going to keel over right this second." Annie forced a smile. "Really. I'll be fine."

Charlotte squeezed Annie's arm with her free hand. "We'll talk more later. Be nice, James."

"When am I not nice?" James smirked at his sister before she left the room. As the dark settled in, he spoke again, "Where you headed?"

"You don't have to babysit me, James." Her defenses snapped back into place. The way James kept popping into her periphery only to turn around and run off left her feeing raw. "Unless that's what you were sent here to do."

James snorted from beside her. "Don't flatter yourself."

"Right." Annie reached for the door panel only to have her fingers close around his arm. She snatched her hand back as if she'd been burned. "Stupid of me to think anyone wants to actually be around me." Without any apology, she pushed past him and stormed into the hallway.

At least out here there were some lanterns hanging on the wall to light the way somewhat. She took off down the hall, away from all of it.

"Hey! Where do you think you're going?" James' voice chased down the hall after her.

"Leave me alone, James." She followed the paths she'd come to know over the past week, toward the one she hadn't been allowed near all week. The one outside, away from the suffocating tunnels.

"All I asked was where you were going." The pace of his steps increased in an effort to keep up with her.

"Go to hell!" The urge to freeze him in place grew strong. It would show him that weak or not, she still had her powers. Maybe then they'd listen to her. Maybe then they'd see her.

"What the hell is your issue?"

"At the moment, it appears to be you. Go play tall, dark and angry for someone else." The stairs to the upper levels loomed just ahead of her. The surface called to her. Fresh air, a few minutes to collect her thoughts, that's all she needed.

James' hand closed around her wrist at the same moment her fingers reached the door panel. "Would you stop?" His words were punctuated by a growl that vibrated through the corridor.

Annie glared at him in the dim light. She tugged against his grip. "Let me go."

"You can't go up there." His grip remained firm on her wrist, but wasn't rough. He tugged her toward him almost gently.

"Why? Am I your prisoner now? You can't tell me what to do." She remained perfectly still. If she gave even a tug of resistance, he'd be prepared for anything she might try.

"Actually, I can. Now let's get you back to the main area until it's safe." He made the two mistakes she'd been hoping for: he let down his guard, and released her wrist.

"I don't think so." She left behind a breeze as she tapped into her other mutation. In a blur, she burst through the door and up the stairs so fast he wouldn't be able to catch her.

Once she escaped the tunnels and made her way through the house that hid the compound below, she slowed. She burst through the front door into the sunshine where she paused to take a deep breath.

"Wanna explain what the hell you think you're doing?" Under the annoyance in his voice, she thought she detected a hint of admiration.

Sunlight cascaded over her. The cool breeze in the air felt like heaven after the stale, recycled air of the tunnels. With her face turned up toward the sky, she blew out a breath. "Let me guess. No one ever got away from you before."

"That didn't answer my question."

"I don't owe you an explanation. You've made your feelings quite clear this past week. You don't want to be around me." The warmth of the sun on her face eased some of the tension.

"When the hell did I say that?"

"You didn't have to." One shoulder rose in a shrug. "The way you act says it all."

"We need to get inside." Tension crept back into his voice. "I'm not kidding, Anne. Come on now."

"I told you—" She yelped when his arm snaked around her waist and he spun her to face him. His proximity sent her nerves tingling as his lips hovered so close to hers she thought he might kiss her. Instead, he moved fast to toss her over his shoulder. "Put me down. Damn it, James. Put me down now!"

"Woman, would you shut up?" James stormed back into the house. He moved fast through the rooms to a back bedroom.

He set her on her feet there, but continued to maneuver her toward the closet. "I'm not kidding."

"Get off me." Annie struggled against him, intent on putting some distance between them. Unfortunately, the use of her powers earlier had left her weak and all attempts failed.

A low growl resonated through James' chest. "You just don't listen, do you?" His arm wrapped around her again. He lifted her mere inches off the floor to carry her the last few feet to the closet. The door clicked behind them so they were left again in total darkness.

"Why the hell are we in a closet?"

"I have reasons." He rummaged above their head. A moment later she heard a click and a piece of technology sprang to life. Small, and yet so complex it would take her hours to figure out at full power.

"This isn't exactly the time for seven minutes in heaven." What the hell had gotten into him? First, he wanted her to stay downstairs, and now he had her pinned in the back of a small closet.

"There are soldiers approaching the house. That's why…now shut up." His breath danced across her ear in a harsh whisper.

"What did you turn on?"

"Something to block their devices. Now I won't tell you again, shut up."

Even though she couldn't see his face, she didn't doubt he glared at her through it all. When the struggling between them ceased she became acutely aware of just how close they were. His body pressed hers into the wall. Her fingers rested on his muscular chest where she swore she could feel his heart beating against it. His hand gripped one of her wrists tight, like he feared she might run away again. She whispered, "James."

"Do you just not like to listen or is it just me you don't want to listen to?"

"If you weren't cutting off the circulation to my hand I wouldn't have said anything." Her whisper came out just as harsh. When he let go, she took a shaky breath. "Thank you."

"Welcome." The apology was gruff, and probably forced. So long as he hadn't snapped at her again, she'd take it.

Without thinking too hard about what she was doing, she laid her forehead on his shoulder. She stifled her yawn as best as she could.

"Tired?" This time there was no harshness to his tone. She could have sworn she heard the warmth of concern.

"Mmhmm." She nodded against him. Her response was just as quiet, "Using my abilities wears me out. Could be the whole dying thing."

Another low growl rumbled against her ear where it lay.

She yawned again. "If you're going to keep me in a closet, can we at least sit down?"

James guided her to the floor with a gentle touch she didn't remember feeling from him before. "Close your eyes and get some rest. We could be in here for a while."

"Not going to argue." Annie leaned back against him easily. His warmth added to her drowsiness. "Thank you."

"Don't mention it."

"Tell someone you were nice to me? I wouldn't dare ruin your reputation as the resident jackass."

A low chuckled carried under his breath. "Get some rest Anne."

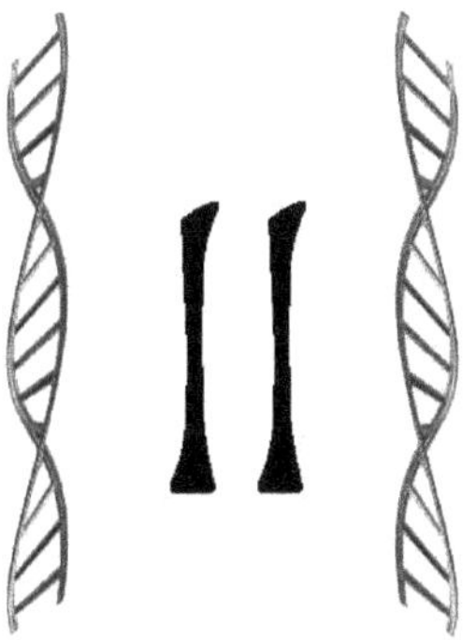

"We've been working on this for a week. Tell me we've made progress." Chance scrubbed his hands over his face to focus. A headache throbbed behind his eyes as it had been for over a week thanks to all the chaos.

Leave it to Talisa to turn his world upside down from captivity. His biggest regret now was that she wasn't there. They had no idea where she could be, even after his multiple intense meditations. At the very least they knew she was alive, and hopefully that meant Roark had survived as well.

"I wish. I've looked through all of my old notes and there's nothing else I can think of dealing with the card from Talisa." Abby sighed. "All I can get is that they are alive, but there's nothing as far as location or anything like that. The symbols weren't that specific."

"Knowing Tal that won't be the only message we get from her. We'll have to keep our eyes out. If she got something out once, she'll do it again." Chance raked a hand through his hair. "What about the fly over?"

"We shut down the grid in time. No noise from Steele's soldiers." Warren rubbed Abby's shoulders as he stood behind her. "One of my nullifying devices was triggered so there was at least one person above ground, but the device seemed to have worked."

"Everyone else made it inside in time." Abby took a shaky breath.

Chance clasped his hands behind his back to stretch some of the rising tension from his shoulders. "And I know Charlotte was beginning Annie's testing when we shut the grid down."

"I was—sorry I'm late." Charlotte kissed Chance on the cheek before she moved to the chair next to Abby. "James was with Annie when the grid shut down. She got away from him. They're both down here safe now."

Abby placed a hand on top of Warren's. "Basic DNA sweep shows she's our daughter."

"Plant?" Chance frowned when Abby tensed in front of him. He didn't like to ask, but he had to. The mental detox Elan and Kat had gone through had been hard enough for all of them. They didn't need to go through it again. "I'm sorry, Abby. You know I have to ask. It's the last thing I want to be true."

"I know," she whispered. "I'm praying it's not true, but I do know it's a possibility."

"We're all hoping for that Gail." Warren kissed the top of her head. "Have you gotten anything else back from the tests yet Charlotte?"

Charlotte squirmed in her seat. "I want to get James to run some tests. So, we have the whole picture."

"What aren't you telling us?" Warren's jaw clenched.

"Let me get a definitive answer first Uncle Warren." Charlotte pulled her bottom lip between her teeth.

"If you give me an idea what's going on Char I can start looking into treatments for whatever it is that is making her sick." Abby gripped Warren's hand.

"Only thing I know for sure at the moment is using the molecular manipulation made her really tired. James said she fell asleep a few minutes after he got her back inside." Charlotte shrugged.

"Where is James? Why didn't he come with you since Annie is down here safe?" Chance frowned. James never missed a briefing. Especially when a fly over occurred.

"He's sitting with Annie. They were stuck in a closet for a few hours during the flyovers. Brought her down as soon as he could. I did a quick exam." Charlotte glanced between the other three in the room. "Right now, it's like she's sleeping really hard. Once she fell asleep James couldn't wake her before he tried to bring her down."

"Is she, all right?" Worry creased across Abby's forehead.

"Her vitals are holding for now. If she doesn't wake up soon I'm going to do another round and we'll make a decision as far as an IV." Charlotte leaned forward. "We're going to take care of her, Aunt Abby. She's your daughter, and you need to be her mother, not her doctor."

"So, our new addition has James riled up?" Chance pursed his lips. That never happened. If anything, James was detached from everyone. He was only interested in their abilities as warriors to help the cause.

"You could say that. He's been a yo-yo this past week. Spooked, angry, and…hell, I don't even know what he is at this time. I'm seeing things I've never seen from him before. He's making me dizzy." Charlotte shook her head. "His aura and I are not friends right now."

"Did you and his aura have a fight?" Chance couldn't help his own chuckle.

"Something like that." Charlotte smirked back at him.

"How long has she been out?" Chance's eyes darted back toward Abby and Warren and Abby. Annie joining them had already turned his friend's world upside down. James' world tilting even the slightest could lead to unexpected results.

"About four hours, since shortly after we shut down the grid. We'll see how long it lasts, but there's no sign of her letting up yet."

Chance nodded. "Keep us posted on her progress, and any progress you make with the tests."

"Will do, Popsicle."

"Please...." Abby's voice strained. "We need to help her."

"We will, Aunt Abby. We'll do everything we possibly can."

"If James is with Annie, who took care of the security checks after the flyover?" Chance didn't fault James for staying with Annie. If any connection existed between the two, he wouldn't discourage it. With Talisa gone it took more and more to reign in James' anger when necessary. However, they did have protocols to follow.

"RB took point. All worked out, Pop. Don't you worry about it. Everything is secure. RB made sure of it." Charlotte smiled at him. "You know Mom is going to pluck you in the forehead if you get worry lines from all the mental pacing you're doing."

"Stay out of my aura, kiddo. I have enough on my mind right now." He smirked at her.

"Would if I could but I'm stuck with my constant acid trip." Charlotte pushed on her knees to stand. "I'm going to drag James into the lab by his braids if I have to. Do you and Aunt Abby want to sit with Annie for a bit, Uncle Warren?"

"Of course we do." Warren nodded. "We'll come with you."

"Oh, wait. Before I forget." Charlotte paused at the door and turned to Abby. "I told Pops last week, but didn't think to mention it to you. Maybe you'll know what's going on."

"What do you mean?" Abby looked almost relieved to have something to focus on.

"Last week I was with Lucas to seek out Mom and Dad's threads. I found them, but something happened to Mom's thread. I think she's up to something."

Warren laughed softly. "When is she not?"

"True." Charlotte smiled. "But her thread went all wavy and then dimmed out for a minute. I honestly thought she was gone, dead. Then a moment later it flashed really bright before it went back to normal."

"What could that mean?" Abby's frown returned.

"So, no ideas?" Charlotte sighed. "I was hoping."

"No, none." Abby shook her head. "I can't even begin to imagine."

"I'm sure we'll find out soon enough, but not before Tal is ready." Warren held out his hand to Abby to help her stand.

"All I'm sure of is that it means Tal is up to something." Chance folded his arms across his chest. "You guys go tend to Annie. I'm going to meditate some more and see if the Spirits have any answers for me this time."

"We'll see you later Pop. Be careful." Charlotte kissed his cheek before she left with Abby and Warren in tow.

Chance let his head drop back. He stared at the ceiling as if it would give him the answers. "Whatever you are up to Kajah...may the Spirits guide you home safely."

Ilana stood at the top of one of the tunnels Chance had created over the past few days. They'd decided to build down instead of out to keep their footprint small. Before Annie had arrived, Warren had been hard at work to create something to shield their energy signatures, but now she knew he was too distracted for such a task, even if the man's mind never stopped running, ever.

She knew in the northernmost corner several Exceptionals were making that tunnel into a stairwell with metal walls and air ducts. The eventual goal was to build a functioning societal structure with up to twenty levels serving multiple tasks. They were currently working only on the second level, which would serve as little more than another living space level. Chance had built eight spiraled tunnels that went down twenty feet so they could begin the next level.

The tunnel she stood over, however, should have been empty. While most everyone else was running around panicking about Annie or Elan, she knew that this tunnel wasn't, in fact, empty. She stepped into the dark and snapped her fingers. A flame flickered on her fingertips, and she flicked it to the ceiling of the tunnel where it spread into a rope of light to brighten her path.

With every step, she took roots lifted from the smooth dirt of the tunnel to form a staircase over the slick, cool mud. She slowed as she got three quarters of the way down, sending the flame ahead of her to warn the person down there of her arrival.

She wouldn't interrupt, she was far too respectful of what Chance was doing to do so.

Chance's voice echoed up the narrow tunnel. "Come on down, Illy. I knew you were coming. I appreciate your warning, though."

"I didn't want to interrupt." Ilana took the last ten steps around into the open space he'd created. Candlelight flickered on the dirt walls, and a mix of herbal scents still wafted through the air. "Your meditations are too important."

"Funny, according to others they're useless." His lips were turned down into a frown, a crack of frustration in his voice he usually tried to keep hidden. More than anyone, Ilana knew how much Chance kept hidden from others. Part of the good, and bad, that came with her particular mishmash of gifts. Far as she knew only Lucas was as aware as she was, because as the only other telepath, and the medicine man, he would have to know.

"Elan was scared, she didn't mean it."

"She did. You do not have to defend her, and she was not all wrong." This time Chance smiled and shrugged. "She reminds me of your mother so much sometimes. I just wish I could have foreseen her leaving. I thought once she had it out with me she'd calm enough to see reason, or at least see Danny, who would help her see reason."

Ilana ducked her head to hide her grimace. She should have known Chance would see her lie for what it was. Elan was scarred worse than any of them, and was skilled at even keeping herself and Lucas out of her head to see all that had wounded her. Ilana wondered if she was delusional to think that was Elan's way of protecting them. "I hoped she would, too. Old instincts came up instead."

"Do you know where she is?"

"No. Lucas is top side in hopes of having better luck. I tried flying, but she's been well out of my range for days. I think she brought in help to get her somewhere faster. By the time we knew she was gone, we had no hope of finding her."

Chance blew out a harsh breath and shook his head.

"There is something else, isn't there?" Ilana stepped closer. While she loved her family and worried for them, she took her role as Guardian seriously. She'd failed to protect many of her people from death during the worst battles of the War, but she'd do whatever it took to protect what was left of them now. Especially since the Lenape tribe had folded the Exceptionals into their world before, during, and after the major events of the War.

Part of protecting the tribe meant keeping the Chief on an even keel. Between herself and Lucas, they did all they could to maintain his mental and physical health. For Ilana herself, that meant being a friend in the absence of her mother.

"Speaking of reminding me of your mother." For the briefest second another smile tugged the corner of his lips until it faded into a grimace of sadness and grief. "Why don't you believe that my current state has to do with all of the chaos we've been handed in the past few days?"

"If you're accusing me of nosing around in your head, I wasn't." She smiled to soften what might have been taken as a harsh statement if he wasn't in a good state of mind. "I have come to learn your body language, Chief. Something has happened that I don't know about."

"I think so."

She pinched her brows together and tilted her head. "You think so?"

"It happened just now during my meditation. I'm not yet sure if it actually happened or if the Spirits were just confirming what we believed to be true, that your mother is alive."

"What happened?"

"I heard her. I heard Talisa call my name."

"Heard her?"

"In here." Chance pointed to his head. "Not in my ears. In my head, just like when you or Lucas speak to me. There was a nudge, a creak like a door opening, and then she spoke."

"Mom. Mom spoke to you telepathically? But she's not—"

"A telepath, I know."

"May I?"

He stepped closer and nodded. "Yes. I wouldn't mind clarification."

Ilana opened her mind. Telepathy was one of the two talents she'd naturally been born with, along with shapeshifting. The Spirits had gifted the rest during a crisis, when she'd been revealed as the tribe's Guardian. The two talents she'd been born with were always present, the rest had to be called upon as she needed them.

Because of this she'd had to learn to close off her mind as much as possible or the thoughts of others became too much. She'd learned to focus it so closely that she could direct it just at Chance as she opened up.

His confusion over the event hit her like a ton of bricks first. She picked over the pile of thoughts and got back to the actual moment when he'd heard the voice.

Chance.

The sound of her mother's voice cut right through Ilana's heart and she pulled free of Chance's mind with a gut-wrenching sob. "Mama."

"Illy." Chance's arms went around her as her knees buckled.

"It was real. It was her. I don't know how, but it was her."

Caiman leaned against the cold metal wall. After living a good portion of her life in this compound, she knew precisely where to go to avoid a full-on view from the cameras. There were only two or three places to hide, and she knew every one of them.

Figuring out what compound Steele would use to hide her parents in was a matter of simple deduction. This particular compound was the most secret of all of his bases. Here was where she'd been hidden for most of her life, where she'd been kept from her true family, where she'd been lied to for years and told that her parents didn't want her.

If Caiman ever cried, she would right then. The pain etched on her real father's face when he'd seen her in that room, the deep crevices of pain that had lined his features when she'd shown affection to the bastard that had raised her, it cut her deep. For so long they'd worked to free her of Steele's brainwashing, and here she was back voluntarily.

There was no other way to free them. With her on the inside it was more than likely she could get both of her parents to safety, and keep all the Exceptionals safe. She'd fought on the wrong side of the cause for so long, she would now gladly give up her life for their safety.

Even if Danny would never forgive her.

Elan.

Caiman grew still. She darted a glance up and down the corridor, looking for anyone that would have dared to impersonate her mother's voice.

Baby girl. Why are you doing this?

"Momma," she whispered.

Did you think your dad and I couldn't handle this?

"How? Momma, how are you doing this? Where are you?" Elan put a hand to her forehead. "Not even Lucas or Illy can get in my head. How are you?"

I am your mother. We're connected too strongly for you to completely block me out, baby. It isn't easy to make you hear me, but I wouldn't ever give up trying.

"Momma." Caiman had never been so close to actual tears. She sank to the floor and wrapped her arms around herself. "I'll get you out of here. I swear it."

Get yourself out. Now. Before it's too late. Go back to Daniel. Tell them we are alive. We will find our own way out. We would never be at peace if we got free at the cost of our own daughter. I lost you once to that man, I won't do it again."

"I'm sorry Momma. I have to do this. If you're in my head, you know it too."

Elan, no.

Caiman forced out her mother's voice and rose. There was no way she'd fail in this mission. Steele forgot one very important thing.

She'd grown up in this compound, but more importantly, Steele had raised her as his ultimate weapon. Her intense, brutal training made her the best. While he'd searched for ways to create super-soldiers under the guise of destroying the threat he'd created—he'd grown his own little super-soldier in the package that was Caiman herself.

Worst of all for him, she knew all the ins and outs of his organization. In the end, the so-called military would suffer a huge blow. Roark and Talisa would be free to return home and save Annie.

Everyone would win.

Except Steele.

If this proved to be her last mission, it would be the best damn mission she'd ever run. The best executed and the only one she'd ever done for the right cause, the right reasons, to save the right people.

If she did it right, Steele would be dead along with a chunk of his military.

"Caiman, my dear." Steele's smile was warm as she entered his office. "Thank you for not killing my men. Talisa and Roark actually made improvements with their latest experiment. My project is finally seeing the progress we'd always dreamed of."

Caiman forced forward a bright smile. She could kill him right there and then, but he had safeguards in place that would mean instant death for her parents. First, she had to play his game until he let her close enough to disable those mechanisms. "Good to know. Curious they were together like that, though. I thought for sure you'd never allow such a thing."

"Oh, that. Talisa had a heart attack or some nonsense. She's too weak to do much of anything right now. Also, it can't be said that I'm heartless. I suppose a couple of hours once a year is allowable." Steele smirked. "They can consider it incentive to do well. I might let them see each other again."

"So, you're done pursuing Talisa as your own personal genetics factory and bedmate?" She picked up a gun from his large display of weaponry. All of them were empty of ammo, but she pretended to admire the new addition to his collection, wishing it could be so easy as one bullet.

"She's been too disagreeable this time. Pretty as she is, I don't care for such attitude. Having this disease has really changed her."

Disease. She tried not to curl her lip over the fact he still called their mutations a disease, or his levels of denial that anything changed her mother but her losses. The genetic alterations only made her stronger. Steele would never change, though. The fact that he and military leaders from all around the world were the cause of this 'disease' didn't matter to him, he only wanted it eradicated because he wanted to control the super humans, not be defeated by them. "You'll still let me remain infected, won't you Poppy?"

It was a good thing he couldn't see her face, because this time she did grimace at calling him Poppy again. He chuckled behind her. "I'm not insane, Caiman. You are the best soldier I've ever had. So long as you remain loyal to me, you'll stay just as you are."

"Good to know."

"On that note."

Caiman's stomach did a sickening flop. A lifetime in the man's presence left her familiar with every nuance of every tone of his voice. She knew what he was thinking before he said it, and while she'd expected as much, it didn't make it easier to face. He wouldn't trust her, not yet. She'd have to endure one more test of faith first, the most brutal and soul crushing. The one that could well end her marriage to Danny if it wasn't already over. "What sort of test are you throwing at me, Poppy?"

"You should pluralize that. You've been out of the fold a long time, my dear. Who knows what they've brainwashed you to believe." One firm hand planted on her shoulder. "You've endured these tests before. It should be no trouble this time.

Caiman couldn't deny the scream of Talisa in her mind, proving she hadn't truly shoved her mother all the way out. Of course, her own grief and guilt over what Steele's plans would mean to her life, her husband, and how much she would betray her own wedding vows. She had to focus on the end game. "Of course, Poppy."

"That's my girl. I have a few new toys to play with you, but first you can go visit your old friend. He'll be thrilled to see you again. You both did so well mixing business and pleasure." Steele's smile when he turned her around was cold and hard as his moniker. "Once you've adjusted back to our way of life I'll be able to send you on your first mission."

Caiman nodded and pulled away. After a brief glance toward her parents' labs below, she left the office. There was no point in delaying the inevitable. Maybe in the end her 'friend' would be able to help her.

Chaz had been as warped as her when she'd left. There'd been seven more years for Steele to warp him further. Unlike her, Chaz was treated like an actual animal. To Steele, he was no more than a tool and a way to get money. Chaz was regularly sold off to rich benefactors for hunting, or for women to play with in their own sick way.

First, she would have to deal with the animal. Perhaps then she could get through to the human she knew lived underneath. That meant doing something she hadn't done since she'd met Danny, she'd have to let another man abuse her. If there'd been any doubt before, it was a sealed deal now. Danny would never forgive her.

Outside the door to Chaz's quarters stood two guards. She waved them off. Last thing she needed now was an audience.

The door slid open at a touch of the keypad. Humidity wafted over her, and birds chirped somewhere inside. Her sharp ears picked up other animals scurrying and slipping through the foliage and trees of the jungle Steele had created in the room. If she hadn't known its purpose, she might have called the scene before her pretty.

Instead, it was a sick elaborate cage for an Exceptional that deserved far better. Of course, that particular Exceptional didn't know it, and had been conditioned to not think like most humans. After a few deep breaths to brace herself, she stepped into the woods.

The path to Chaz's cage had become overgrown. Since the War it was probably difficult to find the wealthy individuals that had once fueled Chaz's purpose as money-bait. It seemed the War had spared Chaz from some of his worst duties.

That also meant he'd been penned in for a very long time. Which meant the upcoming re-initiation could be very painful as Chaz would likely have little control over his animal instincts, as if he ever had.

"Chaz?" Caiman crept over the large log that held his cage. "Cheetah?"

A low growl greeted her, feline, and nasty as hell.

"Cheetah, it's me. It's Caiman." She dropped down in front of the cage. Yellow eyes glowed from inside. She was surprised to find her hand shaking as she reached for the lock. The code was complex, which bought her a few more minutes. "Cheetah."

"You left." It was a snarl, difficult to understand. Of course, his use of English had never been great, but based on those two words it might have devolved some.

"I had a mission. He sent me away. I'm here now. Maybe together we can get out."

He growled low again. "Let me out."

"I am." Caiman hovered over the last number. "Cheetah. Remember, I'm your friend."

"You always help."

She swallowed against the uncharacteristic fear of what that meant. After pushing down the fear as she'd been trained, she hit the last button. She stumbled away from the cage.

A flash of pain triggered her mutation.

Soon it would be over.

Then he would listen.

He had to.

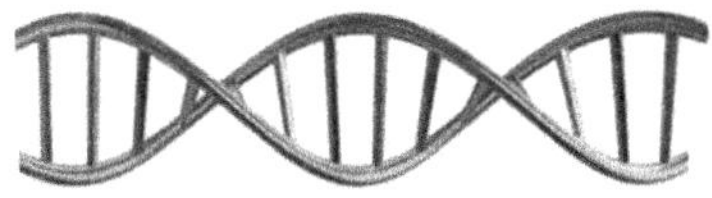

Warren leaned forward, his brows puckered in a perplexed stare. "What do you mean, you heard her in your head? Tal is a great many things, I admit—but telepathic isn't one of them."

"I had Ilana confirm it before I said anything. It's just like I said. We *are* talking about Tal here. If anyone can find a way to make that happen, she and Roark would be able to do it." Chance perched on the arm of the couch. He still couldn't believe what he'd heard, even if he'd had it confirmed. "Fact of the matter is, they are alive. Now we have to figure out how to get them out of there."

"So now you believe me about the card?" Abby's snarky tone didn't match the way she calmly sipped her tea. The past few days since they'd gotten the test results on Annie had done a number on her and Warren. Both looked exhausted with dark circles under their eyes.

"I do." Chance blew out a breath. He knew Abby's attitude had much to do with what they were going through rather than the matter at hand. "Just like I have always believed Charlotte. The ties are still bright. Tal's dimmed briefly a week ago, but it returned and they are both still there. I'm wondering if what Char saw is when Tal gained her telepathy."

"Maybe we are finally catching a break. If only Charlotte could give us some good news about Annie the day would be even better." Abby glanced over her shoulder toward Warren.

"Charlotte and James, you mean," Chance corrected her.

"Right. I keep forgetting he's actually stepped foot back in the lab." Abby took a shaky breath. "To help Annie."

"I haven't seen him this determined in a long time. The past couple of days he's barely left the lab. RB has been running point on security while he's in there. From what Charlotte tells me, he only takes breaks to check on Annie just as she does." Deep down Chance knew the situation with Annie had thrown both Abby and Warren.

He remembered how it had felt when he'd found out Charlotte's DNA had been altered and a part of him had been added to her. It felt like a punch in the gut to say the least. In an instant he'd had a daughter, one he loved as if she'd always been his.

This situation was different, though. "How is Annie doing? Not the tests, I'm getting updates on that. I mean, how is she?"

"Sleeping a lot." Abby's voice hitched. "Any time she uses her mutations she gets tired. She slept for over ten hours after she used them to get away from James the other day."

"They will find something." The entire situation screamed Steele. The man was a monster and anyone who had the audacity to rebuff his plans paid the price in one way or another.

"Charlotte managed to get James working now, but what if he gives up again? Right now, he might be focused, but what happens when the anger returns? You know it always does. What if he refuses to work on it again?" Warren poured himself another cup of coffee, even though all the caffeine in the world couldn't possibly help his levels of exhaustion.

"He cares for Annie." Chance shrugged. "According to Charlotte, the anger is buried so deep when he's with Annie that she can barely see it. There are threads forming between them where James doesn't often form attachments."

"That's all well and good Chance, but what are we going to do?" Warren's fit of anger sagged back into exhaustion in an instant.

"We are going to continue to do whatever we can for Annie. Lucas is meditating to see if he can glean anything from the Spirits to help. As far as Tal and Roark go, we are looking. Mostly we are looking for Elan, because if we can find her, we'll find them."

"The Spirits? The *Spirits*, Chance?" Warren slammed his mug down hard enough to slosh the hot liquid over the side. "This is our daughter we're talking about. One we didn't even know we had—and now she's dying! How the hell are some burning herbs and hallucinations going to help her?"

"Warren…!" Abby shot to her feet. She crossed the room to her husband, her hand running along his back.

"Don't try to calm me down, Abigail! She shouldn't have to suffer like this." Warren brushed aside her touch.

"Warren," Chance tried his hand. "We understand—"

"Understand? Really?" Warren spun around, fury swirling in his eyes. The TV that stood in for a window on the wall became snowy. "There is no way in hell you could understand this."

"Baby, they are doing everything they can." Abby tried in vain to reign in Warrens' anger.

"It's not enough. We are losing her before we even get to know her." Warren drooped against the wall. As he slid to the floor the screen went black.

Chance took a shaky breath as he slipped off the arm of the couch onto the cushion. "I may not know exactly how it feels, but I can see how it is affecting the two of you and for that I am sorry. I know that's not enough, and never could be."

"They need to do more. That's our little girl." Warren's arms wrapped around Abby as he held her close. "Can't lose her. We just can't."

"It's so hard to watch her slip away like this. I'm a doctor, not an idiot, and I know what is happening." Abby wiped at a few tears that slipped down her face. "When she first arrived, there was such a fire in her eyes. Every time she wakes up it has dimmed."

"How bad is the degradation?" Chance knew the answer before he even finished the question by the flinch from Abby.

"It's bad." Abby pushed on her knees to stand. She struggled to get to the closest chair, her hands shaking as she took it. This time Warren moved behind her and began to comfort her. "She maybe has two months if things keep going the way they are right now. Less if she continues to use her abilities."

Warren cleared his throat. "Charlotte said every time she sees Annie the threads between Annie and us have dimmed some more. We're losing her a little more every day."

"They are keeping us updated as they can. The lack of equipment and resources are making it harder to find the answers." Abby wiped at her tears again. Her hands raked through her hair as she blew out an exasperated breath. She surprised him with a subject change. "What about you? Hearing Talisa? What did she say?"

"Charlotte will be the best gauge for following her progress, even better than any test they run." Chance rubbed his hand along the back of his neck at her question. "Talisa said my name, nothing else. I mentally screamed back at her but I don't know if she heard me or not. Like I said earlier I had Ilana confirm it so I know I didn't just imagine it. We're looking at me sitting with a telepath to boost the signal, so to speak."

"So, either Lucas or Ilana, then. I don't know that Ariel will be up to that." Abby leaned back in her chair.

"Ariel isn't up to much these days. She was doing better but the anniversary of the attack caused her to regress again." Chance rested his elbows on his knees, his fingers steepled together. There had been many losses on the day of the attack, but when they lost Joe they'd essentially lost Ariel as well. The couple's deep telepathic connection severed so violently that it had left Ariel catatonic for a month.

"Unfortunately, right now all we can do is wait. Hurry up and wait. My least favorite thing." A frown tugged the corners of Chance's lips downward.

"That doesn't bode well. You're the patient one." Warren smirked across the room at his friend.

"Tell me about it."

James stormed up to Annie. "There you are. Where the hell have you been? We've been looking everywhere for you."

"Hello to you too, James." Annie blew out a breath. Before she snapped back an ugly retort, she took a deep breath to gather her thoughts. When she spoke again her voice escaped in a shaky whisper. "Didn't think I'd be missed."

"You can't just run off like that." A low growl laced through his words.

"No running. Just sitting." Her eyes stayed locked on the sunset as she swung her legs against the low stone wall she sat on. She continued without giving him a chance to get another word in, "It's odd. Knowing that the end is fast approaching. The bucket list gets longer—filled with things you'll never get to do."

"You aren't going to die."

Sadness marred her attempted smile. She turned toward him. "You can't guarantee that, James. No one here can. Weeks ago, I only had a sense I was dying. Now I can actually feel it. Bit by bit as each cell dies off."

James laid his hand on top of hers in a surprisingly gentle gesture. "I'm gonna find a way to help you. I know this isn't easy but—"

"Please God don't finish that sentence." Her lips trembled in a sign of her slipping control. She squeezed her eyes shut so she wouldn't see his pity. "If one more person tell me they understand how I feel or what it's like I will scream. No one knows what this is like. No one could possibly know."

"We all face death every day here, Anne."

"That isn't what I mean!"

"Then what do you mean?"

Annie swiped her hand across her face in a futile effort to wipe away the tears she could no longer control. "I'm not real. What was that Charlotte called me? Right—a clone. I'm a clone. Created as some mad man's plaything. All made up of parts. Scraps and leftovers of Abby and Warren held together by a tenuous thread that happens to be unraveling. No one on this planet is going to understand that."

"That's not true." A gentle touch came to her cheek as James brushed a tear away. There is at least one person that understands. Me."

"Stop. You don't have to make things up to try and make me feel better." Annie jerked away from his touch. Truth be told the gentleness of the touch startled her. Butterflies flitted around her stomach. She fought against them. The last thing she needed now was to make any sort of short-lived connection with anyone. Funny since she'd worked so hard to find her family.

"I'm not making anything up. I'm a clone, too."

"James, really. Just sto—wait. What? You?" She shifted to turn toward him. Her eyes were wide in disbelief. "You're a clone?"

"Of Lucas." He nodded. "The same guy that did this to you forced my mom to create me. Don't see me sitting around with a chip on my shoulder about it."

Laughter bubbled up through the sadness in her heart. "Seriously? No chip? Most of the time you are a giant ball of anger. Hell, just about every time I see you, you either snap at me or yell at me."

"Can't help it." One of his shoulders rose in a shrug. "Part of the programming I received, I guess. They gave me brains and I'm angry as hell. Not much gets rid of it. When I really get going only Mom could ever calm me down. I'm just permanently pissed off."

Annie shook her head. "No. Not permanently. There has been a few times you haven't acted like an ogre."

"Oh, really now? When was this?" James tilted his head. The smirk that curved his lips wasn't snide, in fact she'd have to call it sexy.

"You let me sleep on your shoulder in that closet." She mentally shook off the thoughts of how sexy his smirk was. The last thing she needed was to have any thoughts about James beyond his help. Something about him always pushed past her defenses, though.

"Didn't have a choice, remember? We had to avoid detection and I didn't feel like listening to you complain about standing. Try again."

"You barely left my side for ten hours."

He snorted and turned away. "Whatever. What makes you think I did that?"

"Char told me. And I woke up a few times, every time I did you were there. Thank you. You didn't have to do that." She reached over to rest her hand on top of his.

James muttered something under his breath, his eyes remained diverted but he didn't pull his hand away. After a few minutes, he met her eyes again. "What are you doing out here anyway?"

She turned her gaze back to the sunset and the darkening sky. "I wanted to watch the sunset. We'll never know when tomorrow could be it for me. Staying in that room is about to drive me batty."

"Claustrophobic?"

"No, just having someone constantly watching you gets to be unnerving after a while." She played with a lock of her hair. It twisted and twirled around her finger as she kept her focus anywhere but him to get the nerve for her next question. "Did you ever wonder what it would be like if we had been born and not created?"

"Not sure what you mean."

"I have years of memories that no one remembers but me. Clear as day I can remember Warren teaching me to ride a bike. Or Abby braiding my hair when I was little. None of it ever happened, though. Not one bit of it was real." She turned back to hold his gaze again. "You're apparently stuck channeling a combination of Oscar the Grouch and Bill Nye the Science Guy."

"Who?"

A short laugh slipped out. All his knowledge and he hadn't been given early twenty-first century pop culture. "What it means is that you're pissed off and smart. Or maybe you're just pissed off because you're smart. Hell if I know. I mean don't you wonder how things would be if we'd grown up like we should have instead of just one-day existing."

"I've never been treated any different than any of my brothers and sisters. They don't think of you as a clone, they think of you as their daughter." James' hand rested on her shoulder in a comforting gesture.

Annie gripped the wall beneath her. Her nails dug into the crumbling stone. "Maybe Abby does. Warren sees me as a possible threat. Danny has other problems to worry about, and Ethan avoids me at all costs."

"Why do you think that?"

"It's amazing what people say when they think you're asleep."

"So, here's a question?"

"What's that?"

"Do you think they made you to be a spoiled brat, or is this a new development since you got here?"

"What?" Annie straightened in surprise. Air huffed from her lungs as she faced him, ready to retaliate, but he interrupted.

"So, you heard a few things here and there. Whoop-dee-doo. A few words here and there don't give you the whole picture." The chiding didn't hold the usual venom she'd become accustomed to from him.

"Does it matter? I mean, in the end does it really matter what I think? Won't be too long and I'll be gone. If I use my abilities enough it'll be sooner rather than later." She couldn't keep the helplessness from seeping into her tone. She pushed off the wall and took a few steps forward.

"You can't think like that." His hands rested on her shoulders with a shocking gentleness.

"Why not? If I die none of it will be an issue anymore. You can go back to being angry and looking for your parents instead of wasting your time with me. At least then I won't be constantly going over all the things I'll never do in my head." Silent tears slipped down her cheeks. Without meaning to she found herself leaning back against him. She soaked up what little comfort she could before he would inevitably shove her away.

"Anne…!" James turned her around to face him. His lips turned downward into a frown as he wiped at the tears on her face. "We are going to figure out a way to fix this."

A sad smile on her face countered his frown. "No, they aren't James. I'm going to keep degrading; the pain is going to get worse and in the end, I'll be gone."

"Wait you're in pain? Why didn't you say anything?" His frown deepened as he cupped her cheek and his thumb played lightly across it. "We need to know these things. If we don't we can't—"

Indecision ran through her but in the end what did she have to lose? She cut him off by pressing her lips to his in a soft kiss. Her lips lingered against his, the shock of the immediate flip-flop her stomach did was not lost on her. She swallowed hard when she pulled back. "I-I'm sorry. I shouldn't have done that. I'm not…I mean I don't.…"

James' eyes were as wide as hers as he stood there and blinked back at her. His own shock and indecision reflected back at her. Both stood there for what felt like an eternity. When he did move he crushed his lips to hers in a desperate kiss, his fingers slid into her hair holding her close.

Annie gasped when he pulled her close but didn't fight him. She molded her body against his shocked at how good it felt and how well they fit together. Any doubts or thoughts that dealt with her impending death blew away in the breeze around them. For the first time in as long as she could remember she felt something other than despair.

When he pulled back James leaned his forehead against hers. "What were we talking about?"

"If I say I don't remember will you forget our previous conversation for a little while?" A genuine smile graced her lips.

"But Anne the pain…?"

She silenced him with a quick kiss. "Later. Please. That was…."

"Yeah what was that? Not complaining but…."

Tears welled up in her eyes. "For the first time in a long time I felt alive. Whatever it was I'm not sorry." She laid her head on his chest in order to hide the flash of pain she felt building inside of her. Any second now her faulty DNA would betray her and suck away the brief respite she had been given.

"Not sorry huh?" He pressed his lips to the top of her head a hint of cockiness in his voice.

"Not one bit." A shuddering breath escaped as the pain built and settled in her chest. Her body stiffened in his arms. "James…!"

"Anne? What's happening?" His arms tightened around her.

A cry of pain emerged as her nails dug into his arms. His name came out in a pained whisper.

"I'm taking you downstairs. Try and relax. It's going to be okay Anne." He scooped her up and held her close.

Annie felt his lips pressed against her forehead before everything went black.

Charlotte rushed into the room right as James laid Annie on the bed. "What happened? Where was she?"

"She went to see the sunset." James didn't bother to hide the snarl that had returned to his voice. He was angry that she'd had another attack so fast. More so that she actually thought she was less of a person. And the pinnacle of his anger lay with the bastard that had done this and so much more. "I'm going to rip that son of a bitch into tiny little pieces."

"Stand in line," Charlotte muttered. In quick succession she hooked the monitor back up. She replaced the IV, with new medicine added. "Her pulse is weak and thready. At this point I don't feel safe taking another sample, but it's safe to say from looking at her aura she's deteriorated further."

"Maybe Elan was stupid, but then again maybe she was the smartest one here. We need Mom. You sure as hell can't think outside the box like she can."

"Stop it James. Stop taking your confusion out on me. You care about Annie. You want her to get better. I get it. Just admit what I can already see so we can move on and fix her."

James stopped mid-pace, a low growl in his chest. There were many things he was capable of, many horrible, cruel things. Caring wasn't one of them. "Nice try Shorty. I don't care. I'm a not-so-natural born killer, remember?"

"Blah, blah, blah." Charlotte rolled her eyes. After checking the monitors and making notes in the chart she stepped away from the bed. "Go ahead and sit with her. I know you want to. I'll get back to work on trying to think outside the box."

"What happened?" Warren raced into the room ahead of everyone else. "What was she doing? Is she okay? Damn it. I thought she was up, doing better."

James couldn't stop the growl that shot through him. "She's dying. She thinks her parents don't trust her, and there is no hope for her. Yeah. She's *stellar*."

"Easy James." Chance walked in behind Abby. "Charlotte? What's the word?"

Charlotte didn't respond. When James glared toward her silence, he realized she'd paled so much, she looked like a white woman instead of the native she was. Whatever her distraction, he couldn't be bothered with it."

"Shorty!" James snapped his fingers in front of her face. "What the hell is up with people anymore?" They can't focus long enough to actually help someone. Since Char is out of commission and can't be bothered to think creatively, I guess I'll go back to the stupid lab."

"James." Chance didn't have to speak loud to put the power of his role behind his words. When James was smart enough to keep his lips shut, Chance turned to Charlotte. "Is everything okay in there?"

Charlotte's head shook violently and she took several steps backward. "Caiman." She said nothing else, just stared off toward the west.

"Great. Caiman's thoughtlessness is making Char useless as hell." James snarled.

Chance pointed to the door. "Hall. Now."

James didn't have to be told twice. He barely made it to the hall before his fist connected with the metal wall with a resounding tone that half-deafened him. "As stupid as I think Elan is—at least she took action! Nobody else is doing a damn thing."

Chance showed no reaction to the outburst beyond a quirked brow. "That's two broken hands today. At least yours will heal faster than Danny's."

"Stop trying to be clever, you're not mom." James dug his fingers into his hair, ignoring the pain from his hand. "Sorry, Chief."

"Getting tired of apologizing to me yet?"

"Yeah."

"Good. I'm damn tired of needing to hear it." Chance's hand landed on James' shoulder with a firm grip. "I am your

Chief. I've always had faith that you could get past this wall you've deemed exists. You're the one struggling with it."

"I know what I was programmed to be."

"Then why do you care about Annie? Why do you love your mother? Your father? Why do you protect your sister even when you're being a jerk to her?" Chance sighed. "You're as stubborn as your mother always was. She actually thought she didn't know DNA once. It took Roark beating her over the head a few times for her to get the picture."

"Yeah. I've heard the story." James sighed and turned to lean his back against the wall. "About a million times. Doesn't mean I'm not what I was created to be."

"You were created to be a strong center for your family—to be everything your mother imagined her children to be. Do you really think Talisa would ever do anything exactly as ordered? That anyone, even Steele, could bully her into making you nothing more than a killing machine with no real heart?"

"Mom never did anything as ordered, she hates being ordered around." James glanced up when the door opened. When Charlotte emerged, her skin almost green, he frowned. "Char. What is it?"

"I'm not sure." Charlotte's blue eyes were still wide. "Can you handle the lab for a little while? I think I'm going to be sick."

"Charlotte?" Chance wrapped an arm around her shoulder and kissed her temple. "Anything I can help you with?"

"I'll be okay. Caiman isn't blocking as well as usual, or I'm not. I don't know." She gave Chance a strong hug. "I'm okay, Popsicle, I promise. It's been a crazy couple of days and I think I just need to get my head on straight again."

"You aren't the only one." Chance smiled. "Go take some time and get your head together. You can't work twenty-four-seven. Not even Tal can do that. Then you can come back refreshed and ready to work."

Before she took off, Char barreled into James. He grunted, but held her close in a hug. "Easy Shorty."

"Let yourself care before you explode."

James sighed. That was the problem, wasn't it? He couldn't. The girl had kissed him, and then proceeded to collapse. She was going to die, so what good would caring do? He kissed the top of Charlottes' head. "Go on, Shorty. I've got work to do." He pushed her off him and then down the corridor.

Chance smirked. "If she was feeling better she might have smacked you harder. She wants you to be happy, James."

"Well maybe if someone came up with a way to save that girl so Abby and Warren could live without suffering like the rest of us."

"If you want to claim it's for Abby and Warren, fine. Just keep something in mind, James."

"What?"

"Your demeanor changes around Annie." Chance met his gaze levelly. "Just think about that while you're working on her. It's not a bad thing to care. I promise."

"We'll see."

Caiman stayed low and still on the ground. Several feet away Chaz paced and panted. He had to have been locked up for a long time, his attack of her body lasted only twenty minutes by her calculations.

"I hurt you." A low growl carried through the underbrush. The bushes shivered as he passed by her just out of sight. "You cried."

"No." Caiman pushed aside her mutation with a good deal of effort. The recent attack and instinct wanted her to keep the thick skin in place against a renewed attack. "You know you can't hurt me, Chaz."

"You cried."

"I don't cry." She got to her feet, ignoring the tattered remains of her clothes. "And if I had, why would you stop? That isn't how you were raised, how you were trained."

"You left." He remained out of sight, but paced a circle around her she could easily hear. "Gone long."

"I had no choice." Caiman pondered her best course of action. She had no idea what Chaz had faced in the time since she'd been gone, but something had caused this change in behavior. He was trained to be the animal first, not turn away. To kill without caring, not shy away due to some tears. "Chaz."

"Long time." A rustle of leaves behind her, then silence. The animal had gone still.

Talk about a crapshoot. She figured she had a fifty-fifty chance of being attacked if she approached. But what else could she do? With each step closer to where he'd gone still she fought the urge to give in to instinct and let her skin thicken.

Several feet into the forest she caught her first glimpse of the man she sought. Unlike most of those with animalistic mutations that maintained their human appearance, Chaz was unique. Whether by virtue of luck or genetic manipulation, Caiman couldn't be certain, but Chaz carried some of his animal on the outside.

In the flickers of shadow and light his bare shoulders made an appearance. Spots like those of the cheetah covered his bronze shoulders, and up along his hairline. She knew from far too much personal experience that they covered down his waist and legs right to his feet. Yet the skin of his belly, chest, and face where pale as any regular human, maybe paler.

He'd been born looking like an animal—the first Exceptional to do so. For that special gift he'd been rewarded with this horrid life. Caged, used, and abused until his humanity was all but destroyed to create an almost pure animal.

She'd hated it even when she'd believed Steele's brainwashing propaganda.

With a sigh, she tentatively touched his shoulder. "Cheetah. What have they done to you without me here? What has happened?"

The muscles under her hand twitched, but he didn't attack—a small victory she'd take. Out of the silence came a quiet sound she knew to be rare for him—a purr. His head turned and he rubbed his cheek on her hand. "Nothing."

"I know you're incapable of lying, but I don't understand. What do you mean by nothing?"

"Food. Every day. Cage." A sandpaper tongue ran along her hand, another purr rumbling between them. Amorous could be just as dangerous as attack mode, but he pulled away before she could try to stop him. "Hunt little. Cage. Cage. Cage."

The cage he stayed in was like a dog run, not long enough for an animal meant to run and hunt. "I'm sorry. Chaz, I want to help you. In order to do that, you have to help me."

"You always help." Fast as Cheetahs were known to move he had her pinned to the ground. "Do not cry."

"Then don't do this," she whispered. Roots from a tree bit into her back, and her skin thickened in response. "You are more than the animal. Remember? I told you that. I'm the one that taught you to talk. Let me help you Chaz."

"No help." He sniffed gingerly along her throat before his breath huffed on her ear. "You smell of man. One man."

"My husband." She swallowed against the lump in her throat. "If he'll still have me after what I've done."

"Husband? What?"

"Mate. I know you understand that."

He growled low and moved until he was nose-to-nose. "You have a mate."

"Yes." The fact he hadn't attacked her again helped her relax even as he continued to keep her pinned. "I can help you. I will make it so you can kill all of those here that have teased you."

"Why? You left. Leave again."

"Not without you this time. I promise."

His nostrils flared and he tilted his lead like he was looking for more.

"You are my friend. I promise this time I won't leave without you. Or my parents, he has my parents." Her hand was released and she opened and clenched her hand to restore blood flow. Once the feeling was back in her fingers, she pushed back his scraggly long hair. "I won't let them hurt you again if you help me."

"I am animal. You are not."

The insinuation pissed her off, and she let a growl build from her belly. The moment it emerged as a feline yowl she moved, shoving him back and letting her mutation spring forward. Poisonous claws swung toward him. Despite his super-speed retreat, she knew his moves too well and clotheslined him when he circled her.

The second he hit the ground she pounced on him, her deadly claws right by his jugular. "I am just as much animal as you. Just because I don't always wear it makes it no less so."

He nodded once.

"You will help me?"

"How?"

"You'll know when. Soon as I see you're released, you kill. Don't let them see you coming. I don't want you shot." She kept her claws where they were, but let her skin return to normal. "Despite what he makes you do to me, I know you. You don't deserve what he's done to you. I will help you be free, if you help me do the same."

"Free? I cannot."

"I thought that once too." She released her hold on him to sit beside him. "You can be free. You learned to speak. You can learn to be free."

"I kill."

"Only the bad guys. The ones that kept us here. All of the guys here but my parents are the bad guys."

"Free." His muscles relaxed, his gold eyes focused on the trees above them. "Free?"

"Free."

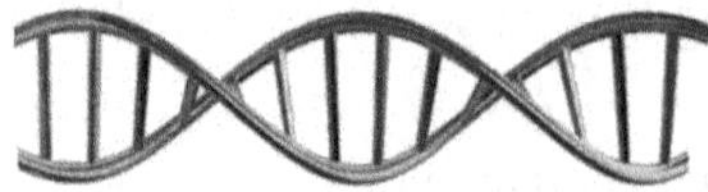

Ilana shifted in her spot across the fire. "What did you have in mind, Chief?"

"Well, if we are right and Talisa did tap into telepathy— I'm hoping with the three of us working together we should be able to contact her and get some information." Chance hoped that would be the case, anyway. With Elan gone and now word from her their best hope of getting any information would be this way.

"I believe Ravenhawk is correct." Lucas ground herbs with a mortar and pestle. "With our combined abilities and all three of our connections to her, we have a better chance of making contact."

"What do the herbs have to do with it?" Ilana asked her brother.

Lucas didn't look up from his work as he spoke. "We are going to seek assistance from the Spirits as well."

"You think they will help us with this?" The skeptical question passed Ilana's lips in almost a whisper, as if she thought better of asking the moment the words left her lips.

Chance offered a sad smile as he squeezed her shoulder. "Even when we think they have abandoned us, they are still waiting for us to listen again. Everyone has moments of doubt." He nodded to Lucas when the man looked up at them.

"Let us begin, then." Lucas held the herbs over his head as he offered up a prayer. Moments later he tossed the herbs into the fire, which cracked and sparked until the flames turned blue. "Great Spirit watch over as we commune with you and the ones we seek to speak with."

The trio linked hands around the fire, all three closing their eyes. A gentle warmth washed over Chance, not from the fire but the presence of the Spirits. It was a sensation he always welcomed, especially now that they'd seemed so far during the War. "Talisa, can you hear me?" The words may have tumbled from his lips, but he knew innately that Lucas and Ilana aided in sending them telepathically.

Sani? Talisa's voice cut into their minds sharp as a knife.

"It's me, Kajah. I can't tell you how good it is to hear you call me that." The tension that had seated itself in Chance's shoulders for so long lessened a tad.

H-How? How are you doing this?

"With the help of your children, of course. Lucas and Ilana are with me." Chance squeezed Ilana's hand at the tremor he felt run through her.

"Mama," Ilana whispered.

"We are here, mother. I am unsure how long we will be able to keep up the connection," Lucas interjected sadly.

"Lucas is right. As much as I want to just talk to you as we always have, we need to make sure we find out what we can." Chance frowned despite how ecstatic he was to hear Tal's voice, even if it was only in his head.

Damn you and your logic. Fine. First things first—how in the hell *could you allow Elan to come here by herself like that?* Anger tinged Tal's previously calm tone.

Chance snorted at the absurdity of the question. "Right. Of course, I *let* your daughter do that as much as I let her do anything. She took off not long after the card showed up for Abby." No one *let* Elan do anything, the girl had a mind of her own, always had.

Well she's here now. Watching her with Steele killed Roark and I. I might know she's just playing the part, but I wish she didn't feel the need to put herself in danger like this.

"Sorry, Tal. We were distracted with Annie when she chose to take off." Chance blew out a breath of frustration. There were so many things he wanted to talk to her about, to ask her. But he knew the time they had to talk would be limited either by the connection or unforeseen issues on her end.

Annie? Who the hell is that?

"Well, that answers one of my questions. We don't know all the details but what we do know is she's biologically Warren and Abby's daughter—and she's a disintegrating clone." A frown puckered Chance's forehead. He had hoped Talisa would have been the one that created her and had some answers on how to help her. Then again, the fact that she hadn't held a small measure of comfort that she hadn't been involved.

Are you fucking kidding me? When did she show up? How did she know where we were?

"She didn't. We identified an Exceptional and the extraction team went in to pull her out of New York City." Chance understood her concern. Privacy was a big part of what kept them safe while they built their numbers and planned to fight back.

I didn't think there were any Exceptionals left in the city after the battle.

"We didn't either. Warren caught on to her when she tried to hack his jumble. I have to say I wish the only complications we faced were her relation to Warren and Abby and the rate of disintegration we're battling."

What other complication could there be besides Roark and I being stuck where we are?

"If I interpreted what the Spirits showed me correctly, she was meant to be James' mate."

Lucas cut in, "I have seen the same thing when I communed with the Spirits. I fear for James' spirit if they are unable to save her."

You can't be serious? A growl rented through their link, deep and almost pure animal from the woman. *When I get my hands on that pudgy, smug, self-absorbed, egotistical—*

"I know, Kajah. There's a long line for that." A question not as important as their other issues, but that had been burning him up with curiosity pushed its way to the surface. "How the hell did you end up telepathic anyway?"

Roark and I have been working on our own project over the top of what Steele wants us to do, right under his nose. Roark now has the ability to control water as well. We're hoping to take him by surprise with it.

Chance noticed Lucas straighten up next to him at the revelation that Talisa and Roark had altered their gifts. As interesting as it was, he had to retain the focus of the conversation. "Any idea where the two of you are?"

If I knew *where the fuck we were, don't you think I would have passed that along first thing?*

Ilana's laugh burst through her futile attempt to keep her composure. "She's got a point, Chance. That would have been the first thing she told us."

Chance couldn't help but laugh as well. "Kajah, I have to tell you. Being here is like living with several mini versions of you, each with a different part of your personality."

I miss you, and I miss them all.

"We know, Mama." Ilana sniffed.

Chance blew out a breath as the laughter faded. "We have a small edge now. With Elan on the inside and an ability to communicate, hopefully we can get you three home soon. Any idea what Elan is up to?"

I have an idea. After knowing Talisa his whole life, Chance didn't miss the shaky, nauseous edge to her voice. *I don't know everything, but I know enough. There will be no mercy when we kill this man, C.*

"We aren't dealing with a man, we are dealing with a monster. There is no mercy for him. It will be slow and painful." Chance straightened, no guilt or shame for his dark statement. The man had helped alter the human race, and now lived to torture anyone that had become special because of it. Spirits forbid if you were someone that worked for him.

I'll see if I can find out anything about Annie. We haven't been working on anything with cloning around here, though.

"James and Charlotte are working on it now. Abby is trying to help some, but she's been too distraught. We'll keep searching for your location. Please be careful, Tal. We all know what this monster is capable of."

When am I not careful, Sani? I wish I could continue this, but I must go before I'm caught. Let's plan to check in again in a few days and see where we're at. I love you all. Ilana and Lucas, tell your brother and sisters I love them.

"We love you too, Kajah. Talk to you soon."

Ilana sniffled, her hand gripping Chance's. "Love you, Mama."

"We love you as well, Mother. Spirits protect you and father," Lucas added as the connection dissipated.

"Now we have an advantage we can work with." Chance opened his eyes as the flames flickered and died down.

"I wish I could make it all better. Be able to snap my fingers and make you whole again." Abby smoothed Annie's hair away from her face. It didn't matter to her that technically the young woman in front of her was a clone. In her mind Annie was her daughter and to watch her child suffer like this tore her apart inside.

A soft whimper of pain escaped Annie's lips as she shifted. "James?" The name came out so low Abby almost didn't hear it.

"Easy Annie. Try and relax. James is in the lab working." Abby brushed her lips along her daughter's forehead.

"Tell him to stop. Not going to find anything." Coughs wracked the younger woman's body.

"Stop? He's going to find something to help you. You can't think like that." The thought of her daughter giving up broke her heart all over again.

"Why not?" Annie's voice became raspy, her eyes remained closed. "I'm the one dying alone."

"That's not true. Your Dad and I love you and want you here with us. We want to get to know you, to be a family." Abby wiped away a tear that cascaded down her cheek.

"He thinks I'm a threat. A plant."

"He loves you, Annie." Unfortunately, what Annie said held some truth. Warren did think of Annie as a daughter and he did love her. After years of dealing with Steele, Annie's arrival and the revelation of who she was and how she came to be had him on edge. It had them all on edge when she first arrived. It hurt him just as much as it hurt her though.

"Then why is he still searching for my mission? I don't have a mission." Annie said with a wheezy breath.

"Are you using your gifts? Annie, you know that makes it worse and speeds up the degradation." An edge of panic entered Abby's voice.

"Quicker I go the quicker the pain stops," Annie muttered.

"You're in pain? Why didn't you tell us that? Let me get you something for that." Abby wiped away another tear that slipped passed her control.

"Save your medicine for someone who needs it. Danny might need it for his hand."

"You are our daughter too, damn it! I don't care if I didn't get to carry you and give birth to you. We are going to find a way to help you and we are going to save you. Don't give up baby. Please don't give up."

"Don't cry, Abby." Annie's hand trembled as it came to rest on top of Abby's.

"You can call me Mom if you want." She picked up Annie's hand between her own and gave it a squeeze.

"Don't cry, Mom." The faintest hint of a smile tugged at the corners of the young woman's lips.

"Let me get you something for the pain please." Abby begged as she brought Annie's hand to her lips and kissed the back of it.

"Shouldn't waste the medicine. Hard to come by. I'll live…for a little while longer."

Abby frowned with a shake of her head. "I don't accept that."

"We weren't really given a choice in the matter." Annie gave her a wry smile. The cough returned and she took another wheezy breath. "Does Warren like chess? I remember playing chess with him."

"He does. He hasn't played in a while though. Your brothers don't play much." Perhaps there was hope for Warren and Annie to make peace with each other and the situation.

"He was a good dad…the memories I have." Her eyes closed again and she fell silent for a moment or two before opening them again. "You were too…great Mom…."

"You have good memories of us?" She asked and took the slight shift of Annie's head as a nod. "At least you have something good to remember."

"We used to bake…taught me to cook…."

Abby ran her fingers through Annie's hair taking as much comfort for herself as she hoped she gave her daughter. "When you are all better we'll do all of that again. I promise."

"Don't promise…won't fix it…." Annie's breathing started to slow.

"Don't push. Save your strength. Dad will be in soon." Tears welled up in her eyes again.

"Think he'll want to play chess?" Annie asked as she took a deep breath. The wheeze had become more prominent now accompanied by a rattling in her chest.

"I bet he would love that. He was complaining the other day about not having anyone to play with other than his computer. Said it wasn't much of a challenge." The small smile on Abby's face turned to a frown at the sound of Annie's breathing.

"Computer…is too…predictable…boring.…

"He would probably agree with you on that. I bet the two of you playing will be a sight to see."

"Just…like…my…dad.…" Annie's voice trailed off for a full minute before she spoke again. "So tired."

"Sleep baby. I'll be here when you wake up." Abby's voice shook. She adjusted the covers around her daughter before she stood. Losing Annie when they had just found her hurt more than anything she had ever felt before in her life. The fact that Annie doubted that they loved her doubled that.

"How is she?" Warren asked as the door slid shut behind him.

"Holding steady for the moment but she's declining fast. She's been using her computer mutation." Abby ran her hand through her hair.

"Why is she using it?" A touch of wariness crept into his voice.

A shuddering breath ran through her as she leaned back against her husband. "She knows you are still searching for her mission. All she wants is her father before the end."

"There isn't going to be an end. James and Charlotte are going to find the answer." He snapped at her.

Abby shook her head before he finished his sentence. "Annie doesn't believe that. She's in pain and doesn't want us to help."

"Why the hell not?" He yelled.

"Easy honey." She turned to face him and slipped her arms around his waist. The pain in his eyes made her heart constrict that much more. "Stop looking. It doesn't matter. What matters now is Annie is our daughter."

"But what if…."

Abby cut him off with a soft kiss. "It doesn't matter. Our daughter is dying. That is all that matters right now. She asked if you played chess." Her lips trembled with a small smile.

"Chess?" His voice caught at the question.

"She asked if I thought you might like to play. She remembers playing chess with you. Said you were a good dad." Her fingertip danced across his cheek to catch a tear.

"I'll bring the board down from my office when she wakes up." His voice shook as much as hers did now.

"I think she'll really like that."

"When I get my hands on Steele…!" Warren growled.

"There's a long line for that baby. We all have a reason to want to strangle that man." Abby laid her head on his shoulder and looked down at Annie. "They have to help her. We can't lose her."

"Annie?" Warren asked quietly.

"What is it?" Abby stepped closer to get a better look. Annie's body stilled, her breathing shallow and rattling. Her skin paled even more and the beep of the monitors slowed.

"Something is wrong." Warren leaned in next to Abby.

Abby checked Annie's vitals. "Annie?" As a trained medical professional, she should have known what to do, but with her own child in turmoil all the knowledge disappeared. Everything moved in slow motion. Things that should have been second nature in a situation like this flew out the window.

"Abby what's wrong?" Warren spun her around to face him. "Breathe Gail. Focus. Breathe."

Abby's gaze darted around the room unable to focus on anything. The intercom button crossed her line of sight and she ran over and hit the button that connected them to the lab. "James…Char…something is wrong."

No response came through at first. It crackled in silence. Charlotte's voice finally came through. "James is on his way."

James raced through the hallway cursing everything from the sun that rose out of their sight every day to Annie herself. The woman was an unwanted, yet powerful, distraction. Every time he thought too hard on the destruction of her very being under the microscope he saw nothing but red. When the anger took hold, he couldn't think straight enough to add two plus two. Worse, when he got into Annie's presence he nearly forgot how to add one plus one.

The very idea that Char thought he could fix this was laughable. His mother Tal was brilliant and may have given him some smarts, but they were nowhere near hers; the fierce temper of the beast she'd worked into his genetic makeup sealed the deal. He was meant for battle, not any of what he was facing now.

Not the science.

Definitely not the confusing emotions Annie caused.

He narrowed his eyes and did what he could do to push everything back. All he had to do was face this like a battle. Battle he understood.

At Annie's door he skidded to a stop and glared at the metal in front of him. He would eradicate the issue with Annie one way or another. With one tap to the control panel the door slid open to a sight he refused to let hurt his heart in any way.

He rushed to Annie's bedside. Abby was still panicking, so he gripped her shoulders and shoved her toward Warren. Abby's protests barely fazed him, even as she beat at his back. Warren himself appeared to be in shock, just staring at the bed. James ignored them both as he injected a syringe into her IV.

"What are you doing? I have to be with her!" Abby tugged on his collar. "She can't be alone. I won't let her."

"She's not going to die." James set his hand on Abby's hand when it stopped hitting him to grip his shoulder. "I won't let her. Just let me work."

"Sorry." Abby whimpered and sank onto the bed behind him. Soft murmurs from Warren filled the room under Abby's quiet sobs.

James reached into the bag to withdraw another syringe. In his head, he counted slowly until three minutes had passed. Soon as he got to three minutes, he injected the next syringe. The cocktail they'd created was meant to slow down the degradation.

Every other thing they'd tried had failed immediately, but James had tailored this one to every inch of her ailment. In tests, her degradation had shown signs of repair.

When Annie stirred, he moved out of the way to let her parents go to her. He stood back across the room even as his sensitive ears picked up her whisper of his name. Need burned through his veins. The need to return her whisper, to comfort and assure her.

Lucas had dared say the word James couldn't acknowledge. *Mate.* Surely their mother had disrupted that gene in him, the one that would have need for a mate. He'd been built for war, as Steele's perfect soldier, under duress.

"Thank you." Abby's teary features came into focus moments before she hugged him tight. Her insistent need to draw him back to the present and out of his own thoughts itched under his skin. "For saving her."

"She's not saved yet." James spoke quiet, glad Annie didn't have the same benefit of an animal mutation that would allow her to hear his whispered words. "We've only managed to slow the process for a little while. We're still working on the saving."

She nodded weakly, her hand holding onto his arm tight. "I know. But thank you anyway."

James gently peeled her hand from his arm. "I need to get back to the lab."

"She's asked for you."

"I can't help her here." He slipped from the room before Abby could protest more. The whole way back to the lab he fought the rising force of desire to return to Annie's room and sit helpless to aid her in any way.

Char didn't look up from her microscope when he entered. "Did it help?"

"She woke up." James dropped in front of the nearest laptop and brought up the test results. The words burned in his mouth. "It won't help her be satisfied in what a shitty hand she's been dealt, but whatever."

"We've all been dealt a shitty hand, James. This War almost destroyed us all."

James' fist unclenched at the catch in his sister's voice. The protective streak he'd always had for his sister flared against his anger, and itched toward concern. "You're right."

"Joe, our parents and whatever they're suffering through, now Caiman."

"And Neil." Guilt flared when she flinched at the mention of her husband.

"He's not dead. Just like our parents weren't dead. He's not dead, James, so don't you dare put him in this."

"Hey." He got off his stool to go to her side. "Alive or dead, he's not here and I know that hurts, Char."

"And I'm going to kick our sister's ass for whatever she's doing. Whatever it was hurt enough to wake me out of a dead sleep."

He frowned and studied her. The twin effect wasn't a factor for him and Lucas since they were clones, but he'd witnessed it with Danny and Ethan as well as Char and Caiman. "Care to elaborate on that?"

"Not really." Char let out a heavy sigh and shook her head. "Let's just get back to work. We can't do anything about Elan now, but maybe we can do something about Annie."

"Maybe." James dropped back onto his stool. As he tapped through the screens to examine the results, his heart sank further. Even with the cocktail he gave her, Annie wouldn't last much longer. Already their sample test was showing signs of degradation yet again.

"I swear I've seen this before. I just don't understand." Char ran her fingers through her hair as she stared at the screen. "James, look at this. Tell me it's not familiar."

All too eager to walk away from the disappointing results, he went back to her side. From what he could see on the screen, she was looking at Annie's original DNA strand, at least what they'd been able to piece together from her first blood test on arrival. By the time she'd gotten to the compound she'd already had such severe degradation, it was hard to piece together what she'd originally had for her DNA.

"This here." Char pointed toward the basal formula. "I can't put my finger on it."

He studied the computation she extracted out of the strand and shook his head. "I don't know, Char. It's awful damn complex, unnecessarily complicated. There's something off about it. Something so not right, it almost had to be intentional."

"Unnecessarily complicated. Who does that sound like, James?"

"Most women, but specifically, Mom."

"Where are Mom's old notes?" Char spun around as if they'd magically appeared. "What if this is Mom's? We have to find her notes."

"Her notes? Are you insane? You really think she kept them after the battle?"

"Sure she did. We have to go to their room."

"Char." He gripped her arm before she could take off. "Mom wouldn't make it that easy."

"So, what would she do with them?"

"I don't know."

Tal didn't even flinch when Steele got in her face. A low growl rumbled through her chest as she bared her teeth at him in a sneer. "I told you, it's impossible. I created you one perfect soldier, no make that two. However, they're both Exceptionals which you despise."

"You made one. I made the other, or have you forgotten that fact?" Steele narrowed his eyes. "In fact, she's back here now, isn't she? What a shame, you lost your precious Elan. She is mine and will always be mine. I made her the soldier she is today."

She lifted her chin in defiance. Much as she wanted to reveal her ace in the hole, and his own doubts over his statement, she couldn't. If he knew she could hear his thoughts, all bets would be off. "Attacking my relationship with Caiman won't change the fact that your experiments, your dreams of the super soldiers will not work."

Twenty-five blown experiments. Twenty-five. She's screwing them up on purpose, but how? Steele's hard gaze flickered to the clear wall between Tal and Roark's sides of their cell. His eyes narrowed. "I know you two have figured out how to deceive me."

"Really?" Tal snickered, despite the imminent threat of Steele's clenched fists. Of no surprise to her, Roark snickered behind her as well. "You watch us twenty-four-seven with your cameras and your men. I bet anything you have code-crackers working every inch of our conversations. How, pray tell, are we deceiving you?"

Steele's cheek twitched, a tic denoting his suppressed rage, at least that's what Tal had always believed. This time it was accompanied by his own tumbling thoughts of doubt. Unfortunately for her, many of his thoughts were still locked to her, and the rest a jumbled mass. She'd have to get a better hold on her new mutation if she ever hoped to unlock Steele's secrets as she'd hoped.

"Just as I thought." Tal wrinkled her nose when she touched his hands to pry them off her shirt. "You've found nothing. I told you, just as we told you before we left your little program. What you want isn't possible, not long term. Not without mutations that make them Exceptional."

"You mean infected and defective."

Tal bristled under the turns of phrase, but only sneered instead of the full-on snarl she wanted to emit. "If I'm so defective then why do you covet my assistance, and me for that matter? Why kidnap me when there are human scientists more easily bent to your will?"

"Just because your mutations make you defective doesn't mean your brain isn't the most brilliant out there. I know an asset when I see one. Just like Caiman. She's infected, but I know just what parts of her to use. A perfect assassin, she would have been spectacular before this War, but will be even more so now with the world in shambles."

Tal alone knew that Caiman was watching them from the observation booth, hearing every word. "Your perfect assassin is only perfect because of the alterations caused by your initial experiments. The so-called 'infection' that made her what she is. Perfect."

"She's still one of the infected. Little more than a tool. I want my soldiers to be more than tools, I want them human."

"You can't have your cake and eat it too." Tal did her best not to flinch at the string of curses in her daughter's head. Even though they'd managed to break through most of Steele's brainwashing in Caiman, the girl had still been raised by Steele and had looked at him as a father in her youth. "No human can be altered to the extremes you want."

"Talisa." Roark stepped up to the glass behind her, his tone carrying a warning. Years ago she never would have suspected her husband such a good actor. Their time in this rat's maze had shown her different.

"I'm tired of lying in hopes of saving my skin." Tal and Roark had both agreed, with Caiman there, the time for acquiescence was over. A rescue plan was in place, it was time to show Steele just what he was asking.

"So, you want to kill us." Roark hit the glass. "Don't, Tal."

"This is what you want." She grabbed a wood box on the desk and popped it open to reveal four syringes inside. "This will give you your supposed super soldier. It will also show you what will happen to a human you alter. Go ahead, try it. One syringe every twelve hours. Good luck with your results. When they fail, if you live, come on back and kill us if you want. I'm done bending to your will."

Caiman's voice entered her head in a rush of panic. *Forty-eight hours? That's all?*

Tal tried to soothe her daughter's worries. *You already had a plan in place, you are brilliant at this, baby. You will save us and we will all go home together. Just promise me you'll be coming with us.*

Danny won't want me back.

While Steele stroked the syringes as if they were *the one ring*, Tal backed against the glass between her and Roark. She glanced at her husband and then turned her attention to the observation room above them. *Love is not so easily broken. He loves you.*

Caiman didn't reply, and in fact shut her mind down to further conversation. A skill Tal hated the girl had been taught. How could she have such skill in blocking Tal out, and how did Steele himself have parts of his mind Tal couldn't reach?

"You've sentenced us to death," Roark spoke through the glass, his head right near hers. His words and voice reeked of disappointment. His thoughts weren't ultimately much surer. *Are you sure this is right? Shouldn't we have waited?*

Tal turned to face him, her hand pressed to the glass. When his hand settled across from hers, she nodded. "In death, we will be together again. We have done our part. From here on out, our path is clear."

Roark held her gaze. "I love you, Talisa."

"Forty-eight hours, Roark. I'll meet you on the other side."

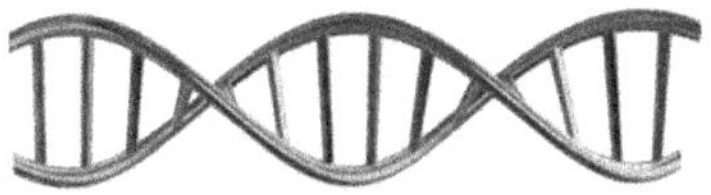

Annie chewed her thumbnail, every inch of her concentration on the chessboard in front of her. As she moved the piece across the board, she flashed a grin at Warren. "Check."

"Again?" Warren chuckled with a shake of his head. "I think that's a new record. I've never been beaten that quick before."

"Hey, I learned from the best." A pang of sadness ran through her at the statement. "I mean, in my version of memories."

"Easy Annie." Warren's hand covered hers where it sat on the table. "We may not have the same memories, but from what you've told us they are pretty accurate. At least close to what we would have done had you always been with us."

"Sometimes I wonder if it would have been better had James never pulled me out of New York. You and Mom wouldn't be going through this now. Everything would continue to fade for me, and you never would have known about me. It would have been so much easier for us all." She wiped at a tear that slipped past her control. The medicine James had given her might have stabilized the degradation of her cells, but deep down she knew there would be no miracle cure. The end result would be the same.

"Don't say that. I don't want to hear that again. James and Charlotte are going to find a way to fix this. They will. And no matter what you are our daughter and we love you." Warren had come around after her last episode and stopped the search for any mission that might have facilitated Annie's presence at the compound.

"Yet I can't tell if you want to cry or throw up every time I call you Daddy." Annie squeezed his hand back with a smile.

"And here I thought I was getting better at my knee-jerk reactions." Warren smirked. "You have to know it's not that I don't love you. I do, I'm just not so good at processing things like this. It's hard. For us all, worst for you. I am your dad and I should be able to fix this."

"You are getting better at the reactions—and I know. It is hard. It's so frustrating for me being the only one with these memories. I guess that doesn't make it easier for you, though."

"Not even close." Warren frowned at the insinuation. He moved a piece on the board before he returned his attention to her.

Annie followed suit. "Check."

"You have no intention of letting me win, do you?"

"If I let you win and don't make you earn it, you wouldn't learn anything."

"I think I said something similar to your brothers when I tried to teach them how to play." Her parents and brothers had gotten used to her references to things they had no memory of, though she did. Warren concentrated on the board to figure out his next move.

"You told me that when I was ten years old and I was so mad that I could never beat you." Annie looked up as the door to her room slid open and Abby walked in. "Hey Mom."

"And how are you two doing in here?" Abby placed a kiss to Annie's forehead before following it up with one to Warren's lips.

"I'm getting my ass handed to me by our daughter. She's ruthless. I haven't won a game all morning." Warren moved his piece across the board.

"Mainly because he keeps making moves like that. Check mate, Daddy."

"Did you expect her to let you win, honey?" Abby's brow quirked at the question.

He sighed. "No, but I expected to win at least one or two."

"Perhaps you need to try a little harder." Abby laughed as Warren pulled her onto his lap.

"Hey now. I don't need both of you ganging up on me." Warren scowled at the two women, but his underlying smile disrupted the severity of it.

Abby studied Annie. "How are you feeling?"

Annie lifted her shoulder in a shrug. "Okay, I guess. I mean, a little better than I did yesterday. I can still feel it, though. Worse, things are starting to feel a little jumbled."

Abby straightened. "What do you mean—jumbled?"

"I don't know. Some of my memories are starting to overlap. The details are all mixed up and hazy anymore. Honestly, my brain feels like a hard drive in need of a serious defrag." Annie busied herself by resetting the chessboard. With an empath for a mother, she doubted she could hide her own trepidation.

"Have you told James about it? It might be a side effect of the medicine they gave you." Warren's brow puckered, his hand running along Abby's back.

"Nope. I haven't seen James since…." Her voice trailed off at the thought of her last conversation with James. The kiss they'd shared right before she'd passed out. She figured that answered what he thought about it, and by extension, her. Not that she could blame him. In the end she would be dead, so what point was there in getting attached?

Abby prodded her daughter to continue, "Since when, Annie?"

Annie's throat suddenly felt as though she had swallowed a pound of sand. She cleared her throat. Maybe if she forced enough indifference into her voice her mother wouldn't pick up on how she really felt. "I guess since I passed out outside. Why would I see him anyway? Tall dark and angry doesn't exactly strike me as someone that would stop by just to chat. I mean, come on. He has to be forced by his sister to work on this."

"Annie? What happened?" Abby's concern was clear, and a wave of calm came from the woman as if she could calm Annie.

"Nothing happened. Do you want some tea? Daddy, do you want anything?" Annie pushed on the table to steady herself as she stood. She focused on the task of pulling out mugs and tea bags. Anything mundane to distract herself. "I'm sure James will be much happier when I'm gone and he doesn't have to stay chained to the lab anymore."

Warren's voice took on the edge of an overprotective father. "Did James do something to hurt you?"

"No, Daddy. Really? James hasn't done anything to hurt me. I just don't get the impression that I'm anything more than an annoying task to him." Despite her best efforts, the gripping sadness that came with the sadness crashed into her heart as if someone had parked a truck on it.

"Baby?" Abby's hands rested on Annie's shoulders.

"I'm fine, really. Everything just hits me hard sometimes." It took considerable effort, but Annie managed to force a smile onto her face. In truth, finding moments of happiness in her situation had become almost non-existent. While her parents still held hope that a miracle cure would reveal itself, Annie knew better. The kiss she'd shared with James had allowed her to forget for a brief time, but she didn't have the energy to keep up the pretense.

"It will all work out Annie. You have to believe that." Warren joined the pair in front of the sink.

"Let me know when the white knight shows up with his horse." Annie leaned into her father with a sigh.

"James will find something, I don't think you are an annoying task to him." Abbie ran her hand along Annie's hair.

"I think I'm going to lay down for a bit I'm getting tired again." Annie leaned up and kissed each of her parents on the cheek.

"Get some rest. We'll bring some dinner by a little later." Warren hugged her to him as he kissed her forehead.

Annie managed a nod as she extracted herself from Warren's arms and made her way to her room. In truth, she wanted to avoid any other questions from her parents. Yes, James had kissed her back but she didn't want to dissect it with her parents. Instead she curled up under a blanket with her back to the door and let the silent tears fall.

17

Charlotte slammed a notebook on the lab table with a growl. "Nothing but this and it doesn't come close to what we think we're looking for."

"What's that, Shorty?" James sat back from the microscope in front of him.

"Only thing I could find in Mom and Dad's room. Some stuff from when everything started with the asshole but doesn't give us anything to go on." Her fingers gripped her hair as she leaned on her hands.

"You went and looked anyway didn't you?" James smirked at her.

"Yes, James." Charlotte snapped back as she narrowed her eyes. "I had to. I had to give it a shot. I had to try. I must do something. We both know what you gave her isn't going to hold her long. I just checked on her and she's…we're going to lose her."

"We're not going to lose her." The words left James' lips with a predatory snarl.

"Well I don't know what the fuck to do. Like you said I can't think outside the box. We need Mom and the best this notebook has is a possible cure to cancer and possibly one for

ADD but not a damn thing to help us." Charlotte gripped the notebook so tight her knuckles ached. A scream worked its way up from her toes as she let it and the notebook go flying across the room.

"Shit, Shorty what the hell has gotten into you?" James yanked her close to him. "Breathe."

"Right. I'll go ahead and breathe because me breathing is going to help your mate live." A squeak escaped when James's arms tightened enough to threaten her lung capacity.

With everything going on, that it was it came down to in the end. After a discussion with Lucas and watching for the signs they had no doubts left. Annie and James were mates—and her death could kill them both. No matter how hard James tried to play off Annie's deterioration, she knew it put a strain on James as well.

James scoffed, his hold on her loosening again. Though he'd relaxed some he didn't let her go. "Mate? Seriously? Don't know what the hell you're talking about, Char."

"Don't try to play it off with me. You know Lucas and I are right. You're burying yourself in calculations and hypotheses to avoid letting yourself feel anything for her. She's down the hall feeling like she's going to die alone and debating on doing it herself just to get it over with all because…."

Chance opened the door, effectively interrupting the conversation. "What happened? Is everything okay in here? I thought I heard you scream, Charlotte."

"A little better now, Popsicle. Still having trouble blocking out Elan and frustrated as hell with everything in here." Charlotte forced a weak smile as she took a step back from James.

"Are you sure?" Chance's brow furrowed in concern.

Charlotte blew out a long breath to try to release some of the lingering frustration. "Positive. Well, pretty sure anyway. I think I just need to get back to work."

"When was the last time you slept?" Chance glanced toward her brother. "James? What about you?"

"I've slept, Dad—don't worry about me. We're either going to find an answer or it will all be over soon. Either way, I'll be taking a break soon enough."

James tensed next to Charlotte as she spoke. His hands clenched into fists by his sides. "I'm fine, Ravenhawk."

Charlotte kept her gaze on Chance to avoid James misinterpreting her sympathy as pity, which would surely set him off again. "We took another look at her basal strand. The tangled mess that it is, is actually so elegantly complex it has Mom written all over it."

"I'll see if Talisa can think of anything when I talk to her next. Lucas, Ilana, and I are going to try to make contact again once Lucas is done meditating. I'll keep you posted." The door closed behind Chance as he left the room.

"Because what?" The question passed James' lips in a tight whisper.

"Huh?" Charlotte blinked a few times to clear her head. She tried to figure out what James was talking about.

"What you were about to say before the Chief interrupted. Why would she want to end it herself?" James carefully avoided her gaze. "Abby going the optimistic route?"

"Trying to anyway. She and Warren genuinely want her to get better and be a part of the family, Danny is midway on that one and Ethan can barely look at her. She feels bad about keeping me from whatever work I would be doing otherwise and that you would have other stuff to do if I hadn't forced you to be work on this since being around her is your least favorite place to be." She pulled up the last set of test results on the screen but watched her brother out of the corner of her eye.

James kept his eyes on the microscope in front of him. "Can't work on finding an answer if I'm sitting there staring at her while she sleeps."

"It's not helping that with the medicine we gave her messed with her mind. She said her brain feels like a hard drive in need of a serious defrag." Charlotte turned to watch her brother as he spun his chair towards her.

"What do you mean? Shit Shorty we need to know these things. What if we just fixed the degradation temporarily and made other symptoms worse? Any details on what's happening?" The aura around James shifted at a dizzying rate. Reds, yellows, and greens, followed by blues, grays and a hint of pink, laced throughout it all.

"Brief but nothing solid to go on. Remember when we tried to hone in on a frequency on the radio and there were overlapping signals?" At James' nod she continued. "That but it's her memories. The overall degradation may have temporarily halted but I think it might be focusing on her brain in the interim."

"We have to do something to fix this. I messed up her mind with the cocktail I gave her. You think meditation would help?"

Charlotte's heart broke as the thread that shot out from her brother in Annie's direction pulsed pure white before it receded back to the murky grey of a thread that had started to fray. "We're so out of our league here James; I'm up for trying anything but that's more Lucas' department than mine."

"I'll go see what he thinks. Can't hurt, right?"

"I don't think a few herbs and some meditation will hurt. Might do her some good and it will force her to relax if Lucas has anything to say about it." Charlotte waited until James left the room to focus on the threads of her parents once again.

One by one the others disappeared from her sight. She lingered on the one connected to Neil and sent all the love she could muster toward it. There had been no indication that something like that worked but if it did she wanted him to feel her love even if from afar.

Neil's faded from her vision leaving only her parents. With all of her focus and concentration she reached out as if to pluck the thread like a guitar string and curled her finger around it. "Mom if ever there was a time I needed you…now would be it."

Caiman stood in the supposed safety of the observation room outside The cell-like room where they were testing Talisa's formula on a soldier. Based solely on her mother's words, she knew that once the final dose of the drug was administered the bullet proof glass between the rooms would have no chance against whatever the soldier inside became.

For the time being it was moderately safe. The tech administered the third dose while Steele stood nearby. For all appearances, the man had become an imposing sight. He'd grown several inches, and his already impressive and hard-trained build had bulked up further. She could almost hear her sister Kat in happier times, if there was such a thing, muttering something along the lines of 'His muscles have muscles'.

The syringe emptied into the super-soldier's blood stream. He didn't flinch, but gritted his teeth and snarled against whatever it did to him.

"How are you holding up, son?" Steele clapped him on the shoulder.

"Excellent, Sir." His teeth still clenched, the soldier saluted. "The initial burn is nothing compared to the results."

"That's what I thought. Twelve more hours and you will be perfect, soldier." Steele turned toward the glass, a maniacal grin as he nodded in her general direction. He walked from the room, and less than a minute later his hands pressed on her shoulders. "Of course, he'll never be the perfect assassin you are, will he?"

Caiman pointed a finger toward the ceiling. The nail reshaped into a pointed claw, the flesh of her finger thickening as it turned gray like the animal she'd claimed. She could feel the poison flowing toward her claw, and pondered how easy it would be to kill him right then and there. "No, he won't."

"Put that away before you hurt someone." Steele clapped her shoulder. "I still think Talisa is up to something. Why don't you pay her a visit and see what you can get out of her, hmm?"

"What?" Caiman flew to her feet, throwing a snarl in for good measure. "Why would I want to be in a room with her? Are you insane?"

"No. If anyone can get the truth from her, it's you. If you fail," he grabbed her hand to hold up the extended claw, "Throw in a little taste of what her end game will be."

The very thought of poisoning her mother turned her stomach as much as lying to her when she'd arrived had. Caiman narrowed her eyes, half-tempted to rip her hand away so the poison would course through his veins instead.

No, baby. Not yet. Her mother's voice entered her head with quiet, but firm insistence. The stronger she got, the more difficult it would be for Caiman to shut her out. *Wait until the soldier's descent. I won't stop you then if the chance arrives, even if I pray you never have to kill another man as long as you live.*

Rather than respond to her mother, Caiman flexed her hand until Steele released it. "She's not up to anything. I don't have to see her to know that much."

"Is that so?" His eyes narrowed in suspicion. "Know your mother that well, do you?"

She rolled her eyes as dramatic as possible. "Give me a break. You sent me to infiltrate, of course, I know her damn well. I also know that when she's done, she's done. If she was lying, she'd keep dragging you along for shits and giggles."

"This is fun for her?"

"I doubt that, but when you keep them penned up like caged rats, Talisa has to find a way to get her jollies. She's probably been playing you for a while, knowing her. She's decided to stop. I recognized the look she gave you."

"You were watching, then."

Caiman lifted her chin in defiance, a growl rumbling through her. "You taught me to observe, by whatever means necessary. You were confronting the prisoner, I was observing for signs of deception, just like I was trained."

He appeared to consider for a minute, then nodded. "Go on."

"It's the same look she gave me when she learned of my deceptions. She threw me out, remember? I left, and had to go back and try again." Caiman fought to keep her gaze firm and unwavering as Steele studied her, to recite the memory as if it was a military tactic when the whole event had been painful and almost meant her death.

"Yes, I remember. That's when you cut off communication with us, destroyed your own implant with an ice pick. I was always curious how you managed that with your defense mechanisms—and why you would unless you wanted out."

"No." Even as her mind screamed yes, she kept her voice schooled and cool. "I wanted in. You told me to get in at all costs. I had to pretend I'd left to truly see what they were about. You're the one that trained me to do whatever it takes, even causing potential brain damage."

"And yet, my dear, you've given me nothing upon your return." He tapped his finger under her chin, and the flesh thickened in a radiating pattern in response. "No location, no word on the new infected among their numbers. I know they've been collecting."

"I did tell you. They're in Canada hoping the remnants of a border would keep your troops off their land. I don't know the exact coordinates, very few actually got those. Any time I came close, one of their stupid telepaths wiped the memory before it left short term and I could store it in the vault." She tapped her head. One of the first things she'd been trained in was how to keep out telepathic snoopers.

"Ah yes, the vault. That's right." His eyes brightened and he smiled. "I'll have them set up the extractor. In twelve hours I'll have the two things I want most—a super soldier and the Infected's secrets."

Caiman tried not to panic as he strode to the door. Extractor, what extractor? She thought of the chemical injections she'd received in her spine to create her resistance to telepaths, and the cybernetic additions that had required a computer genius to create.

"Report to the chamber in twelve hours, Caiman. I'll bring the soldier down there and we can have a celebration as both things come to pass." He chuckled as he left, the bone-chilling noise disappearing as the metal door closed.

The soldier standing guard in the room stared at her as she stood there. Rather than let him, or anyone, see her fear, she strode out behind Steele. She turned corner after corner, winding through the maze of the complex before she found one of the few areas not covered by a camera.

She let out a deep, low breath and sank to the floor. The chamber was where Steele had taken a simple Exceptional with a kick ass mutation and turned her into his assassin. That's where her programming had begun, the first steps taken to numb her to real feelings and feed her fake ones.

The last place she would go again was to that room. She closed her eyes and leaned against the wall, allowing her mind to open to her mother. *I can't go back there.*

You don't have to, baby. In twelve hours, we'll find our own way. Get out while you can. Talisa's voice soothed her mind. *I won't let him hurt you, neither will your father. You go.*

Caiman shook her head. *I have a promise to keep. I must free Chaz, and you won't be able to control him. In twelve hours I'll be with Chaz, not in the chamber. Steele won't lose his chance for the perfect soldier. He'll send underlings to find me. He'll fail.*

In all his endeavors.

Lucas walked toward Chance's meditation room with everything he needed to try to contact Talisa again. Even from halfway across the compound he could hear James' internal debate on whether to join. The extra confirmation of Annie being his mate hadn't made the situation any better. In the end, James was too conflicted to be of much use to anyone.

Against his usual rule, Lucas sent a subtle suggestion that James visit Annie before it was too late. The last thing he wanted his brother to suffer with was regret. Too many in their midst were suffering with regrets already. No one had dreamed the whole world would blow up in the battle for equality.

Then again, Talisa had. She'd known from the start if they went to war the world wouldn't be the same on the other side. That's why she'd tried to end things otherwise, to keep away from battles and skirmishes and focus on the human heart.

In the end, her words had not succeeded where Steele's propaganda had. The War had found itself with many extra soldiers joining the fray. Untrained, and unused to battling Exceptionals, whole cities had been destroyed, much of the country left in ruins. By all accounts they'd managed to obtain from around the world, it wasn't much different anywhere else.

The irony that the governments had banded together to create the super soldier, only to try to destroy anyone with the so-called infection, wasn't lost on any of them. He wondered if his mother had ever found where the whole thing had started. Who had been the carrier of the virus that woke up mutations in so many humans.

Talisa's voice entered his head without warning, harsh and impatient. *Lucas. I'm really busy here, what is your problem?*

Lucas nearly dropped his supplies, staring down the hall, but seeing his mother's face in his mind. *Mother. You've gotten strong, quickly.*

Maybe, or maybe I've always known when my children are out of sorts. She sighed, and he could see the table she stood over, covered with test tubes and beakers. *We're in the middle of a bad situation here, I don't have time for games, what is going on?*

It's Annie. Charlotte discovered something she says has you written all over it. She can't find your notes to confirm.

Annie? Be quick, and tell me.

Lucas sighed. *First, we have confirmed our suspicions. She is, in fact, James' mate.*

His mother's silence echoed through his head worse than her cutting tone possibly could. When she spoke again, it was with the cautious tones of a whisper. *Are you certain?*

Lucas nodded even though she couldn't see him, and continued on his path toward the meditation room. *Yes. Charlotte has agreed, she sees their thread. It's dying along with Annie—and with James' fear of believing it's true.*

He never was good with anything but anger.

He is when you're here.

For a moment, Lucas was sure he'd heard her sob. He refused to comment on it, and in a moment, her mental voice returned as strong. *So, what is it you and Char are so panicked about? What is this thing she discovered?*

"Just a moment," he muttered aloud as well as in his head. Inside the meditation room he set down his supplies and reached for the paper tucked in his waistband. He held it up so she could see through his eyes. *Look. I cannot explain, I haven't got the knowledge.*

You would if you tried, my stubbornly native son. If the words hadn't carried so much affection, he might have bristled. *Now hold it steady near the light so I can see.*

Lucas moved closer to the beam of sunlight filtering down into the room. Soon as he was there, he held it steady and could sense her sudden intensity in his brain. Her gasp came so loud it startled him enough to rattle the page and almost rip it. *Mother?*

It couldn't be. How did he? Shit. No one is with you, are they?

Even though he was certain they were alone, he scanned the room. *I am alone.*

Don't tell James, not yet. Shit.

Mother, what is it?

She can't be saved.

The words fell like a bomb into his brain. He sank down to the dirt floor. *That cannot be true, Mother. You can fix her. Just help Char.*

No, son. In his mind, he could see her white knuckled grip on the desk in front of her. *I designed that formula, as a lark. I thought I'd burned the evidence long before I came in contact with Steele. I knew it was unsafe.*

What do you mean?

The formula for the basal strand is a self-destructive one. It was designed to trick my schoolmates. Everything they tried to rescue the strand would make it die faster. I was going to use it in a final to make them all fail, but thought better of it.

Lucas stared at the sheet of paper in front of him, not understanding. *There must be something, Mother. She's James' mate. This could kill him, too.*

It won't. It might come damn near close, but it won't. His Exceptional healing abilities, along with the ones I added in his DNA will keep him alive—or as close to alive as he can be torn in two like that.

He knew she was trying to hold herself together. If she showed any sign of her internal conflict she'd be in trouble with whoever was watching her. *Mother, it is not your fault.*

I wish that were true, Lucas.

Mother…!

Tell your sister what I've told you. Make Annie comfortable. Try to get James to stay near her, it will help her strength and pain if they truly are mates. I will do everything in my power to get back before it's too late. There are six hours left before we make our attempt.

He flew to his feet. *Six hours until you attempt what?*

Steele is here. I love you all, now leave me be.

Mother! Lucas searched his mind, but she was gone as quick as she'd entered, her words of love echoing in the sudden emptiness. When the door slid open to reveal Chance, Lucas could only stare at him.

"Lucas? What is it? What's wrong?" Chance drew near, concern puckering his brow. "You look as though you've seen a ghost."

"I wish it were that mundane."

"Lucas?"

"We will lose Annie, and it will destroy James."

Charlotte squeaked, then shrieked from the door. "No!"

Charlotte shook her head at Lucas' declaration. "I don't believe that. It can't be true. There must be a way to save her. Mom has to know something."

Lucas gripped Charlotte's shoulders. His gaze held a deep sadness, but he kept it centered on her. "I just spoke with Mother. As you suspected, she recognized the formula. The more you attempt to heal her, the faster it will collapse."

Chance stood next to the siblings. His arms folded across his chest, he frowned. "Is there nothing we can do for her?"

Lucas sighed. "I am afraid not. Mother said we needed to make her comfortable. If they are truly mates as we have agreed they are, then James should stay close to her. Him being there will aid her strength and lessen the pain."

"We could lose James as well, given that they are mates." Charlotte wrung her hands together. She wanted to collapse and cry, but it wasn't the time or the place. "And she's sure there's nothing we can do to save her?"

"I can show you both, if you will allow me." Lucas waited until they'd both nodded, and then the memory flooded Charlotte's mind.

"Fuck," Charlotte muttered as the memory faded. She cringed with a glance toward Chance. "Sorry, Popsicle."

"You are a grown woman, and considering the circumstances I believe it fits." Chance pinched the bridge of his nose. "We will have to make her comfortable as best as we can, then. Fuck, how are we going to explain this to Abby and Warren?"

"I wish I knew." Charlotte pressed her lips together. Her nerves couldn't be more on edge. She had no idea how the situation could be any worse.

Lucas rubbed his hand along Charlotte's arm in a soothing gesture, no doubt fully aware of how on edge she was. "Right now, I believe we can only see to her comfort and prepare for whatever attempt they are making at the compound. As I am sure you saw, they gave the impression that they would be attempting an escape soon."

"I'll get RB to coordinate the scouts and see if Kat can help them with the visuals in case we have incoming." Chance set his hand on Charlotte's shoulder. "We will figure this out."

"How in the hell are we going to make her comfortable when the last treatment scrambled her brain? It's getting hard and harder for her to focus. It's not fair." Charlotte stomped her foot like a petulant child. She didn't care how it looked. The key to one of her brothers' happiness would die and there wasn't a damn thing she could do about it.

Chance did a double take, his confusion seeping into his voice. "What do you mean, it scrambled her brain?"

"While the majority of them are not real, her memories are all scrambled together. She's starting to forget things and this morning she couldn't remember how to tie her shoes. Dad, it's heartbreaking to watch." Her words couldn't be truer. It had taken every ounce of strength Charlotte had to not break down in tears as she'd watched Annie struggle that morning. A simple task stumped Annie so badly, Charlotte had found her sitting on the edge of the bed with a shoe in her hand just staring at it.

Lucas frowned. "Perhaps I can speak with her. Maybe even assist her with a meditation session. It can only help her mental state, and cannot hurt her further."

"I think that's an excellent idea Lucas." Chance somehow managed a smile. "Maybe you can ask the Spirits for some guidance for her as well. I find it hard to believe that the Spirits would bring James' mate into his life only to rip her away."

"I will go see her right after this. I have made an attempt to steer James in Annie's direction. I believe that even with the finality of all of this it will do his spirit some good to be around her. As much as he denies it, he feels the connection to her already." Lucas pursed his lips, going silent for a moment. "There are herbs I can use to assist in her meditation."

Charlotte folded her arms across her chest, releasing a snort. "All James does is deny their connection. He's not noticing how much better she was doing when he spent time with her. Her first significant decline didn't happen until she passed out and he buried himself in the lab. He was trying to help, but it made an impact. When she fell asleep and he sat with her she was much more coherent. The attacks she had were less frequent, too."

"We have a plan of attack then. Lucas, go talk to Annie and see if she'll agree to meditate with assistance. If you're thinking about the herbs I think you should check my cabinet and take whatever you need." Chance held up his hand to silence any protest from Lucas. "I realize we are running a little low on things but this is too important. Charlotte, go see if you can extract your brother's head from his ass and get him to sit with Annie either during or after her meditation. I'll go check in with RB and figure out how to tell Abby and Warren about all of this."

"As you wish, Ravenhawk." Lucas bowed his head in Chance's direction and kissed Charlotte's cheek before he left.

"Thanks Dad." Charlotte hugged Chance and headed in the direction of the lab. She leaned on the doorframe and watched James hunched over the microscope. "Hey James…got a minute?"

"What's up Shorty? I'm still working on everything." The only move James made was to jot some notes down.

"Lucas talked to Mom about Annie." She cleared her throat as it went dry. The mere mention of what had made Annie's DNA the way it was could send him into a tizzy.

That made his head snap up. "What did she say? Did she give him a way to fix this?"

Charlotte shook her head as tears burned her eyes. "No nothing to fix it but Lucas is going to try and get her to meditate to help get her head together again. She did mention something that could help her with the pain though."

"Really? What did she suggest?"

"You." Charlotte inwardly cringed as the initial spark of hope she spotted in her brother's eyes shifted to something entirely different.

"Me holding her hand isn't going to help her get better Shorty." A growl vibrated through his chest.

"Yeah about that…."

"Don't start that damn mate talk again Char. It's not true." He glared at her across the room.

One look at his aura made her nauseous. The colors shifted and changed so fast it didn't stop on one for long. "For fuck sake James, your aura is making me dizzy could you please stop trying to talk yourself out of it and just accept that this is real. You care about her. It scares the shit out of you but you do. And as much as you annoy the shit out of each other she is better when you are around. She has refused any pain medication and if you really are her mate the pain will lessen. You want to help her. This is how."

"Did you and Lucas coordinate your guilt trips?" He snarled at her.

Charlotte's shoulders sagged. "No, I just hate to see you hurting too." She walked over and placed a hand on his arm. "See if it helps at all."

"Char…she's going to die. My mate is going to die." The words came out in a shaky whisper.

"I'm so sorry, James." She wrapped her arms around him and hugged him tight. "Go help her with the meditation. I'm sure she'll be nervous about it."

James cleared his throat as he nodded. "Yeah, I'll go check the meditation room."

"Good. Let me know if you guys need anything." She placed a light kiss on his temple.

"Thanks, Shorty."

"Anytime." Charlotte forced a smile as best she could.

"I'll deny we ever had this conversation if anyone asks."

"What conversation?" She squeezed his hand before he stood up to leave. "Never happened."

"Thank you, Lucas." Annie mustered enough energy to give Lucas a weak smile.

Lucas continued to help lower her in front of the fire. The smile he wore held warmth and peace in it. "I am pleased you agreed to my assistance. The Spirits say it will aid you in your journey." Lucas set a cup of tea beside her before he joined her on the ground.

"The Spirits?" Despite the effort it took, she lifted an eyebrow. The simplest of tasks pained her now. Not so much in the physical sense, but the fact that she couldn't remember little things, everyday things, broke her heart almost more than dying. At least when she was just dying she was still herself. Losing her mind before was killing her spirit. "You said you might be able to help me get this tangle of memories straight in my head."

"You have only been with us for a little while, most of which has been spent in the clinic or with your family. You have not had much time to learn our ways. This group still has its' heart as a Lenape tribe. Those people are the ones who still live above with the land."

"Lucky," Annie muttered.

"Agreed. However, not all of us Lenape live above ground, as we are Exceptionals. All of us still follow much of the old ways. Ravenhawk is our Chief, our leader. I am the medicine man." Lucas inclined his head toward the mug in her hand. "Drink. I promise it will not harm you."

"Ravenhawk?"

"Chance. His Lenape name is Ravenhawk, as mine is Silver Wolf, and James is Night Hawk. My parents, along with yours and Ravenhawk formed the rebellion in an effort to assist the Exceptionals and ensure our survival."

"Modern day cowboys and Indians—got it." Annie inhaled the steam that wafted from the mug before she took a sip. Whatever the contents might be, the components didn't smell or taste like any tea that she remembered.

A low chuckle emanated from the man she'd pegged as always serious, if far kinder and calmer than his brother. "Something like that. James mentioned you had spunk."

The smile she'd worn wavered as a pain shot through her heart. "James mentioned something about me other than me being a pain in his ass? Sounds like a Christmas miracle." She cleared her throat as her thoughts turned back to James and the kiss they'd shared. Other than the time he'd come to her room to give her the injections there had been no sign of him, and that had been days ago. Perhaps it was best that he stayed away. In the not too distant future she would be gone, and forgotten.

"You will not be forgotten, Annie. I promise you that much. As for James, he is on his way here to help you."

Annie swallowed hard and tightened her hands around her mug. There had been mention of a few telepaths in the compound, but knowing of their existence and having a thought plucked from her head were two entirely different things.

"So…the Spirits you mentioned? Do you truly think they can help me?"

"I believe they can. From what I have seen there is a journey ahead of you. The path will not be easy, to say the least. There will be twists and turns in the road, but in the end, it will be worth it." Lucas smiled.

"Lucas has anyone ever told you that sometimes you sound like a fortune cookie?" Despite the severity of her situation, and her own imminent death, she couldn't help but giggle.

James stepped into the room, tension radiating off him. "I tell him that all the time."

Lucas smirked, a hint of the wicked gleam his siblings exceled at seeping through his calm exterior. "And it is still annoying when you say it, brother. Annie, on the other hand, has earned the right to say such things."

Annie tried to avoid paying much attention to James' arrival. She certainly wasn't about to let him know how much she'd wanted to see him. "So, um…what do I need to do besides drink this?" She downed the remaining contents of the mug in one gulp. Slow warmth spread through her body, easing away every inch of her initial trepidation.

"Just relax. I promise no harm will come to you. How do you feel?" Lucas took the mug from her lax grasp and set it aside.

"Feel? I feel…." The warmth coursed through her like a wave crashing against the shore. Her hand wouldn't move from the ground. She couldn't lift it, and it seemed as though an unnatural force of energy was pulling down her whole body.

The flames in the fire changed. Shapes and colors formed within them. As she inched forward, the images shifted and overlapped into the one before.

"Easy, Annie. Do not fight the visions. You will see all that you are meant to," Lucas' voice wove through the voices that spoke to her from the fire. Wait a minute, the fire had spoken to her. What the hell did he give her?

"Let's lay her down before she falls into the fire," James' voice spoke from the fire, warm with a concern that had to be her imagination.

Annie's limbs refused to obey her commands to lie down. She remained frozen in place despite her best efforts. Then her body lowered to the ground, her head nestled against something. Fingertips ran through her head in a soothing, relaxing gesture.

James' voice washed over her, "It's okay, Anne. You're safe."

The images before her shuffled and mingled until one emerged clear and strong. The Daddy-daughter dance when she was a little girl. A tear slipped down the side of her face as it took form strong and clear. As the memory finished, several more played out in front of her from the childhood she remembered.

Then, in an instant, everything changed. The scene that rushed forward was not a memory from her past.

"Anne. Please stop. Could you try to slow down for five minutes, please? You don't have to do everything." James's brow puckered in his attempt to look fierce. He folded his arms across his chest to add to the look.

"I love you for worrying." Annie stepped as close to him as she could with her growing belly. She placed a soft kiss to his lips. "In case you hadn't noticed, I'm not dying—it's called being pregnant. Many women go through this."

"I love you too, but I'm going to worry regardless. You and our child are my priority." The growling grumble of his words didn't match the gentle smile on his features.

"And we are both in perfect health." She wrapped her arms around his neck, glad when he slipped his arms around her waist in response.

"I worried the whole time you were in your vision quest."

"We have both returned, unharmed."

"I thank the Spirits for that my little Wdee."

"And I thank the Spirits for you my Pischk."

Annie blinked at the images she'd seen. Could you even call that a memory, after all before James had shown up at her door they'd never met. She'd certainly never been pregnant. How was the possible?

The images shifted again, not remaining on any one memory too long. Some of her childhood with Warren and Abby emerged, others with James and other members of the rebellion as if she'd always been there. There had even been a man with Charlotte? Was that her husband?

The shifting images ceased. Where she ended up was a place unfamiliar to her. She appeared to be standing in a medical facility.

A large gentleman stood before her with a stern expression. "Tell me your mission."

"Gain entry to the compound, gain their trust and set off the homing beacon." The words felt cold and foreign. A glass window across the room afforded her a perfect reflection of herself. What she found was a cold, unfeeling version of herself. No expression on her features, no inflection in her voice as if she were a robot.

"Good. And who are they?"

"They are the enemy, General Steele. To rid the earth of the abomination we must be scorched from the earth."

"Excellent. What are your orders once you have infiltrated the compound?"

"Fight alongside them when you attack. At your signal I am to turn and kill the one closest to me."

"You are ready." General Steele handed her a hard drive, and wrapped a bracelet identical to the one she remembered Warren giving her the night of the daddy-daughter dance. "Plug this into your pod. It contains everything you will need to gain their trust. Never remove the bracelet. When the time is right, push the amber stone to signal us. You may go now."

"Thank you, General Steele, for allowing me to serve."

Annie startled out of the vision under the force of an enormous shriek. She flew back until her back hit the wall of earth. Her eyes remained half blind, half stuck in the visions so much she held out her hands to ward off attack.

"Anne. Anne, easy." James' voice filtered into her awareness. "You're okay. Breathe. Calm down. We can talk about what has you so spooked."

"No. It's not okay. I'm not okay. Nothing will ever be okay." Tears streaked down her cheeks too fast for her to wipe them away. No amount of conversation could change what she had just seen—or erase what she truly was. She wrenched herself from his grip and tore from the room fast. With no regard to what it could do to her, she tapped into her mutation to speed from the underground.

James called after her, but it didn't deter her from getting to the upper levels as soon as possible. She burst through the front door of the house and ran through the old suburban neighborhood until she reached the stream that ran along the edge of the cemetery where she skidded to a halt.

She collapsed into tears, her knees hitting the ground hard. Abbie, Warren, and her brothers had been her only goal before she died. All she'd wanted was to find her family. Or so she'd thought.

Instead, she'd only found out that Warren had been right all along. The knowledge that she'd been sent to find them, only to destroy them, shattered her heart into a million pieces.

She had to leave. There was no other option. No harm could come to the people she loved.

"Anne!" James raced toward her.

Sorrow choked her voice until she could barely get the words out. "Please leave me be."

"I'm not going to leave you be. Using your gifts makes the degradation worse." James knelt next to her.

"Good. The more I use them the faster I die. Better yet just kill me. That's what you do to a traitor, right?" Annie turned towards him pleading with tear-filled eyes.

"What? No." James jerked back. "Why the hell would you think you're a traitor?"

"If you won't than I will." In a blur she grabbed the knife from his belt and held it to her own throat.

"Fuck! Anne, stop." James inched towards her.

"Stay away, James! I can slit my own throat before you can get the knife away from me." Her body shook with sobs.

James' eyes widened in fear as he shook his head. "Anne, please." Before she could react, he closed the distance between them and crushed his lips to hers. Unlike their last kiss he didn't wait for permission and his tongue swept past her lips.

The moment his lips connected with hers her grasp on the hilt of the blade loosened. It tumbled from her fingers to the ground. Annie griped the front of his shirt and pulled him close. "Please...." She begged not entirely sure what she begged for at the moment.

"I'm not going to kill you, Anne." He tucked a lock of hair behind her ear.

"You didn't tell me how cruel your Spirits are." The fight left her body.

"They aren't cruel, Anne. They teach us lessons, but they aren't cruel about it. What did you see?" James pressed his lip to her temple and held her close. A deep sigh escaped him as he sank to the ground to pull her closer.

"Tons, but only one thing actually happened." With her eyes squeezed shut a shudder ran through her body. "The rest was just a teasing of what will never be."

"If they showed you something of the future they believe it's possible." James ran his hand along her back.

"Somehow me pregnant when I'll be dead soon doesn't feel all that possible." Another piece of her heart broke off when James stiffened. "I'm sure it won't make you feel any better to know that I'm pretty sure that it was you that knocked me up."

"I'm sorry what?" James jerked back and looked down at her as if she had grown another head.

"Doesn't matter. Remember, I'm dying." A tired sigh escaped as she put a bit of distance between them. Any time he touched her rational thought flew out of her head. For the moment, they were wrapped up in each other it almost felt like there was hope. Almost. "I'm leaving. I will not put anyone else in danger for that manic."

"You aren't putting us in danger, Annie. Beside you are too sick to leave."

"Warren was right. I'm a plant. A spy." The tears continued to zigzag down her cheeks. "General Steele sent me to infiltrate the compound and send him the location so he can attack. You need to kill me now."

James took a step towards her, a growl escaping when she took a mirrored step away from him. "Why the hell would you think that?"

"The last memory that came into focus. He gave me my orders, a hard drive full of memories to download into my brain and a homing signal to send him the location. It was a bracelet. Save everyone the trouble and run me through."

"Your parents would kill me if I did that." James smirked back at her.

"Or I can just use my gifts enough and it will be over. Look at it this way…you would be rid of me and could get back to your life."

The growl that erupted between them this time was nothing compared to the one from earlier. Annie could feel James' entire body vibrate from where she stood. "Stop talking like this."

"It's the truth, James. If it wasn't for Charlotte you wouldn't be anywhere near me."

James' arm shot out before she could blink and snaked around her waist as he yanked her towards him. "Does this feel like I don't want to be anywhere near you?"

"I…um…James…." She stammered. "You've been avoiding me since I collapsed. After you gave me the last dose of medicine I asked for you and you left. The only time the pain ever got better was when you were there and you left. What am I supposed to think?"

"I was looking for a way to save you." He said in a whisper. The grip he had on her loosened but he didn't release his hold on her. His eyes were squeezed shut tight.

Annie studied him as he stood before her, her heart breaking in an entirely different way. This was the James she wanted to know. The one without all the walls and forced anger but she would never get the chance. "Would be better if you just ended it now."

"Not going to do that. We'll go talk to the Chief and the others about what you saw. Then maybe we'll talk about me getting you pregnant." A sad smile marred his face as his eyes opened.

"It wasn't real James. Me being pregnant, what you said to me, or the names we called each other that I don't understand." Annie soaked up what comfort she could standing here in his arms. She couldn't explain it but the near migraine headache she had earlier had diminished to a slight ache.

"What names didn't you understand?"

"Wdee and Pischk. What do they mean?"

James stood there, his mouth hanging open dumfounded. "Pischk is the Lenape translation of my Spirit name. Night Hawk. Wdee means heart."

"Oh." The meaning of the word tore through her.

"What else did I say in the vision?" A hint of nerves laced his question.

"You told me you loved me." As the words tumbled past her lips she focused on the ground. It didn't matter that she had accepted her fate, she couldn't see the rejection in his eyes when he denied it.

James rubbed the back of his neck with one hand. "I…uh…I said what?"

Annie forced herself to shrug to play it off. "It's fine. Really. Hard to love someone that's going to be a corpse soon."

"Anne."

"Just facing reality." She leaned up and pressed her lips to his in a soft kiss. "This isn't a fairy tale. I don't get a happy ending."

"You don't know that." He cupped her cheek as he searched her eyes. "We'll find something."

"Sorry, James. Something tells me the revolution is all out of fairy godmothers and glass slippers."

After the huge expenditure of power, Annie had been exhausted. For an hour James held her while she slept off the power hangover. While having her resting in his arms helped some with his nerves, he felt like he should be doing more. There had to be some way to fight what was happening to her, something better than what he was doing.

What bothered him more was that after pushing him to help, Char had changed tactics and urged him to spend time around Annie. He wasn't an idiot, he knew there was a reason for it.

Annie shifted in his arms, a soft sigh drifting through the air. "What…?"

"Easy." He pushed aside his distracting, angering thoughts. "You overdid it."

"I actually feel—better. It's weird." She blinked a few times before lifting her eyes to see him better. "I'm still confused by all of this. You're tall, dark and angry."

Amusement pushed away the last of his frustration, but he kept his expression neutral. It wasn't difficult to do, smiles were rare for him. "Get used to it. Life after the War is nothing but confusion most of the time."

"Wasn't that life before the War, too?"

"That's what some people say. It was always clear cut for me. And simple."

Her hand covered his. "What was your life like before?"

"Simple."

She blew a raspberry of exasperation. "Care to elaborate?"

"Okay, simple isn't exactly right. Being a clone created for battle, I struggled more than most. My parents have a virtual football team of children all only physically about 10 years younger than them, not so simple. Having family and friends coming from experimentation and kidnapping and government lies—also not so simple."

"So, then what, exactly, did you mean by simple?" A ghost of a smile graced her lips, but at least she didn't dare to laugh at him.

"Our way of life on the reservation. There was little technology, and most of it was my mom and dad's." He sighed and leaned back against the headboard. "We came back as much as we could. Whenever we weren't out trying to campaign for our rights."

"I couldn't live without it, it's a part of me."

"Just like with Warren. He had his own little command central there as well." He allowed a fleeting smile. "Your parents liked it as well. Nowadays we don't have much either, but out of necessity and lack of any left, not out of how anyone wants to live."

"But on the reservation?"

"The tribe lived off the land, and the families there." He closed his eyes against the welling anger. "The Lenape accepted us as we were, for our differences, not despite them. Exceptionals were welcome. The Lenape were a good people, they shouldn't have been slaughtered like they were. None of us should have been."

She took a deep shuddering breath and buried her head in his shoulder.

He squeezed her shoulder gently. His ears picked up voices in the hall, and he recognized each one easily. "We have company coming."

"Don't want it."

"You and me both." He chuckled. "But it's your parents and the Chief. We'd best let your parents see you since you were out when they popped their heads in earlier."

"I guess." Her arms tightened around his waist. "Don't go."

"I'm going to let your parents have a few minutes. I promise I won't be going farther than the hallway." The door opened, interrupting her protest.

Warren and Abby came in, looking the worse for wear. In the short time Annie had been in the complex they'd been put through the ringer.

He shifted to disentangle himself from her arms, and surreptitiously placed a kiss on her temple in the process. "I'll be right over there. Promise."

Abby watched him quietly as he went to the door, but then turned her attention to Annie.

James stepped just outside the door with Chance, and immediately his fists clenched. Out of proximity from Annie every single nerve stretched taught. "It's not doing anything."

"It's doing a lot more than you think. I see it in you with my bare eye, and I see it in her. In just the past hour she looks healthier than she has. You, you're a different man around her." Chance set his hand on James' shoulder.

James clenched his fists tighter, but managed to not shrug off Chance's hand. Last thing he'd do is intentionally disrespect his Chief that way. "It doesn't feel like enough. I should be doing something."

"You are."

"No, I'm not."

"Yes, you are, big brother." Char arrived with a tray loaded down with tea and food. "Your bond is strong again, which is helping you both. Take that blessing."

James curled his lip. "For as long as I have it? Is that what you're saying."

Char ducked her head and skirted around them. She'd always been the world's worst liar, and these days it was no different.

"So that's it." James sagged against the wall. "What don't I know?"

"All that matters right now, Night Hawk, is that you stay by her." Chance glanced at the nearest screen. "Your parents are attempting something in about four hours. We'll keep you posted, and if you're needed we'll let you know."

"I have to fight—something, anything."

"Not this time. My lead Warrior knows when to fight and when to wait."

"It feels like it's time to fight."

"Best thing you can fight now is despair."

Annie reached for James despite his assurance that he would go no further than the hallway. In her head, she knew it sounded crazy—but she would swear she felt better the closer he stayed to her. Despite the dull ache that began to bloom in her chest again she forced herself to smile at her parents. "James said I was asleep when you came by earlier."

"You obviously needed the rest. You look better." Warren stayed close to Abby, who at the moment looked as if she were about to collapse.

"Not bad for a spy. I told James he should have killed me." Regret joined the pain in her chest at the grief that contorted her mother's face.

"Anna Maria," Abby choked out through her tears.

Warren led Abby to the chair next to the bed. He cleared his throat. "Annie. Where is this all coming from?"

"The fire—I mean with Lucas—the jumbled memories." A harsh breath shuddered through her. She didn't want to relive it, but it was only fair that they knew Warren had been right all along. "Steele made me to destroy you. Destroy all of you. I was dormant in a pod for a while. He gave me memories to download into my brain when the time was right. He connected false memories to the mission to try and ensure I wouldn't misplace the homing beacon. I was so flustered when James came to get me that I must have forgotten it."

"I don't understand." Abby leaned forward to take Annie's hand in her own. "Lucas' fire told you this?"

Charlotte breezed into the room. "Think of it like a vision quest, Aunt Abby."

"D-did he help you un-jumble the memories?" Abby sniffled as she wiped at her eyes.

It killed Annie to see her parents like this. The bags and dark circles under her parents' eyes told her exactly how much sleep her parents had gotten. The change in Abby worried her most. From what she could tell, it took every ounce of energy for her mother to function. "Yeah, he did. The majority of them still aren't real, though."

"What do you mean the majority of them?" Warren rubbed Abby's shoulders, but looked like a caged animal ready to pace.

"I remembered one from Steel's compound. One of his compounds anyway. Anything else either never really happened, or it can't happen." Annie tried to not let Warren's skeptical expression break her heart further.

"Wait." Charlotte handed her a cup of tea. "You said can't—and can't means it was the future. You had a vision."

"A vision? How can that be? It's not possible, is it?" Abby stared at Charlotte with wide eyes. "We're not Lenape, and Annie is a clone."

Annie winced at Abby's statement, true though it might be. She focused on the contents of the cup in her hand. "She's right. It was probably just a hallucination from whatever Lucas gave me. Why would the Spirits grant a vision to a dying clone? I was never meant to be here, at least not for anything other than to cause pain. My own pain, as well as the pain I was tasked to cause to others. All of which I'm succeeding at."

"So what? Whoop-dee-do. James is a clone, and I'm a mixture of four people. Oh, and did I forget to mention that because of this jackass Steele we all grew at an accelerated rate and have powers that rival some comic books." Charlotte huffed out a breath. "I swear Mom needs to get back here soon to kick everyone's asses. What happened to living the impossible?"

"Unfortunately for me, my 'living the impossible' has gone past its sell by date." Annie forced herself to smile.

A soft titter of laughter broke through the solemn expression on Abby's face. "Annie, really? You aren't a carton of milk."

"I'm not even sure there are milk cartons any longer. We get all of our milk from the cow's topside," Warren chimed in.

A full-blown laugh rumbled from her chest. It felt so good to laugh and smile, even if only for a moment. Happy moments were very rare now. Speaking of which, she figured she might as well ask, crazy though it might sound. "Mom? Why do I feel better when James is close by?"

Abby's eyes widened and darted toward Charlotte when the young woman squeaked at Annie's question. "I can't say that I know—but from the sound of it, Charlotte may have an explanation for it."

"I don't know," Annie hedged. "She kinda looks like she wants to puke."

"That's because I do. I mean, I know." Charlotte wrung her hands in front of her as she glanced at the door to the room.

"And the door has the answers?" Annie blew out a frustrated breath. "Why can't anyone just tell me the truth? I mean damn I'm dying. Not like I have much to lose. Whatever the answer is isn't going to change a Goddamn thing. In the not to distant future I'll be fertilizing the grass that the aforementioned cows eat."

"Annie it's not that. I'm not sure it's my place to tell you." Charlotte shifted back and forth; her eyes darting toward the door.

"Oh, for fuck sake. Does it have to do with the Chief or James?" Annie shot off the bed to confront Charlotte, the mug of tea still clutched in her fist. The pain tripled so fast, a headache pounded alongside her regret over the action.

"Annie, your language," Abby chided, though she smirked.

Really, Mom? I'm going to die here pretty damn soon, and you're worried about me dropping an F-bomb? Like there aren't bigger things to worry about?" Annie tried every relaxation technique she could think of in order to lessen the ever-growing pain, but nothing worked. With each passing moment, the pain knifed through her stronger.

"Annie?" Warren's hand came to rest gently on her shoulder. "Baby, what's wrong? Charlotte? What's happening?"

"James…help," came out in a whisper. Her limbs hung like lead, spots danced in front of her eyes, and everything grew hazy. The spots formed into images. A scene played out much like when she had been with Lucas earlier. The faint panicked voices of the others in the room wrapped around her as she felt herself being lowered.

"Anne, talk to me." James' voice, sharp with panic cut through the haze. "Shorty, she's barely breathing. What the hell happened? She was doing better!"

"Where in my medical training do you think they covered this? It isn't medical, look at her. Her eyes are completely cloudy. This is either an immediate case of cataracts or we need Lucas," Charlotte snapped in reply.

"James," Annie managed to whisper.

"I'm right here, Anne. I've got you." His lips pressed against her temple. "Relax, breathe. We'll figure this out."

Images continued to rush before her eyes. Memories, possible futures, more than she could process all at once. Tears slipped down her cheeks beyond her control. She had no idea what had happened, and could do nothing but lie there and hope it passed quickly.

The ticking of the clock resonated through the room thanks to the brutal combination of Roark's animalistic senses and his nerves. Each second that passed marked another one closer to their escape.

He leaned back against the glass that separated Talisa from him. With Elan in the compound with them, and the human experiment Steele currently ran, time grew short for them. One way or another it would all be over soon.

They would get out of this hell hole or they would die in it. Either option released them from the cage they'd been trapped in, and that would be enough.

Talisa's voice filtered into his head. *Penny for your thoughts, lover.*

Just counting down the seconds until we are able to get out of here and I can touch you again, Li. The heavy sigh he'd been holding back found its way free. *Any more news from the home front?*

I spoke with Chance briefly after Lucas, but nothing more than letting them know we are making a break for it soon. Her own heavy sigh filled the air, her head beating a gentle cadence against the glass. *There is a whole new slew of issues when we get there. There will be no rest for the wicked.*

Let's see—we are waiting for an insane super-soldier to go boom, after which we will attempt an escape from a well-known manic. We'll arrive home to our son's mate dying, who also happens to be our best friend's daughter—and a disintegrating clone. Must be Tuesday. Roark ran his fingers through his hair in a renewed fit of nerves. He checked the clock again.

Talisa's muffled laugh came through the partition. No spark of happiness made the laughter light and airy. *Sounds about right. Elan has been feeding me what she can on the layout of this place. It's not going to be easy and a lot will depend on how much destruction the super-soldier manages to cause.*

There's a part of me that is a little jealous that the poor bastard might get to take out Steele. I so wanted to get the opportunity to pull his spine out through his nose. His head hit the glass as he leaned back to focus on the ceiling.

Now, now…that isn't fair of you. No dirty talk before we get out of here.

Sorry, Li. Didn't mean to get you all hot and bothered…yet. Roark chuckled low. He shifted so he could look at her over his shoulder. *Now, once we get home? All bets are off.*

Promise? Talisa turned to meet his gaze, a sexy smirk teased her lips.

Guarantee it. He winked in reply. Despite their dire situation, they needed every bit of levity they could grab. That's how they'd survived for the past year, how they'd managed to remain sane during their captivity. *After that, I want a fucking beer.*

Only one? Something tells me it will be more than that.

Okay, more like a case—or two. His smiled faded as quick as he'd managed to produce it. *No matter what happens today Li...I love you.*

Don't. Don't you fucking go there, Roark. We are going to get out of here. Her gaze bore into his with a sharp intensity. *We will get home to our family and when we get there I'll make sure you can't walk for a week.*

Now who's teasing? Roark laughed low, his hand pressed to the glass opposite hers. Another glance at the clock told him their time was almost up. "Ready?"

"More than I can say." Talisa turned to face him fully, her hand still pressed against his on the barrier. "It's time."

Roark held his position opposite her, grinning in anticipation of what was to come.

The room jolted and shook, alarms blared around the complex. The time had come. They both lingered for another few seconds before they moved in tandem. Lab coats and sheets from the bed had been fashioned into backpacks of sorts.

Chemicals and herbs were placed inside. They stored as much as they could comfortably carry while still maintaining the ability to fight.

Another rumble shook the room so hard dust trickled from the ceiling. Upon a quick glance, Roark could spot the cracks. Elan had to keep up her part of the plan now if they were to survive. All they needed to do next was figure out a way through the barrier. If Elan had to go from one side of their prison to the other, precious time would be wasted and could hinder their escape.

In theory, if the complex shook enough it could dislodge the barrier—it hadn't happened yet, though. Worry welled inside of Roark at the prospect of being buried alive instead. He tapped into his new power to create a wall of water in front of him that rippled and surged stronger with each moment. He threw the mass into the glass in hopes it would force the barrier to break.

An explosion a few rooms down rocked the room so hard it knocked them both off their feet. As he hit the floor, he lost control of the water and it crashed over him. "Li? You all right?"

Talisa scrambled to her feet, using the desk to steady herself. "It's getting closer. Everyone in the damn compound is panicking. Elan says to stay clear of the wall. Whoever she went to get is on their way."

"She is *not* staying behind," Roark snapped. His teeth ground together so hard he swore he heard them crack. There was no way their daughter wouldn't come with them.

"No, she's not. I've already told her as much. This whole damn family is stubborn."

"They come by it honestly." He lifted one shoulder in a half shrug as he secured his makeshift backpack.

Screams and yells echoed into the rooms from the hallway. Whatever fights were happening on the other side drew nearer. The door to Talisa's side of the room burst open with brutal force, the former sliding door landed in a crumbled heap of metal.

A blur tore through the room as it quaked again. The blur bounced off the barrier with such rapidity it sounded like gunfire from a machine gun. Whatever it was worked well enough to leave a crack that radiated as if a rock had hit a windshield. The blur stopped and formed into a man with cheetah-like spots along his temple.

"What the fuck?" Roark stepped closer to the wall. Even though Talisa didn't seem worried, Roark stared at the young man.

"We do not have much time. We must go. Meet Caiman." The boy inclined his head toward the door.

Roark beat his fist against the wall to no avail. He formed a tendril of water in front of him and slipped it into the crack. The more water he forced into all the cracks along the material, the further it spread out like a spider web.

The young man backed up and flew at the wall again hard enough that it shattered. "Now. Must go now."

"Don't have to tell me twice." Roark climbed through and yanked Talisa to him. He crushed his lips to hers in a hungry kiss.

A growl resonated behind the pair. "Mate later. Run now."

"You better finish that thought later." Talisa grabbed Roark's ass as they pulled apart.

"Definitely to be continued."

Lucas arrived just in time, but nowhere near soon enough. James struggled to keep his temper in check as his brother chanted in quiet tones over Annie.

Ever aware of everything, Lucas popped one eye open to meet James' anger. Rather than speak aloud in the room of nosy onlookers, he at least had the smarts to speak into James' head. *Your impatience is duly noted. Rein it in or you'll send Abby into cardiac arrest.*

You not saying anything but chants aren't helping either. What the hell happened? James knew he should keep his anger in check, but Annie had little enough time without something like this happening.

"Her visions were interrupted," Lucas said aloud in that annoyingly calm way he had. The way the room settled down one would think he was the one with empathic powers instead of Abby. "It appears the Spirits weren't done with her."

"Well, according to her and everyone else the Spirits will have her soon enough!" Warren glared at Lucas. "So, give her back. We have so little time."

James kept his gaze trained on Annie when Warren's voice cracked, the ferocity fading in a heartbeat. His own fears were blessedly interrupted by a gentle squeeze to his hand. "She's still here, Warren. Watch what you say."

"Don't tell me what to do, she's my daughter!"

"And she's my mate!" James snarled harshly at the man who'd been his fathers' best friend. The only thing that kept him from attacking was the gentle hold Annie had on his hand, and the fact that the room fell silent at his statement.

Abby's already pale features went almost white. She gasped, her hands clasped over her mouth. "Oh, God."

Charlotte and Chance both reacted in an almost identical fashion, an amused twitch of their lips. For a moment, it put on display the genetic similarity forced upon them. Then they both resumed their business, bustling about the tray Charlotte had arrived with.

Lucas didn't physically react that James saw, but he had the subtle impression his brother approved.

Warren's nostrils flared, and he narrowed his eyes at James. "She doesn't have the animalistic mutation. Don't you dare force this on her to soothe some sort of instinct."

"I'm not." James' facial muscles twitched with the effort he had to put into remaining calm. "She didn't even know until now, you overbearing asshole."

"Takes one to know one, big brother." Char sank to the floor opposite him. A cup balanced in her hand, an aromatic mist rose from the tea inside. "Now help me lift her. Popsicle rarely makes our medicine anymore since Lucas became our medicine man. You know this must be special. Let's get it to her."

"Someone is full of flattery." Chance chuckled. "Lucas was occupied. I wove in no more power than he could."

"The old man has more experience with interrupted visions after our mother had her own once," Lucas verged on both laughter and sarcasm. Something that happened rare enough everyone glanced his way for a moment. "The Spirits felt he would be better suited this time."

Chance outright chuckled, but remained back from the group. "Why don't we all stop crowding her? Abby, will you assist James? Warren, take Lucas' place. You won't need to chant. She is almost returned to us."

As everyone moved around the small room, James lifted Annie so her head was elevated. He placed a quick kiss to her temple, nodding to Abby when he felt they could help her sip the tea without drowning her.

While Abby tended to her, James noted his three family members huddled near the door. Their heads together, their lips never moved, which meant Lucas was facilitating a silent conversation he wasn't a part of. He'd have to press for answers later.

For the moment, his focus was on Annie. After a few minutes of painfully slow sips, Anne stirred. Her eyelids fluttered open before closing again. A heavy sigh caused a flinch of pain. "What does that mean?"

Warren interrupted James' attempt to speak. "What does what mean? Did you have more visions? Lucas is best for interpreting."

"No. I mean, I did, but no." Annie opened her eyes again, and though they remained foggy, she focused on James. "Mate."

James tried to form the words to explain, but too many eyes were on him. He shook his head, looking up at Charlotte.

Char took her cue. "It's a bonding of sorts. Not like marriage, but like marriage. It's both stronger and weaker, and can strengthen and is strengthened by magic. It's our natural instinct to find our match. We can have more than one in a life, but it takes extreme circumstances to cause such a thing." She smiled at Chance.

"Chief is a sort of mate to our mother, but our mother's true mate is our father," James added. "Death, or betrayal, or extremely close connections can create extra mates."

"If I remember correctly from the way Tal described it to me, it's why you feel better when James is around." Abby brushed a lock of hair from Annie's forehead. "And why he isn't quite as temperamental a bastard when you're around, unless you or your connection is threatened, of course."

Warren grunted in protest, but wisely kept silent.

"Death." Annie's white-eyed stare remained fixed on him. Little by little the white began to fade and color returned to her eyes. "What would death do to it?"

"It doesn't matter." James shook his head. "What matters is that you know you aren't forced to return the bond. I am using it to help you, but you are free to refuse the bond."

Annie repeated, "What will my death do to it?" A stubborn set to her jaw reached her eyes with a fierce flash of anger.

James refused to answer, equally as stubborn. She didn't need to know what it would do to him. He shook his head and urged the cup to her. "Finish your tea. Chief made it for you."

"Tell me."

"No."

Annie narrowed her eyes at him, then turned to Abby. "Tell me."

"Sweetie, you shouldn't be worried about such things." Abby's features were strained in tension. In the past week, she'd aged nearly ten years. "You need to focus on taking care of yourself."

"Stop lying to me, stop protecting me. Just tell me the truth." Annie pushed away from them and sat on her own. At least she took the tea and sipped at it.

"It'll sever the bond." Warren hadn't moved since Annie had woken. "Brutally. James will do more than mourn."

Annie ignored James growl to stare him down. "It'll hurt you."

"Yes," James begrudgingly admitted.

"Then I don't want it!" The words carried a conviction that pushed at their bond hard enough to physically knock him back a couple of feet. Annie clutched her knees to her chest. "I have no time anyway, I won't hurt you too."

"Too late," James muttered, rubbing his chest. He tried not to tense at the sudden ache, but his fists clenched, a low growl in his belly.

"Oh no." Charlotte took the risk to move to his side. "Easy."

"Too fucking late," James snarled at Anne. "Pushing me away hurts too. If you don't want me, fine. But let me fucking help you while I can."

Talisa's whole body hummed with life in a way it hadn't in the year they'd been trapped in this rat's cage. Animalistic energy coursed through her veins. Sirens blared through the metal halls, making her eardrums scream in protest, but it only fueled the fire of crackling energy.

Roark's hand on her back pushed her forward, but she stopped before reaching the door. She set aside her backpack, not wanting the items inside damaged in the battle. "Wait. There's a lot out there. I need one that smokes."

"What?" Cheetah snarled. "You are the crazy."

"Always." Talisa stopped at the doorway, and stuck her hand out to stop Cheetah. "Five to the right, six to the left. Move fast out the door, speedy. Roark and I will take those on the left."

Without further ado, they rushed from the room and into the fray. The Cheetah was a blur in form and thought, so Tal focused on the task at hand. Adrenaline coursed through her veins as she confronted the first soldier in her path.

She rushed him hard enough to knock him flat to the ground, flipping away with his gun in her hands. The gun was tossed aside, cracking open against the wall as she pounced again. Her hand chopped across his throat, cutting off his air as she flipped him over and into the soldier heading their way.

Gunfire echoed through the hall, the man she'd been battling went limp. She rolled over him and grabbed the head of the soldier he'd landed on. With a fierce tug, she twisted his neck fast and hard, satisfied with the snap.

A gust of wind burst by, and the last two soldiers were dispatched. She nodded in satisfaction even as Roark continued battling that last remaining soldier. At this point the man was about done for, but she knew Roark was having fun letting loose some of his pent-up rage, so she let him in favor of searching for her fire source.

"He is wasting time," muttered Cheetah.

"You are young and foolish," Tal replied. She scanned the downed soldiers, sniffing the air as she walked among them. The distinct bitter scent of tobacco hit her as she approached one of the men Cheetah had dispensed.

"No time."

"There has to be time. I need this." She glared at the Cheetah before turning her attention to the soldier. There was no way a potent smoker would have his lighter hidden beneath too many layers. She dug through a few pockets of his vest, finally coming up with her prize. "Finally."

"Li, let's go." Roark hauled her to her feet. "How far is it to the exit point?"

"Two levels down and at least a thousand yards with a lot of soldiers in between." She flicked the lighter, stopping short as the flame lit. "Oh, thank the Spirits."

Roark paused with her, rubbing her shoulders gently. "Go ahead, baby."

She grinned and swept her hand over the flame, calling it to her. The fiery energy responded like an old friend and her body shuddered at the missed power returning to life. The flame climbed along her hand, and she tucked the lighter in her pocket.

"Rest of the way we fight dirty," Roark rumbled low in her ear.

"You bet." Tal grabbed the bag she'd discarded, putting it on. "You can vent that pent-up rage on me later instead of the soldiers. Turn on the water, I'll keep the fire and Cheetah…well, he'll keep doing whatever it is he does."

"I do not waste time." The Cheetah glowered.

"There you go." Tal chuckled and took off at a run for the nearest elevators according to Caiman, who was currently occupied with her own battle. "Elan is outnumbered. We must hurry to help her."

Roark hit the button soon as they got to the elevator, but it required a code. The one Caiman gave her didn't work. Roark pounded the panel. "Shit."

"Flood it." Tal spun as he worked with the panel, another group of soldiers headed their way from the left. She lifted her flaming hand and twirled her fingers until a large ball of fire hovered above her hand.

She threw it down the corridor, yelping as she was yanked onto the elevator as the soldier's screams rang out.

While the elevator descended, she turned to Cheetah. "Caiman is outmanned and outgunned. She is the best at what she does, but she's going to need help before Roark and I can get to her, even with our abilities. Soon as that door opens, you go."

Cheetah stiffened to attention at the clear order in her tone. He gave a short nod.

"Good. Roark, this floor is packed. You get to play with your new little toy, and I get to play with mine." She tugged him close and kissed him hard." When he growled, she pulled back with a grin. "Go get 'em, lover."

Soon as the door opened, Cheetah was gone. Tal blasted the hall with fire, spreading her arms as she pushed it both ways. Soon as Roark was at her back, she dropped one arm and swung it around to join the other, creating a full firestorm down the length of the hall.

As she moved forward, Roark moved against her back until they were near the corridor that tee'd off the one they were in. Her focus on the fire wavered when she mentally felt a wall of stone against her constant probes.

Through the firewall came a figure made of pure rock. "Shit. He's got Exceptionals. Roark!"

They spun and Roark went after the man with water, holding him back better than her fire could. Meanwhile she circled back around and, avoiding his water, set her hand against the metal walls, and stoked the flame she held. As it crawled along the walls and ceiling, metal warped, dripped, and reformed on the floor.

She pushed harder and harder, sending the heat along the walls and into the earth around the corridors until the entire structure collapsed on the oncoming attacker. Before she could finish her sigh of relief a white-hot pain tore through her arm.

A yelp that sounded much like a bark slipped from her lips. She didn't need to guess what had happened as more shots echoed through the building as their attackers gained ground from the corridor they'd been trying to enter.

She set her hand on the wound to cauterize it before joining Roark side-by-side in an onslaught attack. They took out soldier after soldier, his water drowning those she didn't burn first. As they stepped over the last of the bodies, she glanced back and forth down the hall they'd come to. "Caiman is that way, but says to go this way."

Roark growled as he looked to the left where she'd said Caiman was at. "We aren't leaving her behind."

"Damn straight we aren't. Come on." Tal turned and rushed toward where their daughter and Cheetah were. "She's still outgunned and outmanned. Tried to make them think we'd be leaving by one of their planes. She can't get out."

"Then let's get her out."

Annie flinched when James snarled at her—more from the sensation that someone had just scooped her heart out of her chest with a rusty spoon than any fear from his anger. Any response she might have formed died on her lips when she realized that it had been her statement that had done this to them.

"Don't fucking speak to her like that." Warren glared at James and took a step toward him. "She didn't ask for your animalistic tendencies to be thrust upon her."

James' lips twitched in a snarl. "This has nothing to with you."

"It has everything to do with me. I'm her father!" Warren advanced on James until he stood toe to toe with the other man.

"Considering you only accepted her in the last few days, how's that going for ya?" James snapped back at him.

Annie shot to her feet. Despite the exhaustion that overtook her at the simple move, she pushed her way between the two men. With her back to James she slipped her hand along his arm to gently grasp his clenched fist. She brought her other hand up and pushed it against Warren's chest. "Daddy, please. He didn't ask for this either. Last time I checked, he didn't plan any of this when he picked me up in New York."

"The only reason this happened is because of his animalistic mutation." Warren frowned down at her."

"You knew Mom was the one for you right?"

"Annie, that has nothing to do with this situation."

"Answer the question." Annie glared right back at him. The contact of her back against James' chest strengthened her enough that she could remain on her feet.

"Yes. I knew she was the one from the moment I met her. That isn't the same thing. What they have is...." Warren pursed his lips, as he appeared to struggle for words.

"It has everything to do with this. You don't need to have a mutation to have a mate—in your case soul mate. You make it sound like the animal side of him means he's going to start humping my leg or something." Annie heard a low chuckle from Char and whipped her head around toward her friend."

"Sorry. Mental image and all." Charlotte covered her mouth to hide the smile that formed. After a moment, she appeared to gather herself. "Uncle Warren, your thread to Aunt Abby is no different than anyone else has, animalistic or not. It's a connection. That's all. Without their connection, Annie would already be sedated to spare her from the pain."

While the connection you share strengthens you, it has been damaged and not enough to sustain you through this argument. Lucas' voice filtered into her head.

Happy for the respite from her attempt to calm down her bullheaded father and semi-enraged mate, he left that task to Charlotte, and Chance, who had apparently joined the discussion. She tuned them all out to focus on Lucas. *If I had known what I said would hurt him...I was trying to avoid that. I want him. I want everything the Spirits showed me. None of it is possible, though.*

They would not have shared these visions if they were not possible.

How is us being together and having a child at all possible when I'll be dead in the not too distant future? Annie swayed on her feet. James' arm slipped around her waist, for which she was grateful.

Lucas' eyes widened just a hair, but it was enough to convey his surprise at her statement. *They showed you a full life. They believe there is a way for it to occur.*

Annie managed a small smile. *You weren't expecting that were you? I know my Lenape name but I'll never have a naming ceremony. I felt what it was like to spend a night in his arms when it wasn't out of perceived obligation. I saw the joy and love in his eyes when he was told we were to have a child. Even through the darkness of this War I saw so much light. I won't get to experience any of it. He will never get to see what I saw. Instead, my dying will hurt him worse than anything I could ever imagine.*

I may not have expected it, but I firmly believe they do not show these things without reason. Perhaps there is still a way to stop this.

No way to stop this. I saw my death. My DNA is killing me. There is no way to change that. I'd need a new body or something and it wouldn't matter because it's not possible and I'm out of time. She sparked a glance at the clock on the wall. *Before morning I will be gone. At least I know it will be peaceful.*

"Anna Maria are you listening to a word we are saying?" Warren's annoyance broke through the mental conversation with Lucas.

"Uh, actually no, Dad. Completely tuned it all out while I talked with Lucas." Annie attempted to look as if she felt guilty even though she really didn't.

"Annie!" Abby cut in. "How could you not listen to what we've been saying? We only have so much time left."

"You're shaking." James grip tightened around her waist.

"Noticed that huh?" Annie cast a sad smile over her shoulder. Her legs shook with the effort it took to remain standing. "Legs are about to give out."

James scooped her up in his arms and cradled her to his chest. "Let me help you."

"If I say no will you drop me on the floor?" She gave him a wry smile.

"James put her down. This isn't funny." Warren glared over at them.

"If I put her down she will collapse to the floor." James snarled at Warren.

"You're right Dad it isn't funny. You're more concerned with some half-assed notion that James will hurt me. When, in the grand scheme of things, I'll be dead soon so what the hell does it matter? James is not the enemy. Steele is."

"If there is so little time why are we wasting all this time arguing?" Abby fretted from her spot at the table.

"I'm gonna go with you started it." James smirked at them.

Annie laid her head on his shoulder and let her eyes shut. "He's got a point, albeit a juvenile one but it's a point. We can keep arguing but I'd rather not."

"Why don't we take a break?" Chance piped up from his side of the room. "Warren, I need to talk with you anyway.

Talisa and Roark may need some help from our side once they are out."

"Break sounds good. I'm too tired to fight anyway. Everyone go do what they need to do. James and I need to talk." Annie popped one eye open to look up at James.

"We do?" Tension still radiated through him and the skeptical look he gave her.

"I could beg but that would involve you putting me down on my knees and then picking me back up again. Way too much work. Can we talk?"

"Will you let me help?" The frown on James' face didn't reach his eyes. Pain and sorrow reflected there.

"Yes, I'll let you help."

Roark ignored the hail of bullets that whizzed down the hallway to yank Talisa close. He kept a firm arm around her waist when she fought him. "You're hit."

"It's a flesh wound, I'm fine. Worry about it later." Talisa pulled herself from his grasp. A cone of fire burst from her extended hand toward the soldiers heading their way.

"How many left, Li?" As much as he wanted to get a better look at the wound on her arm, he knew they had to get to Elan.

"Fifteen, maybe twenty." She stole a glance around the corner.

With a nod, Roark stepped out into the corridor. He locked onto a group of soldiers. A wave of water surged forward, enveloping them, and cutting off their air supply. One by one they dropped to the ground, clearing a path to Elan and Cheetah.

A wave of heat hit his back, and he knew Talisa was taking out more soldiers.

Elan battled in the middle of a large group of soldiers. If they weren't in such trouble, he'd be proud as a peacock over her skill. She dispensed another soldier and spared a minute to glance his way. Her eyes widened. "Daddy, behind you!"

Roark grunted as a blade sliced across his arm. He spun to grab the attacking soldier by the head. One harsh, quick twist brought sickening crack before the man fell to the floor. "Which way, Elan?"

"This way." Cheetah stopped long enough to point down a corridor where more soldiers were flooding into the room.

Roark sighed. "Couldn't have been easy."

"Is it ever, Daddy?" Elan grinned even as she sliced her lethal nails across the throat of an approaching soldier.

Roark chuckled and leapt into the fray, eager to get them out to safety.

One by one, whether by fire, water, strength or speed the soldiers dropped until there were no more standing in the way of an escape.

Roark pulled Elan to him and dropped a kiss on the top of her head. "You okay kiddo?"

"Daddy I can take care of myself." Elan wrapped her arms around him despite her protest.

"I haven't seen you in a year. I'm allowed to worry." Roark pulled Talisa into the hug relishing in the ability to touch his wife and daughter again.

"We do not have time for feeling. We must leave." Cheetah growled.

Talisa chuckled, "Very to the point, isn't he?"

"Always. He doesn't know anything but fact." Elan pulled out of her parents' embrace. "He's right, though. We need to get out of here before more guards come."

"What's that noise?" Talisa turned toward the opposite corridor.

Roark turned with her and picked up the scent of something that was now as big a part of him as his animal tendencies. "Water. Lots of water."

"Shit the destruct protocol has been activated. We need to move." Elan tugged on Roark's arm.

"And that means?" Roark followed Elan and the others down the hallway.

"Flood base. Pick through what's left later. We must move. Don't like water." Cheetah's face scrunched up in disgust.

"He's right. Steele has most of the bases set up like this. There are a few water tight rooms to keep certain equipment safe." Elan stepped over a few bodies as she scanned the hallway.

"What kind of equipment?" Talisa followed the path their daughter took.

"Different things. Does not matter we must leave." Cheetah bristled at the sound of the approaching water.

A wave rolled down the adjacent hallway filling the connecting corridor. Roark tapped into his new gift and pushed the liquid back. Inch-by-inch it rose on the other side of the translucent wall of water he created. "Figure it out later I'm only going to be able to hold this for very long."

"This way." Elan tugged on Roark's makeshift backpack.

"Shit." His control faltered, the force of water was too huge for his new power. The water level rose above their heads until it broke through his barrier and rolled over the group of them. He barely managed to create a box of air around them to protect them as the corridor flooded.

"Interesting way of handling it, love." Talisa winked. "However, you forgot about an escape route. How are we going to get out of here?"

"There's a lab a few doors up that's water tight." Elan pointed in the direction they'd been heading before the destruction protocol kicked in.

"Stay close, then." Roark concentrated hard. Beads of sweat dripped down his face. Still, with each step they took he managed to keep the protective box around them.

"This one, but the doors won't open with the water in the hallway pressing up against them." Elan's brow puckered. "I know you're tired, Daddy, but can you?"

Roark took a shaky breath. He was already pushing it just protecting them.

Talisa rubbed his shoulders. She dropped a soft kiss on the back of his neck. "You can do it, Roark. Just focus."

"Right. That's all. Focus." Roark smirked at his wife.

"Like meditating. You can do it, baby."

Roark let his eyes fall shut. He took one deep, measured breath in, followed by a long, slow one out. Each breath relaxed his muscles one by one, his heartbeat slowing in his focus. In his mind he formed a focal point of a single drop of water. The drop grew into a puddle, the puddle a lake, the lake an ocean. He lifted his hands from his sides toward the door in front of them.

When he opened his eyes the water still churned around them but the protective box he had formed now framed the doorway and the group stood on the other side of it. Roark stepped through, the door slammed shut behind them and he released his control of the water outside the room.

"That was kinda cool Dad. You almost looked like Lucas or the Chief." Elan grinned at him.

"Don't tell them that." Roark chuckled.

"What the fuck is this?" Talisa's yell interrupted their moment of brevity.

"Li? What's wrong?" Roark ran further into the room.

"Steele's experiments." Cheetah snarled from his crouched position next to Elan.

"Are those people?" Roark touched the glass on the front of one of the pods that stretched out to fill the room. "What is this sick fucker up too?"

"I'm not sure I want to know." Talisa frowned.

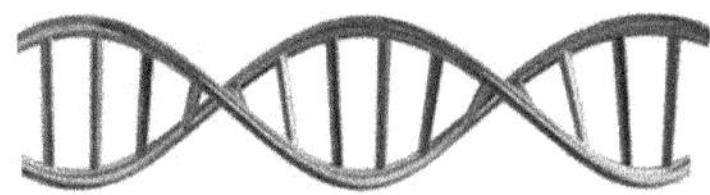

Talisa wiped at the glass opening on one of the pods. Inside a woman's features were lax in the deep sleep of stasis. Much like the young man impatiently pacing nearby, she was more animalistic than any she'd seen before.

Her skin was porcelain white, gray streaks like those of a tiger lined her features in what could have been disturbing, but was deeply beautiful instead. Each line enhanced her features, down the lines of her collarbones. The animalistic features didn't end there, with her nose slightly upturned and pink dark gray like a cat.

To be frank, Tal was surprised there were no whiskers.

"Mama. We don't have time for this, we have to go. You know, lots of bad guys out there and all that?" Elan touched Tal's arm. "Please."

"Shh." Tal waved her off and moved to the next pod, and found the man inside much like the woman beside him, with even more animalistic features, jaguar-like spots on flesh the color of a latte. Whiskers did appear on his pronounced upper lip, and she wondered if he had a tail.

A spark of a long-buried memory burgeoned up and her stomach twisted. "Oh my god."

"What is it, Li?" Roark had found his way to the instrument panel. "This computer control panel looks like Warren's work."

"And this is mine," Tal whispered, her hand on the glass.

"What? What the fuck do you mean?" Roark's head snapped up, but he didn't move from behind the panel. "You wouldn't do this."

"Not willingly, no. I don't remember exactly. I just know, somehow, I did this." When she turned away, Elan couldn't meet her eyes. "Is that right, Elan?"

Elan fidgeted. "We have to go."

"Elan," Roark's voice carried a heavy warning.

"It's too late, it no longer matters. What does matter is we have to take care of them." Tal pushed away from the pods and moved to Roark's side. "We can't leave them to Steele's hands."

"What?" Elan spun, her skin immediately turning gray and growing thick. Her claws grew. "You can't be serious? We must go. *Now.*"

"Not without these people. I did this to them, I have to help them. Don't you worry too much. We have help on the way." Tal's hands shook as she touched the screen before her. Roark must have noticed because he gave her forearm a reassuring squeeze before he returned his hand to the panel. "If we can, we have got to get them out of Steele's clutches."

"I'm more worried about you!" Elan slammed her hands down on the top of the panel. "He'll do more of this to others, with or without you. But if he gets you back? He'll do far worse. We have to go."

"I am *not* leaving without these people, Elan!"

Chaz zipped up to the panel. "We are wasting time." He twitched and spun around.

"There's no one there," Tal soothed the young man as best she could. "That's the panels coming to life. Roark and I are seeing what's going on with these people and if it's safe to move them."

"There are 12 occupied pods." Roark's hand flew over the panel. "Eight empty."

"Three of them are dead." Tal shook her head sadly. "They might have been dead when put into stasis, kept for further testing, maybe. Based on these readings on the person in pod 10, if we took them out of stasis they would die."

"Mom. Dad. Really? You aren't doing this! How in hell do you expect us to get all of them out of here?" Elan's mind screamed in far more colorful detail the extent of her protests.

"I'm not arguing any further." Tal frowned at the screen. "Are you seeing the same thing as I am, Roark?"

"Three very healthy individuals in stasis, maybe two more we could save. The rest look like experiments gone wrong." Roark's voice carried a growl of fury. "Kept to experiment further, I'd wager."

"Agreed. Let's see what we can do to get these pods safe to travel. Ilana will be along soon enough to help us move them." Tal pointed at Elan before she could voice the protest screaming in her head. "You know these machines well enough, help us or go stand by the door and wait for your sister."

"Fine. I'll make sure the waste is taken out." Elan curled her lips and moved toward the pods with people beyond saving.

"They aren't waste, Elan, any more than you or Chaz were." Roark chided her more softly than Tal had been about to. "Treat them with dignity, please."

"Don't tell me that, Mom's the one that'll have to handle making sure they can't be used for more experiments." Elan mentally shuddered at the same time Tal physically shuddered.

"She's right." Tal knew she'd have to burn the bodies to keep them out of Steele's hands, that didn't mean she liked the idea. Hell, she hated every minute of this. Rather than focus on her guilt or the unsightly task of taking care of the bodies, she focused on the task at hand.

Together with Roark, they prepped the five pods for travel. She honestly didn't know how they'd move them, but already Ilana was scoping out locations close enough they could hide out until they could take the pods one by one to base.

"Hey." Roark tugged her close once they had the pods by the door. He placed a soft kiss to her temple and proved he knew her well enough to nearly read her mind. "This isn't your fault."

"Technically, it isn't. I know that. Up here." She tapped her forehead, then glanced behind them at the room as Elan and Chaz finished setting up the bodies and empty pods for combustion. "It's just tough to see what it brought about."

"I know. None of us wanted this." He took a deep breath and focused on the door that led to their exit out of the compound. "Is there any danger out there, Li?"

"There's plenty of danger, but none of it immediate. No soldiers or Steele. I think he fled before the real battle started. Protecting himself, and all." Tal pointed to the instrument panel. "Flood it. I think we need to get out of here soon as we can. We don't know how soon they'll come back to clean up the mess and look for our bodies."

"It's about damn time, too." Elan strode past them and smashed the panel with her fist before Roark could flood it. She ripped out a few wires, and then a few more until the door slid open. "We've wasted too much time on these things."

If possible, Tal's heart clenched into a tighter knot to hear Elan speak that way. It seemed that being around Steele for any amount of time was too much for Elan.

Chaz zoomed past them all, fast down the dark corridor toward freedom.

Tal sighed and shook her head. "Think you got them, lover?"

"I think so." Roark waved his hand and the five pods seemingly floated past them into the corridor behind the others. A bubble of water could be seen below each, rolling them down into the dimly lit hall. "You sure you can do this?"

"Just go. I'll be right behind you." Tal accepted his kiss before turning back to the room. She pulled out the lighter and lit it. Once she had the flame gathered in her hand, she pocketed the lighter. With a deep breath, she faced the bodies lying beside the empty pods.

"Forgive me for whatever role I played in this." She closed her eyes and focused on the flame to make it grow stronger.

Before she could regret or doubt further, she pushed the flame into the room, enveloping everything in it. It would take a lot of heat to destroy everything beyond Steele's use, but she'd stand there until it was done, if it killed her.

Once the door was shut to leave James and Annie to their privacy, Lucas turned his attention back to the other matter at hand. "Ilana is moving fast as she can, but Mother will not elaborate on the complication no matter how hard I try."

"Complication?" Warren spun, his worried gaze widening into panic. "We need her here, not worrying about some complication! Annie needs her."

"Warren." Chance set a hand on the man's shoulder. "Talisa knows exactly what is going on, so whatever it is must be important or she wouldn't allow such a delay. You know how she feels about family."

Lucas knew everyone in the room understood as well that Talisa had also said there wasn't anything to be done for Annie. Even knowing that, Warren would still prefer the reassurance of Tal here working her magic, or at least trying.

Warren sagged, pulling Abby closer. "I know."

Lucas nodded to Chance, then gestured to Charlotte to follow him. Once out of earshot, he spoke low. "Mother is very preoccupied with one mutation, and an injury, she says you will understand if I give you the basics."

"Mama is always preoccupied with ten things. I don't mind if you relay, as long as I get to have her in my hair annoying me very soon." Charlotte's attempt at a smile was weak. "What about Annie, though?"

"Leave her comfort to me. There is little left for white medicine to do. Even Annie knows this now." Lucas followed her into the lab. "What they are delayed with is something beyond what we have had to deal with before."

"If it's been in Steele's compound, I can only imagine. I was one of those things that was beyond belief once myself." A bitter note mixed in as she worked to clean the lab from the mess created in their rush to help Annie.

"There are five of them."

"Five of what?" Charlotte paused with a tray of beakers in her hand. "Exceptionals?"

"Yes. Wait, technically six. One of them is fully functioning and—highly unique. More animal than we have ever seen."

"Mom told you this? Can you show me?" Charlotte moved closer, her features a mix of horror and fascination.

"I can." He easily plucked a memory of Chaz from his mother and shared it with Charlotte. Once she'd seen it, he took a seat and let her return to her cleaning as her mind pored over the implications of the young man.

"Fascinating. Dangerous, but fascinating. He seems— stunted, yet advanced."

"He was kept in a cage."

Charlotte shuddered. After a moment she gasped, a soft whisper slipping free, "Elan."

"Yes. He was raised with our sister, received harsher treatment and was used to—"

Another shudder coursed through her. "Train her to be used by Steele's men. Right."

"Do you want to know the rest?"

"Want to? No. Need to? Yes. If I'm going to be prepared, I must."

"Mother says they are in cryostasis. That is why they are returning slowly. There are five ungainly pods, and despite our father's new skill with water, it is going to be slow going." Lucas frowned. "It would suit us well to have Warren to ensure the pods are maintained well and not booby-trapped."

"Warren isn't going to be much use to us. He is so angry, and in such deep mourning, he is so conflicted it's rather dizzying." Her nose wrinkled, and though she carried none of it in her tone, her eyes reflected her own torment over it.

"I would think you would be used to it having lived with James and our mother so long."

"It's nothing you ever get used to." In what seemed like no time, Charlotte had restored the lab to its usual sparkling state. "I have no idea how to prepare for such technology. This lab isn't big enough for five cryostasis pods."

Lucas smiled when her frown turned into a stern pucker of her brow. Even without his telepathy, he could tell she was thinking hard. Her expression was identical to Talisa's when lost deep in thoughts. "Idea brewing?"

"Yes, actually. Pops recently created that large bay we are using for storage and salvage in hopes of Warren making a better plane for retrieval."

"The future hangar." Lucas rose. "That is an excellent idea. What do we need to do to make it suitable?"

"Warren, but we are going to have to make do without him, it would seem." She hopped to her feet. "Let's go see if we can partition off a portion of it specifically for a lab-type of setting. We can transport our equipment once we have a place to put it."

Lucas was glad that they both had the excuse of busy work, and knew Charlotte was as well. Anything to distract them from the negative events happening elsewhere. They could focus on keeping busy, and the idea that their parents would be returning soon.

"Just tell me something, Lucas."

"Elan is returning with them, Charlotte. She is terrified of our reaction, but she is returning."

"She is terrified of Danny's reaction more than ours." Charlotte pushed open the doors to the large bay, her frown seemingly stuck on her features. "I can't say that I blame her. I would be too, even if he does love her with all he is, she hurt him."

"She hurt herself, too." Lucas rubbed his hands together as he took in the bare dirt walls that encompassed most of the large room. Only a few walls had been set in place at the far end of the bay. "That is destined to be the control room. Perhaps there? There are walls and a floor, and power running to the systems."

"My thoughts exactly." She jogged toward the area and scanned it quietly. "We'll need a proper ceiling. The pods will have to stay out there, and we'll have to use this enclosed area for the lab work."

I will talk to Mackenzie about assisting with the completion of this room as quick as possible. I expect we have twelve hours before we will need it."

"Twelve hours? We'll see them in twelve hours?"

"Thereabouts."

Her shoulders sagged and she dropped her head into her hands. "Thank the Spirits."

"Thank the Spirits," Lucas agreed.

After a moment she straightened, the sadness burying into a business-like countenance. Her brow puckered when he grinned. "What?"

"Sometimes you are too much like mother for your own good."

"Oh, shush." Despite her scolding, she grinned. She rubbed her hands together. "On that note, we need to get to work. There's a lot to do and no time to do it in."

Lucas bowed and took off for the mess hall. Busy work would do for now. Soon enough they would be dealing with loss.

For the time being he was all too happy to deal with hope.

"Thank you." Annie used every ounce of strength she had to adjust her position on the bed after James set her down. If the visions were truly visions and not hallucinations or wishful thinking she would be gone by morning.

"So, you want to talk? Talk." James' bit out. He stood next to the bed with his hands stuffed in his pockets.

"I deserve that. Can you sit with me?" Without the full knowledge of the bond or what it would do to either of them she had pushed him away in the hopes of sparing him worse pain. That plan failed miserably. It made everything worse for both of them.

He flopped down in the chair next to her bed. "So, talk."

Annie beckoned him closer and once he begrudgingly obliged she placed her hand on top of his. "I've put you through the ringer, haven't I? I wouldn't blame you one bit if you hated me or wished you had never come to get me in New York."

"I'm fine." James snapped back but it didn't hold the usual bite.

"Right you're fine and I'm going to live past the next few hours. What do those two statements have in common? Pischk, look at me please."

"What?" When he finally lifted his head to look at her the muscles in his jaw rippled from being clenched so tight. Dark circles had taken residence under his red-rimmed eyes. Had he been crying?

Even without the physical contact between the two of them, the proximity alone lessened the pain enough that she pushed on the bed in an attempt to sit up. Despite how close they were it didn't strengthen her enough. Her arms trembled for a moment before they gave out and sent her crashing back to the bed.

"Anne…you are supposed to be resting." The angry façade fell away to reveal his true concern. There was the James she would have fallen in love with.

"Trying to sit up isn't going to be what kills me. My DNA is already taking care of that." A weak smile tugged at the corners of her lips.

"Ask for help. Amendchewagan." James moved to sit on the bed and helped her sit up.

"I've asked enough of you already." Annie leaned her forehead against his with a shuddering breath. "I've done enough to you."

"I told you I'm fine."

"Haven't realized I can tell when you're lying, huh? And yes, I know I'm stubborn."

"I'm not…wait a minute. How did you know what I said?" He pulled back perplexed but kept an arm around her to support her.

"The visions. You called me that quite a few times…usually under your breath. Guess it was a common theme of our…." Annie pressed her lips together in an effort to stifle the sob she felt welling up inside of her. The visions felt like a cruel joke. As if the Spirits were dangling a toy in front of a small child only to tell them they could never play with it.

"Our what?" James wiped a tear off her cheek that slipped past her control.

"Doesn't matter. I'll be dead by morning. I know that much." She cleared her throat and forced herself to meet his eyes again. "I need to get this out or I won't. I lied to you when I said I didn't want it. I was stupid and naïve. I thought if I pushed you away it would make it easier and all I did was make it worse for you. You will never know how sorry I am that I did this to you."

His guarded expression held no insight to his true feelings. "Anne, you don't have to apologize."

"Yes, I do. A million times. Even right now I'm probably making it worse than before but I couldn't stand it if you died and you thought I didn't want you." Tears coursed down her face unbidden.

"I'll be fine."

"We both know that's not true. I never wanted to cause you this pain."

James leaned in and silenced her with a kiss. His lips played soft and light against hers. He wiped more tears off her face when he pulled back. "Stop worrying about me. Enough of that talk. Can I get you anything?"

Annie shook her head as she composed herself. "Just don't want to be alone right now."

"I can go get your parents if you want."

She grabbed his wrist with as much strength as she could muster. "Please don't. I can't…I can't deal with them right now. Don't get me wrong I'm glad I found them and that I was able to meet them but…."

"You're the one dying. You can't keep comforting them." He finished her thought for her.

"Something like that." Annie didn't argue as he laid her back on the bed. "Lay with me?"

The hesitation in his eyes lingered for a split second before it faded. James stretched out beside her and pulled her close. "What were you going to say earlier? It was the theme of our what?"

"James, it doesn't matter. It can't happen." A hint of a whine tinged her voice.

"The Spirits don't share things without reason. I'm curious as to what they would show." His fingertips ran up and down her spine.

"Our marriage." She sniffled as the words escaped in a whisper.

"Marriage?" James cleared his throat. "I…uh…wow. Marriage and I knocked you up? Did your father happen to kill me in these visions?"

"James." His name passed her lips backed by a growl. "We both know it's never going to happen. It's cruel for your Spirits to tease things that cannot happen."

"The Spirits don't tease, Anne. If they showed you this they believe it possible somehow." His lips brushed along her forehead.

"How is me being a wife and mother possible if I am dead? I'm a clone not a zombie." Annie pulled back to look up at him.

"Did you look like a zombie in the vision?" James cupped her cheek, his fingers thread into her hair.

"No, I don't recall asking for fresh brains." Annie rolled her eyes at him. Zombie? Really?

"Then the Spirits know something we don't. I don't know how to explain it but we have to have faith in them. We cannot question them."

"You sound like Lucas."

"I've been told it's not a bad thing when I sound like him." He pulled her close for another kiss.

"It's hard to have faith when your life is about to end." She laid her head back on his chest.

"Right now, you just need to rest Anne." James grabbed a nearby blanket and laid it over both of them.

"Rest. Right. Rest for my death." A shuddering breath escaped her body.

"Just one question."

"What's that?"

"Were you a good little squaw?" His rich laughter filled the room as her fist connected with his arm.

Roark guided the pod toward the clearing that Ilana would land the plane in. A cushion of water rippled beneath it to keep it off of the ground. While they had still been inside the compound moving all of them at once had taken considerable concentration but it had been doable. Once they were outside and on uneven ground it was a different story.

"Ilana." To see their daughter and soon the rest of their family after being held captive for so long brought tears to his eyes. He held his arms open as she disembarked the plane and ran towards him.

"Daddy." Ilana threw her arms around him and held on tight. "Where's Mama?"

"Finishing up. We have some things we need to load on to the plane." Roark dropped a kiss on the top of her head.

"Is that…?"

"An Exceptional. Yes. We have five total that we need to get out of here. They are all in stasis. We have to be careful." He touched the panel in the top corner of the pod he had brought out with him and checked over the readings.

"What about Caiman?" Ilana scanned the area.

"She's coming home with us. A friend of hers is coming as well."

"Friend?" Ilana's forehead puckered in concern.

"Yes, a friend. She freed him as well. He's…." Roark's words faded as Chaz sped up to them.

"Go. We must go. Before they come back." He dropped to the ground on his haunches and sniffed Ilana's leg.

"Uh…." Ilana's gazed flickered between Roark and Chaz.

"Mate. You have a mate. Smells similar to Caiman." The perplexed expression came across as almost comical with the next question he uttered. "You share a mate?"

Roark pinched the bridge of his nose. "Brothers. They are twins. Worry about who is mated to who later. Right now, we need to get these pods loaded."

Ilana approached the back of the plane and opened the holding area. "We can fit two maybe three down here. The other two are going to have to go in with us. It will be a cramped. I'm sorry."

"Nothing to be sorry for kiddo. I'll take a cramped plane over the way we've been living the last year. Let's load this one up and then we can get the others. Think you can help me with that? We need to keep them off the ground." Roark set his hands on Ilana's shoulders and gave them a squeeze.

"I can do that." Ilana's gaze shifted towards the compound. "Is Mama okay?"

"She will be baby. Just hard to see what Steele did." The pod floated over to them and Roark guided it into the holding area. Once it had been settled in the back he gave the readings another check.

"I don't understand how he could be so cruel."

"I wish I knew. I don't think we ever will though." Roark wrapped his arm around her shoulder, "Let's get the others. Hopefully Mom is done with what she is doing."

"How did yours and Mama's gifts change?" Ilana's questioning gaze met his.

"Short version? We altered them to try and help us get out of there." He steered her back towards the compound where the other pods waited for them to transport them.

"Won't that make the Spirits mad?"

Roark blew out a breath as he thought about the best answer. In all honesty, he had no clue if what they did would anger the Spirits. He could only hope that they would understand the reasoning behind it. "I don't know. We can ask Lucas and the Chief when we get home and settled. I can hope they understand why but I am ready to accept consequences if they see fit. It's a new gift that I don't plan on abusing. I'm not even sure if it's permanent."

"Ilana." Talisa's voice broke into their conversation.

"Mama." Ilana ran from Roark's side and practically tackled her mother.

"It's okay baby. It's okay." Talisa met Roark's eyes over their daughter's shoulder while she comforted her. Her previous task had taken its toll on her both physically and mentally.

"Mom is right. It's going to be okay. We're all going home." Roark pulled both of them towards him dropping a kiss on the top of each of their heads.

"We could be home already if it weren't for these metal boxes." Elan's spit out. She leaned against the side of the building with her arms folded across her chest.

Roark strode over and pulled Elan towards him despite the fight she put up. "Stop," he chided in a soft tone.

She fought another moment before she stilled. There was no relaxation, but at least she stilled.

He kissed her forehead and hugged her tight, ignoring the fact that he felt her skin start to harden in defense. "We've missed you all. This is the right thing to do. Ilana and I will get them to the plane and loaded. Give me a hand loading them?" One thing he knew about Elan is she hated feeling useless. Hopefully asking for her help would lessen how antsy she was now that they were waiting to leave.

"This is stupid. I don't know why we are bothering with this. He could have booby-trapped them or created them to hurt us." Elan yanked herself free of Roark's arms and stomped off towards the plane.

"Dad she didn't…." Ilana started.

He held his hand up to stop her. "It's fine. I know being here again wasn't easy for her and she's worried about facing Danny again."

"Go. Must go. Cannot waste time on…feelings." Chaz breezed up to them before taking off in the same fashion.

"Can't blame him either." Roark scrubbed his hands over his face. "She's right we need to move. Ilana help me please."

Two of the pods lifted off their place on the ground. One holding the feline looking male and the other held a young child. Dark curls cascaded over her shoulders and she clutched a teddy bear in her arms. No other obvious alterations had been made that they could tell but all the pods would need further inspection.

"I'll wait here with the other two." Talisa reached out and squeezed Roark's forearm.

"We'll be right back. Will take less time with two of us. After that…we're going home." Roark leaned in and kissed her soundly on the lips.

"And after we see everyone and get settled you are mine for a few hours."

"Damn straight I am."

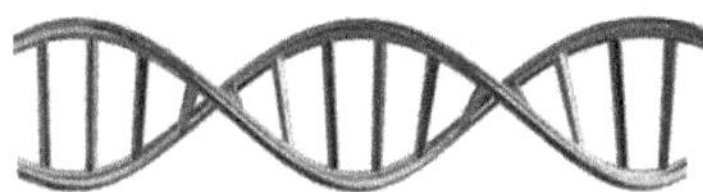

The time it took to get the pods to the plane wore on everyone's nerves. Talisa's newfound telepathy had her in a terrible headache from everyone's thoughts. Everyone except Elan's, of course. Tal remembered Lucas once commenting on how Elan had the odd ability to completely block him from her thoughts without any sign of telepathy herself.

Still, even with such ability, Tal could still sense her daughter's thoughts in fleeting moments. More prevalent, however, was the tension radiating off the young woman.

The extra minutes Tal took to check the pods in the cargo hold before they took off had both the near-silent Elan and the hyperactive Chaz both about to vibrate out of their skin with nerves. When she descended the ramp from the cargo hold, Tal found her daughter right outside, a dark glare set deep into her beautiful features.

Before the young woman could open her mouth, if she'd even intended to do so, Tal cut her off. "That's enough. Do you think I'm not aware of the danger we're in right now? I am not a child, nor am I anywhere near naïve. Your father and I have been trapped here for a long time and we are just as anxious to get the hell out of here as you are, if not more."

Elan rose an eyebrow, her shoulders straightening in defiance.

Tal stepped closer to set her hands on Elan's shoulders. "I know it was tough for you to go back there, that's why I didn't want you to. Though I couldn't be happier to see you."

"There's no time," Elan grumbled. "For any of this."

"Those people, whoever they might be, deserve the best care after what they've been through. I could very well be responsible—,"

Elan's eyes dropped to the ground, her brow pinched tight. A fleeting thought passed right through her shield to Tal's mind. An image, actually, of Tal working over the feline female in one of the pods.

Tal closed her eyes and sighed. "I am responsible for them. I did this to them somehow, though I have no memory of it. They are my responsibility, they are all of our responsibility. No more or less than the Exceptionals back home."

"Mama," Elan all but whispered. "I didn't mean…."

"I know." Tal opened her eyes again to smile at her daughter. "I still have to do right by them. We can't lose them in flight before we can even help them."

Roark appeared around the side of the rickety plane. At her mental nudge to get the plane ready, he simply nodded before he disappeared from sight again. A few moments later the ramp began to rise.

"We're just about ready to leave. Let's get home."

"Mama." Elan grabbed her arm before she could move away. "It's not your fault. It's his. You taught me that. I don't want you to forget."

The simple acknowledgement of Steele being at fault warmed Tal's heart. Tal's biggest fear upon Elan's appearance at the compound was that she'd forget all that she'd learned since they'd freed her from Steele's tight grip, and his brainwashing.

Tal hugged Elan briefly, but tight as possible. Elan returned the hug with a fierce one of her own before they broke apart.

"Let's move." Elan stiffened, whatever emotions she'd been feeling almost visibly being buried deep inside as her features became stoic.

"Agreed. I want to get home." Tal followed Elan onto the plane. She observed the way her daughter moved to help Chaz. It appeared that just her presence calmed him enough to sit still.

"Want to copilot, mama?" Ilana worked with the controls, her focus on the panel before her.

Tal shook her head, making her headache worse. "I think I'll sit with your father." Anything to even just hold his hand for the time it would take them to get home. She knew after that, there would be many reunions and embracing. "I hope that's all right."

"Of course. I got this." Illy glanced back with a bright smile. "Just glad you guys are here."

"So am I."

"Ditto," concurred Roark as she sat down beside him. His hand immediately clasped hers. "One question. Will this thing fly all right with the extra weight?"

"We'll make it work. My biggest worry is extra patrols after the destruction of the compound." Ilana focused briefly behind them, as if to get confirmation from her sister. "It may take us a while to get home factoring it all in."

"That's fine. Let's get moving before they arrive to search for us, or our bodies." Tal leaned against Roark, trying to focus her telepathic energy on him. The stress of the past few hours made her already feeble grasp on the new power weaker.

The constant hum of Chaz's brain, coupled with Illy's undoubtedly unintentional broadcasting of her excited thoughts left little room for Tal's own thoughts.

Within minutes the scrapped together plane took off, the strain on the engines from the extra weight could be heard from the minute they took off. Roark's hand squeezed hers tight. "You good?"

"Chattering children in my head, a plane that could go down, and that maniac likely looking for us? How could I not be?"

He chuckled low, then kissed her forehead. "Try to focus on me and get some sleep. If you think it's possible."

"Don't think it, but I'll take you up on the focusing on you."

"I've missed you," he whispered low. No naughty thoughts accompanied his words. His focus seemed to be laser pointed on their clasped hands.

She knew he meant how she'd felt when she'd gotten on the plane. Being separated so long, the simple act of holding his hand eased a long-standing ache deep in her heart. "Me too."

"Damn. That didn't take long. Looking for a safe place to land. We've got some jets coming in." Ilana's tension at least turned off her mental exclamations of happiness.

Tal lifted her head, her free hand gripped tight on the armrest as the plane dove toward the ground quicker than what might be safe with the extra weight.

"Hey, dad. Could I get some help with the landing? The weight's making the descent too fast."

"On it," Roark replied in tense tones.

Tal closed her eyes, taking a deep breath as the plane rattled its way toward the ground.

James pondered heading to the door to get Warren and Abby in the room, but every time he moved Annie clamped onto his arm. The strength she showed in those moments was surprising considering her current state.

For nearly two hours he'd held her. For a time, she'd been almost strong. Though he knew the facts about improvement before decline in medical literature, he'd not been witness to it. Most of the death he'd seen had been in battle and very sudden.

His heart ached with every inch she moved closer to the end. He knew Warren had to be chomping at the bit to get in with his daughter by now.

Still, he'd been glad for the time she'd been able to speak enough for him to get some knowledge of who she'd been. If he didn't know better, he'd curse the Spirits for bringing her into his life for only a short time.

As it stood, once she was gone he knew he might never be this calm again. The occasional stabbing pain in his chest every time her breathing rattled was clue enough to what he'd go through when she did die.

That was when he'd need others in the room, because who knew what he'd do.

Annie's eyes blinked open again, her normally pale features nearly gray now. Mentally he thought, *cellular decay*. That no longer mattered. There was nothing he could do to help now, not that he ever could. He closed his eyes against the rising streak of anger.

A cold hand set over his clenched one, which calmed him enough to open his eyes to face her. Her brows puckered briefly, and she took a rattling breath from the effort. Her hand lifted, only to point a finger behind him.

"What? Should I get your parents now?" He moved to rise.

"No." The sparkle of laughter her voice had once held had dissolved into a rattling whisper. "Computer."

"What? No." James shook his head. "Using your power will only cause you to degrade even faster. I won't."

"Too late for that." Somehow her voice sounded behind him as her lips remained still. "I can still do this anyway, it just takes more effort to send it out. That'll kill me faster than you letting me touch it."

"Anne. Stop."

"I'm dying, James. Nothing can stop this." The color in her eyes faded a little more. "Let me have this."

He sighed, weighing his options. If he didn't let her have it they might only have ten minutes instead of twenty or thirty. "Fine. You win."

"I always did, so the Spirits said."

James grabbed the computer. Once it was set on her lap, he propped her up by leaning her against him. "You are a stubborn one. I should still get your parents."

"Five more minutes." Another rattling breath shook her body. "That's all. Then we can get them. Until then, you need me more than I need you right now."

"I'm not helping any longer?"

"Not even the Spirits themselves can. Funny, though."

"What?"

"I thought it would hurt more."

He closed his eyes against the rush of pain through his heart and head. "Maybe I am still helping, then. I don't want you in pain. It helps knowing that you aren't."

"Don't lie."

"All right. Nothing helps." He let out a shaky breath. One of her hands settled on his forearm. Cold as ice, but she still controlled it. Her other hand rested on the computer. He rested his chin on the top of her head. "There should have been more."

"Of what?"

"Everything."

"Maybe there will be."

He let out a cold laugh. "Right."

A shuddering breath shook her whole body as he held it.

"Anne?"

"Maybe...."

"Anne!" James moved quickly out from behind her so he could see her face. A gentle smile sat on her blue lips. A cold chill ran through his whole body. "Don't. No. You said five minutes. You were supposed to...."

Out of the corner of his eye he saw her finger twitch against the computer. A slow breath seeped from her still smiling lips.

His whole body began to shake, he took a step back from the bed. "Anne!"

The door flew open, both Abby and Warren flew in asking what had happened.

James couldn't speak, couldn't move, couldn't stop staring as Anne's parents ran to her.

He balled his fists in anticipation of the rage he knew would come, but it never came. Numbness seeped through his limbs.

"James?" Charlotte touched his arm gently. She twitched when he spun on her quickly.

"She's gone." He didn't know how the words formed in his dry mouth. The cold, numb feeling remained in his limbs, keeping him locked in place.

"Why didn't you call?"

"I thought we had time. She said—I thought…" He bowed his head, ignoring the chaos in the room. Why didn't he feel the rage?

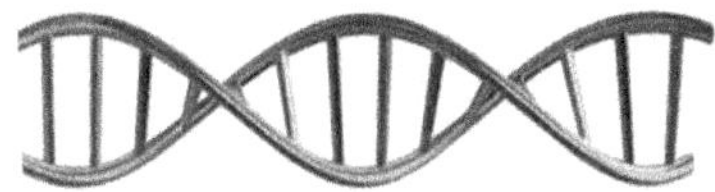

The room that had been still and quiet exploded into utter chaos the moment James had yelled Annie's name. The cacophony of voices that filled the room would have been enough to make anyone dizzy let alone the auras that spiraled out of control. The combination of the two threated to cause her to expel what few contents her stomach held.

Grays interwoven with hints of various shades of pink surrounded Abby as she cried over Annie, clutching her daughter to her chest rocking her. A dark murky gray with frayed lines of red wrapped around Warren as the man knelt next to Abby sobbing along with his wife. James was a surprising myriad of almost every color with red pulsing through and then retreating as if it were being beat back by an outside force.

"What did she say, James?" Charlotte remained watchful for the pain and rage they all expected from her brother at the loss of his mate.

"Five more minutes. She wanted five more minutes of quiet before everyone else came back in." The pained expression on his face told her just how deeply his soul hurt.

"She shouldn't have been alone." Warren bit out through clenched teeth.

"She wasn't alone." The growl that erupted from James shook Charlotte to the core.

"Her mother and I should have been with her." Warren shoved the side of the bed jostling Abby and Annie in the process.

"Uncle Warren it wasn't on purpose." Charlotte attempted to soothe the situation. The last thing Annie would have wanted was the two of them literally arguing over her dead body. She reached in and picked up the laptop off the bed before it ended up on the floor in pieces.

"We should have been the ones with her. We should have been the ones holding her hand when she died. Not her supposed mate." Warren seethed with anger, fists clenched at his sided.

"Anne was my mate!"

"You're still standing. I thought you'd be writhing on the floor in pain and yet here you stand."

"Warren! What the hell is wrong with you?" Charlotte pushed her way between the two men. "Look at your wife and your daughter. What would Annie think about you attacking James right now?" That's when she noticed it. Annie's body still had an aura. Black with white around the edges and laced through.

"I can take care of myself, Shorty." James interrupted her thoughts with a snarl.

"My daughter would never love an animal like you."

"You arrogant son of a –"

"Stop it." Abby screeched. "It doesn't matter anymore. She's gone. My baby is gone. Oh God my little girl is gone." Each sentence punctuated with another sob.

Charlotte set the laptop on the nearest table and wrapped her arms around her mother's best friend. "I'm so sorry, Aunt Abby."

"I've got her Charlotte." Warren gently pushed her away from his wife. He leaned down and pressed a kiss to Annie's forehead. "We should tell the boys. Do not move her until we come back Charlotte."

"No, I can't leave her. I can't." The wail that accompanied the words broke Charlotte's heart all over again.

"We'll stay with her, Aunt Abby. She won't be alone."

"Please she can't be alone. Don't leave her alone." Abby clung to Warren's shirt as they stood up. Her tenuous hold on the garment appeared to be the only thing keeping her standing.

Warren scooped her up with a glare at James as they left the room.

"James, he doesn't…."

"Don't Char. You all shoved this mate crap down our throat and look at me. It's can't be true. I wouldn't be able to function." James looked anywhere in the room but at Annie. The murky green that pulsed through his aura was far from peaceful. The red surged to the forefront again only to dissipate just as quick as it showed up.

"I don't have all the answers. Lucas is more in tuned with the Spirits than I am. But I saw the connection between the two of you." Tears welled up in her eyes.

"Shorty, I can't do this." James walked over to the bed and straightened the sheet around Annie. The words of a Lenape mourning prayer tumbled from his lips in a near whisper. He pressed his lips to her forehead lingering only a moment before he grabbed the laptop and left the room.

"James…." Defeat washed over her as her brother stormed out of the room.

"Let him go." Chance entered the room and knelt next to the bed. He whispered his own prayer in Lenape.

Charlotte met Chance's eyes as he tended to Annie. "Dad…!"

"I know Char. I know."

She collapsed against her father sobs racked her tiny frame. "Why? Why wouldn't the Spirits let me save her? I don't understand. Dad I don't understand. James…she was so good for James. They were connected. I saw the thread. They were mates. I don't care that he's not having the normal reaction when a mate dies. They belonged together." The last sentence came out in a whisper.

"I don't know. The Spirits may have other plans. They have not shared them with me."

27

Roark kept a tight grip on Talisa's hand as he took a deep steady breath in. The speed of their descent along with the consequences if he was unsuccessful both helped and hindered his focus. Each molecule of water he plucked out of the air pooled together under the plane forming a protective barrier between it and the ground.

"You've got it, Roark." The fingertips of Talisa's free hand danced along his arm.

Her reassurance helped, but his mind and abilities were exhausted. Not even his healing could keep up with the amount of exertion he expended to assist in their abrupt landings. This was the eighth or ninth time they had to land to avoid being detected and recaptured.

"One more jump and we should be home." Nerves tinged Ilana's voice.

"What's wrong, Ilana? Something blocking our way?" Elan leaned forward in her seat.

"No, we're clear now." The younger woman flipped a few switches instead of elaborating.

"Than what is it?"

Ilana inhaled a shaky breath past her teeth. "We lost Annie."

"Where did you leave her?" Chaz rocked back and forth coiled tight ready to strike at the first opportunity.

"I don't think she meant misplaced her. All the more reason to get home." Roark ran his free hand through his hair. Losing Annie only meant one thing. The compound had its own chaos at the moment. Just the thought of Talisa hurt sent a stabbing pain through his heart. He could only imagine what James felt like right now losing his mate.

The rickety plane lifted off the ground once more but stayed close to the ground this time. Every time it creaked or shook Roark worried that it might actually fall apart around them. With the hanger in sight the brief thought that the added chaos would delay his reunion with Talisa.

"Only briefly." Talisa's sad smile matched his.

The plane shuddered to a stop in the hanger. "We're home." Any hint of joy vanished from Ilana's tone.

"We'll get through this just like anything else. Right now, let's greet your brother." Talisa stood and waited as the ramp lowered.

"Mother. Father." Lucas gave a short bow as the ramp moved down slower than molasses in snow.

Roark released Talisa's hand long enough to pull Lucas to him in a tight hug. "Son."

"It pleases me to see you both. There is much to discuss."

"Right to the point as always." Talisa chuckled briefly as she embraced their son.

"RB and Mackenzie will assist with our new guests into the new lab area. Let us get everyone else inside before Steele sends another flyover." Lucas made a point to stop and make eye contact with Elan. "Daniel will be up shortly he is tending to his mother."

"Few improvements while we were gone." Roark took in the new security and additional tunnels as they made their way to the lower levels.

"Ravenhawk has been busy with the expansion He has been meticulous with every detail." Lucas nodded in Roark's direction.

"You mean he felt useless and was staying busy." Talisa said with a smirk on her face that made Roark yearn even more for the time alone they had planned.

"Perhaps we really needed to expand." Chance stood up from his seat in the middle of the common room.

"Sani." Talisa fell into Chance's waiting embrace.

"Kajah." The only other man alive that could kiss his wife on the lips and not die for it did just that.

"Chief." Roark nodded his head in Chance's direction.

"I'm not kissing you." Chance clasped hands with Roark and pulled him into a manly hug.

"What am I not pretty enough for you anymore?" Roark blew his friend a kiss.

"As much as I'm enjoying our old banter we're in a bit of chaos ourselves here." The laughter evaporated from Chance's words.

"I'm sorry we didn't get back in time." Talisa wrapped her arm around Roark's waist.

"I'm not sure who we'll need to sedate more, Warren or Abby. She's a hysterical mess and he's in a rage against James." Chance folded his arms across his chest. "The Spirits have only told me to be patient and all will be revealed."

"You're usually the patient one, Chief."

"Ilana and Lucas have been trying to remind me of that but it has been hard as of late." Chance sighed.

"I will take Elan to Daniel and our new companion to a room." Lucas bowed to the group and led the others down the hallway.

"How bad is James?" Tension shot up Roark's spine as he awaited the grim report on their eldest son.

"He's holding his own at the moment." Chance hedged.

"Wait he's not incapacitated?" Talisa looked between the two men.

"Not even a hint of rage."

"But I thought Annie was his mate? He should be seething in anger and barely able to function." Roark puckered his eyebrows in concern.

"Neither do we. Charlotte says she still sees an aura around Annie's body. It's slowly receding but it hasn't disappeared completely as it normally would when someone dies."

"What the hell did that asshole do?" Roark growled.

"I was hoping you two would be able to tell us that."

Elan ignored Lucas to the best of her ability as she got Chaz settled in to sleep. She alone knew the trick to slow him down every time. Thankfully, Lucas kept his back to them so she might handle things without revealing the Cheetah's weakness.

She studied Chaz quietly. "When is the last time you slept, Cheetah?"

"Ignored…many…days…months…you were gone…I heard of War." Chaz blinked a few times when she touched the bio-implant behind his ear. "They did not send me…I thought…fight."

"So they went to war and forgot one of their finest. It's probably for the best, Cheetah. There were no winners, and those like us were killed just for existing. I don't think it mattered to Steele's soldiers whose side we were on." She slid her finger along the implant until he stilled.

A low purr came from the now drowsy man before her. "Death…welcome."

"Some days I would have welcomed it, too." Elan rose the moment Chaz drifted into sleep. She strode past Lucas. "He'll be out for at least 24 hours."

"You seem certain."

"I am. I know what buttons to push."

"What—buttons?"

"Don't ask."

"I would not dare. You would not tell me, either way. I have no need to read your mind to know that." Lucas kept pace with her, though much calmer in many aspects.

Elan slowed only when she heard sobs. Outside of Annie's room, she hesitated. Now wasn't the time, but she had to see Danny, at least.

A mere few seconds after she peeked into the room, her husband spotted her. Grief streaked his cheeks, but a myriad of emotions slid across his features before he went stoic. He stepped away from his family to the door.

"Danny," she all but whispered. "Are you—,"

"Not now." He touched the pad beside the door. With a hiss the door closed in her face.

"Right." She turned on her heel to move back down the hall.

"Elan," Lucas protested.

"Please don't."

"He needs—,"

"Time to grieve." She paused once she'd turned a corner. "I'm not an idiot."

He circled to face her. "You are upset."

"Live my life and tell me I shouldn't be." She squared her shoulders, unwilling to admit the depth of the sting from Danny's rejection. Expected, though it may have been. She shook her head. "If I'd remained, the door would stay closed. Mom and Dad have to do their thing, and God knows where James is."

"Right here." James had managed to sneak up on her, damn similarities to Lucas, she hadn't even noticed him lurking in the shadow behind his twin.

This time Elan did brace for the impact, for the fury. "Why are you hiding?"

"Waiting."

"For what?"

James glared at Lucas. "Everything to hit."

"Wait, what?" Elan wrinkled her brow. "What do you mean, waiting for it to hit?"

"There's been a—an unusual reaction," Lucas hedged.

"Unusual, my ass," James countered.

Elan growled low. "Would someone tell me what the fuck is going on here?"

Chance had walked them to Annie's room slow enough to tell the whole story of Annie, James, and her eventual death. Tal kept a tight grip on Roark's arm the whole time to steady her brain from the influx of words and thoughts.

Though she'd adjusted somewhat to so many minds back at the compound, being here near the epicenter of a recent tragedy, there was much more mental projecting. Of course, she was much closer to many of those within the hidden base of her kind.

By the time they reached the door, a sort of film dropped over everyone's projecting thoughts, effectively dimming them enough to hear her own thoughts.

I would not intrude unless it was necessary, her son, Lucas' words entered her mind. *You seemed to wish for a clear mind by my perspective.*

Talisa smiled, warmth filling her. *You must teach me how to control this better. It's still awful damn new.*

You have the skills, you are tired and stressed.

Good point, she murmured in her mind.

Chance studied her, a quizzical expression on his features.

"Sorry. I was getting some help from our son. I'm ready now."

"If you're sure." He touched the pad.

The door slid open to reveal the grieving family. Abby was the first to lift her head, her gaze fell on Talisa. Tears streaked her normally perfect features. "Tal."

"Abby." Talisa released Roark to embrace her friend. "I'm so sorry I couldn't do more to help. I'm so sorry Steele got hold of that formula."

"I'm sorry I can't be happy to see you."

Tal kissed her friends' forehead, nodding to Warren as he shook Roark's hand. There was a brief, angry exchange that she willfully ignored, sure it had something to do with James. Instead, Tal moved to Annie's bedside near the twins. "She is beautiful, Abby. I'd expect nothing less from your DNA, of course. I'm surprised at Warren's input, though."

"Not the time," Derek all but snarled.

"Bullshit. I have no filter, so shut it. I can hear your thoughts now, and I don't appreciate one of them." Tal knelt, brushing her fingers across the cool skin of Annie's forehead. "I'm sorry I couldn't do more for you, Annie. You deserved so much more than this. So did your family. I'm just glad you got to meet them."

Me too, came the faintest whisper of a voice, as if from a deep, dark tunnel.

Tal lifted her gaze to the young woman on the bed, then to the now silent monitors on the wall. Though they'd been silenced, they still read the young woman's vitals. Nothing, not even a whisper of life.

Tal shut them down, only to see them spring to life again. "Warren, stop."

"She's not…." Warren's response was weak, then faded as the screens flickered again and went blank.

Tal hugged him tight. "Grieve with your family now. We'll have time for anger later."

He nodded against her shoulder before returning to his family.

Tal wrapped her arm around Roark's waist before leading him and Chance out in the hall. She clasped Chance's hand to lead him far from the room. "Privacy," she muttered. "Away from the electronics."

"Wrong way, then." Chance pulled them the opposite direction. Through a few lengths of tunnel, down a set of steps, they emerged into a brand-new tunnel. He took them several feet down into the darkness until Tal had to light a fire to help them see. "This good?"

"Yes." She glanced toward the entrance some ways down. "Roark, could you get any echo taken care of?"

"Got it." Roark's brow twitched in a moment of concentration before a thin wall of water blocked the entrance. "What is it, Li?"

"Something's wrong. Something is very off with this death. I swear I…heard Annie."

Chance shook his head. "That's not possible."

"I know."

Epilogue

James stared down Lucas with a dark glare. "Tell her, Lucas. Tell her how you lied to me."

"Nobody lied to you, James." A frown flickered across Lucas' features. "Like I've already said, there was a complication. Annie was your mate, the Spirits, and Charlotte, were quite certain on this."

"Bullshit. You all just wanted me to help her." James threw up his free arm, the other still holding tight to Annie's computer where he'd last heard her voice. He had no idea why he'd even taken it, all things considered.

"Wait, wait, wait." Elan stepped between the two of them, her gaze on Lucas. "I know Annie was his mate, I smelled it on him before I left. Clear as can be."

"Gross," James muttered.

"Hey, be glad you couldn't smell it. Your sense of smell is nowhere near mine." Elan glared at him. "Why are you saying they lied?"

"She's dead." James glared down at his sister. "Gone. Vamoose. By all accounts I should be near death myself in misery and rage…and here I am only ready to beat the living shit out of anyone who claimed she was."

"But—," Elan's mouth gaped.

"Like I said," Lucas spoke low, even, untouched by emotion, the asshole. James envied his ability to be even all the time. "There has been a complication. One I do not understand. Based on…."

James snarled when Lucas drifted off, his gaze distant. "Lucas, I swear if you don't come up with a better fucking excuse, I will slit your throat and see if that leaves me in the rage I'm supposedly supposed to be fucking in right now."

"I would like to see you try," Lucas' gaze returned to James. "Something is off, but I assure you she was your mate. There isn't a soul here who did not see it. Even Elan."

"Fuck you. Fuck you all. She obviously wasn't." James turned to storm down the hall. When Elan grabbed his arm, he flung her off hard enough her skin turned gray and thickened a mere millisecond before she hit the wall. "Get off, Caiman."

Elan snarled back, but made no move to approach.

James stormed to his room, wishing to the Spirits they had real doors he could slam. Instead he set down the computer on his desk before grabbing the chair. He threw it across the room before dropping to the floor in a heap.

Pain ratcheted through his chest, though he still felt as though he could function. This was not at all how it was supposed to happen.

"Fucking hell. I need a fight," he muttered. "Or a drink."

"Easy there, Tiger." Annie's voice echoed into the room.

James' head shot up so fast his neck cracked. He flew to his feet, scanning the room. "What the fuck? Whoever that is, it isn't funny."

"Okay, got it. We're tall, dark, and angry today." The clarity and strength in her tone sent chills down his spine.

He shook off the chill, doing a desperate search for the source. His gaze came to rest on her computer, which sat partially open. Unable to stop his hands from shaking, he opened the top the rest of the way.

The screen flickered, pixels dancing across the screen in a series of numbers he'd seen in the codes Warren worked. The images of numbers streamed across the screen until a figure appeared walking through them.

"What the fuck?"

"Neat trick, eh? How do I look?" The figure spun through the numbers.

"Anne?"

To Be Continued

Coming Soon

In Chaos Theory

Book 2 of The Exceptionals

Chapter One

Dawn approached too fast. Soon she would have to find shelter. Inessa had been traveling for the better part of six months now. Only at night. During that time she'd kept moving to avoid the risk of being caught by anyone remotely anti-mutant.

Beyond the cities that now lay in rubble people gathered. No. Humans gathered. Trying to rebuild. To grow some food on the land left behind that had not been scorched and destroyed. Some were successful and she's seen the joy of people coming together and forming families out of the darkness.

For the most part she'd avoided settlements, although sometimes the appeal of a hot cooked meal outweighed the danger. She only caved in mutant sympathetic settlements.

Seeing a person's aura gave you an inordinate amount of information once you learned the proper way to read them. Auras were a tricky thing. One color could have a myriad of meanings. Since the ability to see them was the primary mutation she developed, she had made sure to learn fast how to understand them.

Some days it was all that kept her alive.

The horse danced beneath her, pulling her back to the present situation. Few options remained for shelter in the middle of nowhere like she was. While Indiana had mostly come out unscathed, it only survived due to the amount of open land. Filled with cornfields instead of possible hidden groups of mutants.

The ground remained battle scarred, mostly from the after-War skirmishes that still raged between the military and the mutants or their sympathizers. Still, it was wide open with only a few barns to shelter her. The closest had animals inside, so it was still in use.

Somewhere there had to be an abandoned barn. With a kick to the ribs she got her horse moving again, galloping through the faint pre-dawn light in search of a run-down barn, a cluster of trees, anywhere to take shelter for the day. A place to sleep and recover.

A few more miles through the fields she spotted the perfect barn. Not so run down that it could cave in on her, but obviously falling from disuse.

Unfortunately, it was occupied. By one person.

Inessa frowned, studying the aura in the barn with care. It was a mutant. For the most part she left mutants alone as well. Too many were far too paranoid and her general friendliness and understanding tended to freak them out more. It was far too lonely an existence for the people person she'd once been.

Just as she thought she'd have to move on, to leave this mutant alone, her memory caught up to her. There was something familiar about this person.

She knew him.

A grin crossed her features and she led the horse into the barn, slipping down just outside. It was easy to tell he was sleeping and she hated to startle a mutant that was alone. The sun coming up over the horizon left her little choice. She pulled the door open and led her horse inside, pulling the door closed.

As she'd hoped the loud creak of the door had managed to wake the sleeping mutant, but now he hid. His indecision clear in his aura, she moved forward, "Dr. Carter?"

A tiny squeak of surprise escaped, but he didn't move. As expected, suspicion tempered his moves. There was something else too. He was different, something major had happened. An injury, although his pain had been minimal. A side effect of his mutation probably helped.

Dr. Carter, maybe you remember me? I'm Inessa Jelen. Last year you set my leg after the destruction of the city. You saved my leg, you saved me. Do you remember?" Inessa took a cautious step forward, tossing the reigns around a post. "Of course, my leg isn't important now that New York City is nothing but rubble."

"Inessa," he whispered. "I remember."

"Good. Thank you, remember that I'm a mutant too, right?"

"You joked about your name." His voice remained a whisper, hard to hear. "Said it was hilarious. Inessa means pure, and you were anything but."

"That's right."

"Complex displaced fracture of the fibula, complete fracture of tibia. Result of crushing with loose fragments. You needed surgery. I couldn't move you once I was done, left you in the care of a friend of yours. We were supposed to return. Take you back when you were able to travel. I never made it back."

"No, you didn't. I feared the worst for you." She moved around the corner of the stall he hid in. "Don't feel bad though.

Dixon took great care of me. Once I was well enough to fend for myself he left New York to find his family."

"You healed well, then?"

"I sure did. I'm surprised to find you out here in the middle of nowhere. You told me about the compound, I've been trying to get there. It's slow going, just me and the horse. What about you? Where's your wife?"

"Charlotte." A wave of grief crashed over him. Gray with blasts of deep purple consumed his aura. "I don't know. We got separated. Indianapolis and St. Louis were among the last cities hit. We were trying to help some orphaned mutant children. She went to St. Louis. I came to Indiana. I just remember the explosion. The screams. Screams of the children. My own screams."

Inessa knelt in front of Dr. Carter, setting her hand on his arm. "Dr. Carter?" There was no way to stop her gasp when he lifted his head. The right side of his face, mutilated with scars. The eye she remembered as a stunning blue now white and dead.

His left eye moved in her direction, but it was slow and couldn't seem to look right at her. "I was found by a sympathizer. Thankfully, I was able to keep myself out of pain by numbing my own nerves, but I had no medical care."

"Where is the sympathizer?"

"She's gone. I guess she was already sick when the War came. Weak heart. She died a few weeks ago during a skirmish." Dr. Carter's hand shook as he ran it through his hair, "She helped me keep the wound clean, and even stitched up some for me, but there was no way for me to get real medical care. My face and blood are among those tagged."

"How have you survived?" Inessa took a shaky breath and sat next to him. The wounds were bad, but she was relieved his suffering had been kept to a minimum. For her surgery, she'd been appreciative of his unique mutation. Without any access to anesthetic he'd been able to operate while she was fully awake and she hadn't felt a thing. His ability to dull nerves or make them fully alive in an attack had been one she had declared the 'coolest' she'd ever seen. "What about food? How can you go anywhere?"

Tracy had laid me in with some supplies every couple of weeks. I've been stretching them out. Right now, I've been trying to figure out how to get back to the compound when I can only see shadows and light in one eye. I have to find out if Charlotte is alive. If she survived the attack on St. Louis." His breath came out in a long-exhaled attempt to keep calm. "She's all I've got now."

Inessa smiled, "Well then Dr. Carter, I think I can help. I really do hate being by myself and I was heading to that compound too. If you aren't afraid of horses, my buddy Shiksa and I can help you travel."

"Afraid of horses? I was raised on a farm and bred horses." For the first time since she had shown up a bit of hope brightened the layers of his aura. Even still the sadness and longing for the love he remembered kept it dull.

"Good. Then at dusk we'll set out again." She squeezed his arm. "Don't you worry, Dr. Carter. I'm the best at keeping away from troops and snitches. The best liars can't hide the nastiness of their auras. I'll get you home and back to your wife."

"Thank you, Inessa. And please, call me Neil. I'm hardly a doctor anymore."

"Okay, I'll call you Neil. I have one stipulation to that, though."

"What?"

"Don't give up hope. Don't ever give that up. It's all we got."

About the Authors

Sarah Cass's world is regularly turned upside down by her three special-needs kids and loving mate, so she breaks genre barriers, dabbling in horror, straight fiction, and urban fantasy. An ADD tendency leaves her with a variety of interests that include singing, dancing, crafting, cooking, and being a photographer. She fights through the struggles of the day, knowing the battles are her crucible and though she may emerge scarred, she's also stronger. While busy creating worlds and characters as real to her as her own family, she leads an active online life with her blog, *Redefining Perfect*, which gives a real and sometimes raw glimpses into her life and art.

~

Mary Terrani lives a chaotic life as the mother of two boys of the 20 something and teen variety. They keep her on her toes on a regular basis, so she's happy to get lost in other worlds. Her long-standing passion for the written word drives her need to create chaos with her pen that only she can solve. She loves to dabble in many genres, from young adult to paranormal, and post-apocalyptic piece she's co-written with fellow author, Sarah Cass.

When she's not writing, Mary can be found in a variety of activities including knitting, gaming, and anything involving her favorite geekdoms. Mom, author and all around geek she loves spending time with her family. You can find Mary on Twitter, Facebook and her website.

Books by Mary Terrani

Decking the Halls

Books by Sarah Cass

The Tribe Series
The Tribe
The Wolf
The Chief
The Raven
The Dominion Falls Series
Changing Tracks
Derailed
Dark Territory
Runaway Train
Home Signal
The Lake Point Series
Santa, Maybe
Deep-Fried Sweethearts
Stalled Independence
Witch Way
A Thorough Thanksgiving
Eve's New Year
Heartstrings & Hockey Pucks
Luck of the Cowgirl
Stars, Stripes & Motorbikes
Free Falling
Love for Hire
Haunted Hearts
Stand Alone Novels
Masked Hearts
Leap

Divine Roses Ink
DivineRosesInk.com